Dolph's Team:

A Dolph Martinez/Jerri Johnson Mystery

D1553482

Dolph's Team:

A Dolph Martinez/Jerri Johnson Mystery

Jim Sanderson

INK
BRUSH
PRESS

ISBN: 978-0-9839715-0-4
Library of Congress Control Number: 2011937997
Manufactured in the United States of America

Cover Design: Michael Sanchez
cover photographs: Jim Sanderson

Ink Brush Press
Temple and Dallas, Texas

Author's Note:

Characters in *Dolph's Team* also appear in the following books.

Dolph Martinez: *El Camino del Rio* and *La Mordida*
Jerri Johnson: *Safe Delivery* and *La Mordida*.
Pepper Cleburne: *El Camino del Rio* and *La Mordida*.
Pooter Elam: "Potential" in *Semi-Private Rooms* and *Faded Love,* also in "Someone to Watch Over" in *Faded Love*.
Joan Phelan: "Potential" and "Bit by the Metal" in *Semi-Private Rooms* and *Faded Love,* and "Someone to Watch Over" in *Faded Love*.
Walter Boone in "The Truly Talented Writer" in *Faded Love*.

Other books by Jim Sanderson

Fiction

Faded Love (short story collection) Ink Brush Press, 2010.

Nevin's History (novel). Texas Tech University Press, 2004.

Semi-Private Rooms (short story collection). Pig Iron Press, 1995.

Dolph Martinez/Jerri Johnson series:
La Mordida (novel). University of New Mexico Press, 2002.

Safe Delivery (novel). University of New Mexico Press, 2000.

El Camino del Rio (novel). University of New Mexico Press, 1998.

Nonfiction

*Some Ways of Writing—A Writer's Way: A Supplemental Guide To Writing
    For Composition and Sophomore Literature* (composition text).
    Kendall Hunt, Fall 2007

A West Texas Soapbox (essay collection), Texas A&M Press, 1998

For Jerry and Barrie

Other Fiction from Ink Brush Press

Laurie Champion, editor, *Texas Told'em: Gambling Stories,* with an
     introduction by Doyle Brunson

Terry Dalrymple, *Fishing for Trouble*

Terry Dalrymple, editor, *Texas Soundtrack*

Andrew Geyer, *Dixie Fish*

Andrew Geyer, *Siren Songs from the Heart of Austin*

H. Palmer Hall, *Into the Thicket*

Dave Kuhne, *The Road to Roma and Other Stories*

Myra McLarey, *The Last Will and Testament of Rosetta Sugars Tramble*

Jim Sanderson, *Faded Love*

Melvin Sterne, *Zara*

For information on these and other books, go to
www.inkbrushpress.com

Chapter 1

Walter Boone's eyes went googly as he stared at Dr. Oscar Montalvo through his thick tri-focals and tapped his forefinger on the scarred wood of the picnic table: "Now I'm not saying that when they stuck that garden hose up my ass and started sucking out a sizeable portion of my innards, I wasn't upset. They may have gotten that cancer, but I was thinking that I might miss some of what they were pulling out. And I'm not going lie and tell you that I took it all bravely. I yelled, I cried, I screamed. I mean after all . . . ."

Dolph Martinez had heard the story before, so he concentrated on the late afternoon April sun making its way through the sparse shade of the dying mesquite tree. But out of a nearly involuntary sympathy, Dolph twisted his butt on the warped wood of the picnic bench.

Dr. Oscar Montalvo rolled his eyes and twisted in his seat. "Walter, you know that's not what happened."

Walter paid the doctor no mind. "Just the idea of it made my asshole pucker, as though anticipating the humiliation," he said.

"Ask Dolph there about humiliation and pain," Dolph's best buddy, Pepper, said. "Show 'em your wounds, Dolph. Show 'em where the metal bit you."

Oscar Montalvo shook his head, "I see scars all day long. I don't want to see yours."

Dolph swung his attention toward their faces. Old men showing scars, this was what they had come to. So Dolph, the ex-Border Patrol Agent who had squatted in whatever shade he could find out in Texas' Big Bend country, lifted his shirt and showed them where the college kid smuggling a plastic bag full of marijuana had gut-shot him. Then he stuck his shoulder out of the V of his polo shirt and showed them the small scar from the bullet that broke his collar bone. He got that scar in a wild shootout with some tough broncos whose boss was a little old lady bank teller. Pepper had gotten most of his knee shot off in the same stupid fight. After that fight, Dolph and Pepper, the guy Dolph once put in prison, came roaring out of far West Texas looking for shade.

As Dolph maneuvered his shoulder back into his shirt, Pepper had his leg on the table and his pants leg pulled up to show his mangled knee. "Now, Walter," Pepper said. "Show us your ass."

"Oh, for Christ's sake," Oscar said.

"The point is not the scar," Walter said. "Don't we need more beer?"

When Pooter jumped up to run to Big John's Icehouse because it was his round, Dolph's ass jiggled as the wooden bench groaned. Now that Dolph worked in "security" and "investigations," Pooter was Dolph's muscle when Dolph needed muscle. Pooter was aging, but the ex-pulling guard from UT's old wishbone offense days could still intimidate people if he practiced looking mean, and he could do them some damage if he actually got ahold of somebody.

Dolph was glad that he had on a straw hat. It was not yet Memorial Day, but a San Antonio April afternoon trumped tradition. Walter, of course, had a straw Panama covering his bald pate. Pepper wore a wide-brimmed cloth outdoors hat over his few remaining strands of hair. His diamond earring sparkled in the sun and sometimes threw reflections into the others' eyes. Pooter wore a gimme cap on his shaved head. Only Dr. Oscar Montalvo went hatless. His thick salt-and-pepper hair and dark khaki complexion were protection enough against the sun.

"It's actually a pretty simple operation," Oscar Montalvo said. "And you were under anesthesia."

"Leave it to a medical doctor to analyze a good story and ruin it for us," Pepper said. "Truth is not the point when you're bullshitting."

"But I don't think our souls are necessarily in our hearts or brains," Walter retorted. "What if parts of our souls are tucked up between our guts?"

"And some of yours got sucked out," Dolph said. Walter could and would make an argument about most anything. In an age when you couldn't even major in philosophy at most state colleges, Dolph met with two philosophers every day: Walter and Pooter. Philosopher 1, Walter, rapped the table with his finger and flashed his reptilian smile at Oscar. Philosopher 2, Pooter, returned with the beers, five bottles in between his curled hands. Somehow Pooter got a fresh, glistening, sweating bottle in front of each of them. Unlike Walter, Pooter was an introspective philosopher. He pondered mysteries but kept them to himself. Both had Ph.D.s in philosophy.

"I'm just saying," Oscar continued, not to be outdone. "In this case, the exam is technically more difficult than the operation."

"Thanks for the medical advice," Walter said. "Now let me give you some bug advice. It's time for your yearly bug spraying. See, unlike those in the medical profession, those of us in the bug profession keep up with our patients."

"Is Oscar the patient or the bugs?" Pepper asked and pushed up on the front brim of his hat.

"You killing the bugs or feeding them?" Pooter mumbled. And everyone turned to look at Pooter. After considering Pooter's point, the other three returned to their discussion of bugs, medicine, and Walter's rectum.

For Dolph, beer 2 was almost as good as beer 1. So instead of listening to the conversation, Dolph felt the cool beer run down his throat and watched Pooter. Pooter gazed away, no doubt listening to one of the debates he carried on his head. His gaze settled on the slow-flowing San Antonio River down the slope from Big John's Ice House.

Dolph decided to listen. "Okay, Walter, I can feel you leading me places I don't want to go. Enough about your ass already," Oscar Montalvo said.

Walter pushed his straw hat back and cocked his head to peer through his thick lenses. His grin seemed about to release a hiss, like the snake's in Eden. Then he had those eyes behind his thick glasses. You had to listen to Walter. After all, he had been a writer. "But this time I'm talking about soul. I guess an M.D. wouldn't know about a soul."

"No, I guess not. That's what you fuzzy, feely Ph.D.s like to talk about."

"Why don't we talk about something we can all understand?" Pepper asked. "Say pussy and beer."

"We're too old to talk much about pussy," Dolph said.

"Hell, none of us ever understood a goddamn thing about it anyway," Pepper said. "Jesus, look at us, a bunch of old farts. Probably been so long since any of us had any of it, we forgot which armpit it was under."

"We can lie about it," Dolph said.

"Who woke up Dolph?" Pepper asked. "Now somebody ought to shake Pooter. I think he's gone senile on us." Pooter shifted around to smile at them with his passive Buddha look. Walter's smile could charge you up; Pooter's smile could calm you. Pepper mockingly said the comments they had all heard: "'Why do you go out and drink every day and tell the same stories over and over? Don't you get bored?'" They all dropped their heads and nodded.

"That's what my wife says every time I go out," Oscar said.

Walter gently patted his back. "Wives, bosses, do-gooders, M.A.D.D. mothers, social workers, cops, and therapists don't understand. And we get tired trying to explain. The stories, the beer, the location, the shadows, the heat or cold, the way you held your tongue all make the story better and better until you finally got it to be true. Which is to say, the stories are a lot better than the individual real worlds we have to live in."

"The same would have been true for the old Spaniards and the Cohuelticans," Dolph, who had a Master's Degree in history, said.

"That's almost profound," Pooter said.

"I divorced my second wife for that very reason," Walter said.

"Now which one is the second one?" Pepper asked.

That's a tough question," Walter said. "I seem to remember Claudia."

And then Walter started the story about his temporally short but emotionally long marriage to his second wife. Dolph had heard this story many times too. So much for the romance of the conversation. Dolph looked for some romance in the location.

Big John's Ice House was an old Southside ice house just off Military Drive, right before a bridge over the San Antonio River. For years San Antonio had been distinguished by its ice houses: mom-and-pop quick stops where you could pick up milk, bread, beer, and a pack of cigarettes.

Bring the kids along, make a nightly outing, pick up an Eskimo pie or ice cream sandwich for the kids. In the old days, teenagers would run to your car, take your order, and make change from the coin dispensing machines strapped around their waists. And for the beer drinkers, the ice house owners would put a bench out under a tree where the patrons could sip a cool one. That was all in the time when air conditioning was scarce, before Texas went liquor-by-the-drink at county option. But Dolph and his friends met at the same bench under the old cracking mesquite tree at the same time every week day and drank their beers until they had to be home for supper. For Dolph and his friends this old ice house was protection from the oblivion that threatened them. Now, this once-dying part of town had an Anglicized/Nippon/Hispanic corporate growth spurt: a Toyota factory spitting out trucks for Texans. San Antonio, Texas, and the rest U.S. of A were fast forgetting Dolph and his friends.

When he pulled the bottle from his mouth, just to practice seeing, Dolph raised his readers from his chest, where he kept them, bouncing and dangling from a cord around his neck. Settling the slim spectacles on the tip of his nose, Dolph read the label on his beer. Then he looked over the rims at the slow-moving river

The river was mostly a drainage ditch, and across the street was the old Mission County Park extension, which had become a part of Mission Trail National Historic Park, and Mission Park Cemetery. But the tourists rarely made it out to see this part of San Antonio history. San Antonio de Béxar came into existence along this redirected part of the river. Right down the river were Espada and San Juan Capistrano, and upriver were San José—"Queen of the Missions"—and Concepcíon. Those old Spaniards' herds and fields were here. And they probabably squatted near this very bench with the Cohuelticans and told their stories. But a zillion dollor construction project was stretching the Riverwalk from downtown all the way to the Southside. Soon, for the sake of tourists, the river project would erase what was left of Spanish history and what was Dolph and his friends' history—Big John's.

Dolph couldn't tune out Walter for long. Walter had tired of talking about his second wife, so Walter shifted to his first wife, the one, great, true love of his life. Dolph had heard these stories too. But he had to listen.

5

Sarah Boone was the part of Walter's history, and he couldn't get this lesson out of his mind. Sarah Boone had come to see him during his convalescence from his operation and the accompanying chemotherapy. "Sarah and me just had layers. We had raised kids. We had become history. And even though she had cussed me most of our marriage, even though I had destroyed most of my marriage from heeding my hormones—for which prostate cancer would have been a more fitting punishment—we had had kids, we had formed each other. Lying in a hospital bed, drugged up, with the cancer just having been sucked up out of my ass, when I saw her, I cried." Walter waited. Dolph took a drink.

Oscar Montalvo leaned on his elbows toward Walter. "They don't just suck out colon cancer. And you would have been so drugged you wouldn't have recognized her. And you would have been hurting."

"Who's telling this story, Oscar?" Walter said. "I ought to know. I was there."

"Your soul' again?" Oscar asked.

"That's right. Your soul. It can happen," Pooter said.

"Oscar, you got to recognize the importance of what could have happened," Walter said.

Pepper look at Dolph. He too knew the story. "How come you just can't forget the early wives? The last two or three, you can cut and run, but those first three or four . . . Why are they always the pick of litter?"

Walter nodded and said, "Poor Sarah, my first ex-wife, the most prominent chainsaw sculptor in the U.S., will see me through."

"Chainsaw what?" Oscar asked.

"Chainsaw sculptor," Walter said. "Chainsaw sculpting was the province of redneck, tourist-trinket makers until Sarah Boone came along."

Oscar shrugged his thick shoulders, rubbed his mop of salt and pepper hair.

"She made it an art," Walter said, tilted his head back to look through his lenses and adjusted his straw hat to keep the sun out of his eyes.

"Skip this part," Pepper said and tugged at one of the points of one his moustache, which he still waxed and curled. "I don't like your preaching about the attributes of chainsaw art. I suspect you don't know shit about chainsaw art."

"And here is the purpose of chainsaw or any other art: We all have at least one woman who makes our guts ache, even if we've had those guts cut out." Walter smiled. He had them. They were listening. Walter was the snake in the garden. Dolph heard the hiss. Dolph knew that he should guard himself from Walter's hallucinogenic but romantic daydreaming, for Walter could make the moment seem worth all your tomorrows. They had all lost too many tomorrows. None of them had enough left to gamble on Walter's far-fetched plans. "Sarah is still an attractive woman, still could turn even a young man's head, and if I could have somehow seen my way to now, I would maybe have stayed with her."

"I call bullshit on that one," Pepper said. "Young man can't think or remember but with one part of his body. And there you were, in the prime of life, bumping up against Hollywood starlets. Think how you'd punish yourself now if you hadn't taken advantage of those opportunities. You'd be noble and true blue and old."

"I was after the essence of woman back then. I wanted epic proportions. I wanted to know all about women by having all of them."

"That's true, that's true," Pooter said and nodded his bald Buddha head.

"See the trouble your dick gets you into?" Oscar said and pushed his shaggy hair out of his eyes.

"If I'd have had sense instead of a dick . . . ," Pepper said.

"You've had sort of a short supply of both," Dolph said as soon as he recognized an opportunity.

Peering through the thick lenses that made his eyes look bulbous, yet hypnotic, Walter said, "I'm not just talking about that."

"You're an old man with an eat-out ass. All you got is memories of that," Pepper said.

"No, no," Pooter said. "Even then, even then, we can know intensity. We can feel it. I hadn't but seen Joan but knew she had an intensity."

Pepper shot a glance to Pooter as if to warn him not to go there. Pooter had followed Joan, been her disciple and savior. Pepper was now in love with her.

"You guys are full of shit," Oscar said.

Dolph looked at Pepper and nodded. "There's always some woman or

some instance that makes your hand shake the bourbon out of your glass."
Pepper nodded back.

Beneath them, across the worn, cracked jogging path that no one but
Dolph and a few others ever used, was the gray-brown river. It was ugly
now, but to the Cohuelticans and the Spaniards, it must have been as close
to paradise as they could find on this earth. Paradise for Walter was in
Mexico. Small towns, where an old man with his retirement in his pocket
could live like the old rich Spaniards. Could buy what he wanted—booze,
women, memories, fun, immortality. Walter had hissed that plan to Dolph.
He had the towns circled in red on a map tacked to his apartment wall.
Any of those towns would do, Walter had told Dolph.

* * *

Charlie Montalvo liked cleanliness and class a whole lot more than his
brother Oscar did. So while Dr. Oscar Montolvo sat, just as he did
everyday, under a dying mesquite tree at a dirty old ice house, the site of
three shootings, Charlie propped his foot on a proper bar railing at The
Cadillac Bar, an Anglo corporate imitation of a famous Neuvo Laredo bar,
the one where a Texas Ranger was stabbed and killed with a wooden knife.
And Charlie didn't drink beer. He sucked down margaritas and waited for
Oscar's young wife and the the impending seismic shift in his life. He had
been checking his watch all day, and now, after work, his watch checking
became a nervous tic. He pulled his eyes from his watch to his glass. It was
empty. He ordered another.

Charlie's memory and thoughts had just given out. He had gone over
plans, possible outcomes, potential screwups, and regrets so many times
that his mind had just overheated and shut off. Cooling mind, cold feet, he
thought. After all, he was contemplating the impending death of his
brother.

Oscar was older, smarter, more highly respected. Their parents had
doted on Oscar. The community praised Oscar, the doctor (wow, a doctor,
the Mexican boy had done well!). Plenty of Mexican boys had done just
well enough to make themselves lawyers. A lawyer back on the Southside,
back with his community, was nothing special. Southside Mexicans were
used to lawyers, overrun with lawyers, but a doctor, who could have gone

8

on to rich, white areas and made even more money, now that was something else to Southside Mexicans.

Charlie drove a Lexus. It was sitting outside in the parking lot. Oscar drove a Ford pickup. Charlie went to parties with C.E.O.s and corporate officers. Oscar met a bunch of trashy old men at an old, left-over, crumbling, ice house. Oscar was rich. He had gotten into medicine before the insurance companies took over doctors' practices, back when doctors made the fortunes. Charlie's salary from his law firm just barely covered his child support.

Across the bar was a mirror, in the mirror was Charlie, and behind him, frowning and looking all the sexier because of her pouty face, was Lee Ann Montalvo. Charlie turned to see the real Lee Ann instead of the mirror image. Tight jeans held her ass and thighs from spreading out just a bit farther. The navel on her bare, tight belly supported a silver ring. The scooped neckline revealed two perfectly round dollops of vanilla-ice-cream breasts. The nose was long and slender, the lips full. Charlie looked down at her feet. She had on sandals. Even her long slender toes with pink toenails were perfect. The toes were hers. The rest of her was Oscar's creation. For all of Oscar's achievements, she was his prize.

Charlie stepped forward to hug and kiss her. "You kidding? What you thinking, boy? Turn back around to that bar," she said. Charlie did as he was told. "Where you been?"

"I took off early."

"Good thing I knew where to find you. As far as what we're doing, as far as what is going on, we're lawyer and client having a conversation."

"Not brother and sister-in-law having a drink?"

"You need to get serious."

Lee Ann looked around, reached into her purse, pulled out a cigarette. Charlie had his lighter up and lit before she even got the cigarette to her mouth. "This bar is no smoking," the bartender said

"Well, shit," Lee Ann said and crushed the cigarette in her hand, Charlie's lit cigarette lighter still in front of her face.

Charlie turned to the bar, saw his face in the mirror alongside extravagant, sexy Lee Ann. His mind clicked, got warm. He looked at his watch. "It's close to being done."

"Stay calm."

"Oh shit, oh shit. Maybe we shouldn't. I mean my brother."

"Ramón is there, waiting."

"Oh shit." Charlie looked down to see his hand start to shake. "Are you sure he has it all down?"

"I've rehearsed it with him over and over. He's got his story down."

"But he's not the brightest spark. He could get scared. He could change his mind and his story."

"Oscar threatened him. I heard it. Other people too. He's probably told his drinking buddies about the whole thing. Self-defense. Hell, this is Texas."

"Yeah, this is Texas, and Oscar's the one defending his wife."

"And so poor Ramón gets locked up for a long time." Lee Ann looked up at Charlie's face, said, "Besides, Ramón thinks he's getting me," and smiled. Charlie felt his mind turn off. He felt a chill. Being evil didn't feel that bad if Lee Ann was the prize.

* * *

Pooter saw a lone egret wander out from behind some tall grass and a river willow and nervously, tentatively dip its beak into the San Antonio River. "You don't see too many of those around here," Pooter said. He had grown tired of the direction of the conversation, so he began to amuse himself. As they talked around their lives, again and then once more, they all tried to abbreviate how they had arrived where they were. The bottom line, which none of them wanted to admit, was simple: they all should have seen it coming.

Pooter, though, knew he was different. He had always been a lineman and would remain so. He protected the stars. He followed the plays. He didn't make them. Unlike the others, he was steady. After his attempts at rescuing Joan Phelan, now Pepper's woman, he didn't allow himself ambitions. He reacted, and noted. No matter how well you planned, Pooter knew that you couldn't plan for an accident. To Pooter, there was no such thing as emergency planning.

The egret dipped its beak once more into the water, and the river made a barely visible swirl around its legs. The beer tasted cool. There were interesting things to look at, or rather, for Pooter, things to look at and make interesting.

Just down Military, on the other side of Mission Park Cemetery, was a tiny, tacky strip mall made with cinderblocks painted to look like real bricks. And on the corner, with a view of the cemetery, some enterprising soul had put up his sign: *PRE-PAID FUNERALS*. Emily Dickinson "could not stop for death." But now we just didn't have the time to be bothered by my death. And the owner of the strip mall shop would take care of the funeral part of death; let others preplan the actual dying and other parts. Money and convenience, even if you were poor, could help you escape the scariest part of being human. Pooter liked the irony.

But the conversation pulled Pooter away from his considering. Oscar, set to thinking and confessing by Walter's sermon, said, "Any of you seen my wife?" He didn't wait for any of them to answer. None of them had seen her. "She's beautiful. But she didn't start out that way." Pooter's eyes and attention left the egret and settled on Oscar's face. He looked as though he had aged since they had sat down. Crows feet bunched up around the corners of his eyes. The drooping skin under his chin seemed to fall just a little farther.

"Damn, don't tell her that," Pepper said.

"Let him talk," Pooter said. Pepper and Pooter were opposite equals. Pooter had been too restrained, too plain for Joan. Pepper was going to prove too testy, too full of the bar bullshit that drinking buddies like to hear.

"She was just this trashy nurse from West Texas. Born in Odessa, then moved to the big city and bright lights of Lubbock. Scrawny, no tits, bad teeth, crooked nose, and talked West Texas out of that crooked nose." Oscar stopped, looked around him, thought, no doubt, that he had gone too far already. This, though, was new. Pooter had not heard it before. From the looks on their faces, neither had any of the others. "Well, my first wife had left me, my kids were living with her and developing all sorts of problems, so I started fixing the second wife up. First her teeth, then her nose, then her tits."

"All the finest money can buy," Pepper added.

"Let him talk," Walter said.

11

In the moments that Oscar hesitated, Dolph had left and reappeared with another two hands full of bottles of beer. Dolph spread the beer in front of them. "Then I sent her to school. She worked hard and studied. She lost that West Texas accent. The words didn't get caught in her nose no more. So I married her."

"Happily ever after," Walter said.

"See, you guys talk about all these women. But I did different," Oscar said. "I chose one and fixed her." Pooter liked this story. It was mythic. It touched at the core of masculinity. He looked around. The others liked it too. It was a better story than even Walter could have told or even made up.

"Touching story. I'd like to see her," Pepper said.

"Does Joan hear you talk like that?" Pooter asked. Pooter was immediately sorry that he had said that. He had been protecting Joan for so long that he just couldn't stop.

"I don't think he's finished yet," Dolph said.

"Now my perfect woman, the one I made . . ." Oscar started.

"The Frankenstein monster," Pepper interrupted.

"Shut the fuck up," Dolph said.

"Now she's fucking the lawn boy."

Dolph exhaled, then hung his head and just shook it. Pepper looked like a fish out of water—sucking air. Walter patted Oscar's shoulder. And Oscar looked at him like he was an idiot. "And I feel like I want to kill him," Oscar said. He put his elbows on the table, hung his head, then lifted his head to look at each one of them. "Any of you feel like talking me out of it?"

Hypocrisy kept Dolph, Pooter, and Pepper from commenting. So Walter had to say, "Think of some other way to deal with it."

"Then think about this," Oscar said. "My daughter's living with a drug pusher."

"Shit," Pepper said. "You're confusing me. Too many people here need killing."

"He's a small-time Mexican boy dealing pharmaceuticals. She lives with him over north of 35, in that San Antonio College area, off of McCullough, one of those big old mansions converted to apartments." He ran his hand through his peppered hair, shook his head, adjusted his glasses. "She's dropped out of school, stays fucked up. I'm sure he's the reason."

"Are you sure she's fucked up?" Pepper asked.

"He's a fucking doctor," Dolph said.

"There's counseling," Pooter said.

"You really want him killed?" Walter asked.

"Which one, which boyfriend, the wife's or the daughter's?" Dolph asked.

Oscar dropped his head and shook it. "I got a concealed weapons permit. I've got a gun in my car."

"As a former criminal who got convicted," Pepper said. "I got to warn you. Don't be telling us this shit."

Oscar let himself chuckle. "I don't know which son of a bitch I want to shoot more."

"So okay, I got it. Go for both," Pepper said in a serious tone and nodded his head.

Dolph said what they all were thinking, "Sure you wouldn't want to scare him just a little?" Pooter felt himself shiver. Dolph was right. This could be another mission, another chance to fix what fate fucked up.

"What you got?" Oscar asked.

"I don't want to say exactly," Dolph said.

"It's that fucking Taser, isn't it?" Pepper said.

"Oh shit," Walter said. "I've gotten in trouble already over that."

"What's wrong with a gun or a club?" Pepper said. "I'm a conservative in that sense."

"Look, somebody is fucking with Oscar and his wife. All I'm saying is maybe we can help out," Dolph said.

"Who's this 'we?'" Walter asked.

"Give me the word," Pooter said. Pooter wouldn't have minded planting a fist into either boyfriend or holding them while Dolph put his fists into them.

"Oh, holy shit," Pepper said. "If it's a puppy or a kitty, an old lady, a wetback with a hard luck story, teenager with anxiety, a whore with a heart of gold, a woman with a pretty smile and a sad story, then Dolph starts sucking his panties up his ass and wants to start charging wind mills."

"You left out old assholes with prison records," Dolph said. That was mean, Pooter thought. Dolph had put Pepper in prison. They joked about it, but it was still a tender issue.

Pepper smiled. "I'll bet you want to zap one of the boyfriends with your Taser just a little."

"I'd bet you would want to bounce that lead-lined cane off his head once or twice," Dolph said. While his shot-off knee recovered, Pepper had armed himself with this cane. Ingenuity, Pooter thought. In a world with no order, they tried to look out for each other, no questions asked. Pooter was glad they were his friends.

"We could talk to him," Pooter said. They all knew what that meant.

"Or reason with him," Walter said. His hissing grin disappeared. "Sometimes you guys forget the power of reason."

"Oh shit," Oscar said. "This is all just too much. I shouldn't have said anything. I don't need you guys. I need psychiatrists and therapists." He pushed himself up. "All this worrying has just worn out my bladder." Oscar limped away.

Pooter looked back at the river, sniffed the air, and then looked straight up.

"What in the fuck are you smelling?" Pepper asked.

"Daylight savings time," Walter said.

"You can smell daylight savings time?" Pooter asked.

"We have an hour longer to drink in daylight," Walter said.

"It's man-made, artificial, abstract. But we abide by its rules." Pooter said.

"Means summer is coming," Pepper said. "Means roasting our asses."

* * *

Dolph tried to notice this change in the time and feel of the evening, but instead he felt that cold that moved up from his toes and down from his head by way of his blood vessels. Dolph was scared. It was a tingle, a premonition, a slow cold fear, like the time the backpacking hippie toting his stash of pot over from Mexico gut shot him. Like the time he turned his pistol on Reynoldo Luna's henchman, squeezed the trigger, and watched a butterfly of blood spread its growing wings across the boy's white-shirted chest. Like the time he begged his co-conspirators not to shoot Reynaldo Luna, but Pepper squeezed his trigger and sent a bullet through Reynaldo's head.

Then they all heard the shot. Dolph was up from the bench first, and peering over his shoulder for possible backup, he saw Walter, Pooter, and Pepper limping behind him. He got to the door of Big John's outdoor restroom. He hesitated, breathed in, looked behind, and shoved open the door.

Dolph froze in the doorway, and Pooter, Pepper, and Walter pressed up behind him. Oscar Montalvo was lying under the urinal in a pool of blood that was spreading out and around him, staining the cement floor. Dolph knew better than even to check. In between the sink and the urinal, shaking just a little, a puzzled look on his face, was the young Mexican kid with the smoking gun. They all knew, right away, that this was the lawn boy. Echoing in Dolph's head was the laughter of all the people he'd seen killed: ex-priest and ex-professor Vincent Fuentes, Sister Barbara Quinn, ol' Texas Ranger Joe Parr, and the bad bronco Reynaldo Luna.

"Holy shit, it could have been any one of us," Walter Boone said. "Just depended on who had to pee first."

But Dolph knew that the reason the dead were laughing was that this killing was specifically Oscar Montalvo's. Oscar's laugh now joined them. The laughter rumbled around in Dolph's head and put pressure on his brain, making him feel as though there were an ice pick inside his head about to poke a tiny hole through his skull from the inside out, so as to release the pressure. He felt his stomach doing flips, turning the taste of the coppery beer into bile, and he felt his knees growing weak. He stepped back against the restroom wall and felt his back sliding down the wall as his knees gave way. "Hey, what's wrong with Dolph?" he heard Pooter ask. With Pooter grabbing his arm, Dolph got himself outside into sunshine before he lost control of himself.

Chapter 2

Dolph's boss, Jerri Johnson, left her office across from San Antonio's Main Plaza, just behind the courthouse, and headed for the Nix hospital. Like the five drinkers at the ice house, she meant to deal with history too, to follow her traditions and habits. As she stepped into Palo Fuentes's room, she realized that this old man had been an important surprise in her life, a coincidence that had turned into fate. She could no longer imagine her life without Palo. Had she not let him become a part of her life, she would not have had the great luck of finding Joe Parr, her second husband. Sometimes, luck was a part of fate too.

Palo was lying peacefully but breathing heavily under the glow of a single light. Jerri tip-toed to the chair beside the bed. She had errands and obligations to other people, and thanks to cell phones and text messaging, she had almost no time off. But since every moment now counted, she did not want to miss a single chance of seeing Palo. His face was sallow, almost ashen. The I.V. in his arm looked as though it were burrowing into a pale, white vine, not something as thick as the underside of a human forearm. The nurses could no longer find veins.

Moving slowly and deliberately, Jerri patted his forehead. His eyes fluttered and then opened. He sucked in some air, coughed, turned just his eyes, recognized Jerri, and smiled with some difficulty. "Jerri, dear Jerri. I think that I was dreaming . . . ," he said.

"Go back to dreaming," Jerri said.

"I'll have plenty of time to dream. Now I need to see the real world." Palo tried to chuckle.

Jerri still had to live in this real world. And it would be a harsher world

17

without Palo. She suddenly felt guilty for so egregiously thinking of self when Palo was facing the annihilation of self. "Have you had any pain?"

"Breathing is difficult." Palo coughed as he chuckled. "The curse of growing old is that what we used to not even notice, we notice, because it becomes more difficult. I limped on that pendejo cane for years. Now I wish I was back to limping."

"Do you need anything? Can I get you something?"

"What are you working on? I like to hear about your cases. I'm not sure I remember them, but I like to hear about them."

"I'm waiting for the next one."

"What is it?"

"That's why I'm waiting. I don't know what it is, but I'm waiting. I'm busy now. I'm a success. Lots of money, remember? Now cases find me. I'm not sure that is good."

"I remember I was proud of you. You have grown beyond me. Or I have fallen beneath you."

"No, you were never beneath me."

"Oh sure I was. I came to this country a criminal. And I helped you get started, and then you helped me bringing the wets to this country, and then you became the bail bonds lady, and now you have your own detective agency. Maybe your virtues have made up for my sins." He smiled and coughed. "Or maybe it is your legalness made up for my criminalness."

At one time, Palo had been a gangster in Mexico. Rival gangs or the PRI itself had planted a bomb in his car. Palo survived the blast but lost one testicle. He had become a marked man in Mexico. So his son, Vincent, conspired to get his father out of Mexico. Vincent used his lover to get his father out of Mexico. Jerri was Vincent's lover. "Dying is not so hard," Palo said. "But it takes time—and concentration. I don't seem to have enough of either."

"Have you thought that you may survive this?"

"This is simply old age," Palo said. "My body has just worn out. My mind is not too far behind."

"But you still advise me."

"Not for long."

"Take your time."

Palo's chuckle got lost in his throat. He looked at her now with his watery eyes. "If I had had any sense, I would have died in one of my shootouts or explosions. That type of dying wouldn't have been as hard as just wearing out."

"But then I might never have met you. When you came to this country, you didn't get blown up or shot."

"So I will count that as a blessing." If he could have mustered the energy, Jerri thought Palo might have cried. Despite all the great disappointments in his life, despite the frustration of feeling the life seep from his body, his mind and wit were still sharp.

A crack of light appeared at the door. Jerri checked behind her to see a nurse smiling as she entered the room. The nurse tidied the room and checked on Palo. Jerri should spend the night, she thought. Wrest what time she could from Palo's death. But she was tired and had work to do. So self-centered, so trapped by ego, Jerri thought.

"Leave me to my fate," Palo said. "You have work to do. I have thinking and remembering to do."

Jerri stood up to kiss his forehead. "You'll be in my dreams."

"They are not just dreams," Palo said. "They are us, only better. I almost thought of something important. But I can't force it from my mind to my mouth. I think that I should go to sleep again to see if I get to wake up again."

Jerri squeezed his hand, gently laid it down as she backed away from him, then paused in the doorway, next to the nurse, to memorize already sleeping Palo. Then she felt a vibration on her hip and a staccato buzz. She stepped into the hallway, dug into the pocket of her slacks, and pulled out her cell phone.

"Jerri, call that politically ambitious, shyster lawyer friend of yours and tell him to get down to the police station." It was Dolph. "This is the case he says he wants. He can defend the dispossessed."

"You know I could maybe defend him too."

"You'll want help. This guy's just murdered one of my best friends and confessed to it. But the whole thing creates a stench in the nose of the Lord. So get your friend down here."

"Where are you, Dolph?"

"At the police station."

"Be nice, Dolph."

"Don't worry. Pooter, Pepper, and Walter are with me."

"Oh God, you shouldn't have told me that. I'll try to get bail money for all of you."

* * *

After Lee Ann left him, Charlie had several more margaritas. As more people lined up at the bar, Charlie pulled his elbows in while rubbing shoulders with the drinkers and diners. He talked to the nice lady bartender and admired her butt when she turned her back to him to mix a drink. He also admired the waitress who brushed up against him as she fetched drinks for the people out on the patio. A pleasant feeling came over him, one that you feel while drinking with other people, even if you don't know them. Drinking at home was just not the same. But then Charlie shuddered. His brother was probably already dead, and Lee Ann wouldn't want him drinking in a bar. Outside in the dusk, the south downtown streets looked deserted. He walked toward the garage where he parked his Lexus, and in his mind, he made Oscar age from a teenager to today.

He tried to drive himself home, but instead, on autopilot, he pulled his Lexus into his brother's re-topped Alamo Heights driveway. As the solar lights guided him up to the four-car garage, he glanced over his left shoulder at the stone-paved sidewalks and patios, the flowerbeds, the fountains, all darkened by the spreading arms of the oak trees and lit by lights in the trees and more solar lights on the ground. Charlie hit the button on his garage door opener and watched the garage door fold open. Charlie parked his car, closed the garage door behind him, and squeezed in front of Lee Ann's Jaguar. His brother's truck was gone. His classic 1968 Corvette was in its usual guarded position.

As a Mexican new to this country, Ramón was taking up where Oscar and Charlie had been. As boys on the Southside, one generation away from absolute poverty, but believing whole-heartedly in the Hardy Boys and Horatio Alger, Oscar and Charlie started mowing lawns, and then Oscar, the older, figured he'd make more money if could mow the lawns of the richer people. He bummed rides to Alamo Heights, knocked on doors, and got contracts. A cousin and older boys gave Charlie and Oscar rides until Oscar got his own hand-me-down car. They had cut this very yard, and now Oscar owned the house and the yard and was paying another Mexican boy, this one a near-artist with plants and stones, to make the place palatial. Charlie knew, though, that Oscar underpaid Ramón, just as Oscar had taken seventy percent of his and Charlie's fees back when they were kids. Oscar was older; he was smarter; he was a better businessman. He had claimed his birth right back then and was still claiming.

Charlie walked out the side door of the garage that led into the dark yard, made almost creepy by the shadows from the stretching arms of oaks, the tall shrubbery. In the back yard was an expensive greenhouse with attachments to regulate temperature and humidity for delicate and tropical plants. Around the greenhouse were riotous outgrowths of plants and circling paths of stone. Ramón Burgiaga had landscaped this whole yard. The backdoor was suddenly lined with light. Then it opened farther to reveal a vision, a dream, a fantasy that Charlie had been having since his brother had brought Lee Ann to live with him.

His brother's surgeon friends had made Lee Ann perfect. And now wrapped around that perfection were a black push up bra holding her saline breasts; a red corset making her waist nearly wasp tiny, sending one slight roll of flesh over it just under the black bra, and another roll of flesh just under the corset, making her belly button bulge; black panties, which Charlie saw were thongs; and open-toed stiletto heels. He ran to her; she pulled him inside. And they didn't even wait to go to the bedroom. They did it right there on Oscar's tiled kitchen floor.

After their acrobatics, Charlie rolled off Lee Ann to look at her tight face. She rolled to face him. "You should probably go home."

"Oh honey, I want to stay."

"How much have you drunk?"

"I shouldn't be driving. I should stay."

Lee Ann shook her head and rolled away from Charlie. Now he was looking at her back. "It's done," Lee Ann said. "He is surely dead by now. Ramón did just as he said he would."

Charlie turned back around. It was indeed done. His brother dead. He had finally bested him. Charlie should have felt better, or worse. But

21

mostly he felt the chill on his naked back from the tile floor.

The phone rang, and Lee Ann pushed herself up. Charlie watched her sculpted body as she made her way to the kitchen phone. After she answered, almost on cue, she started to cry.

* * *

Jerri Johnson caught just a glimpse of Dolph Martinez as she entered the San Antonio Police Department downtown station. She saw Dolph's graying head, saw his start-up beer belly, saw his sad eyes, and then saw his smile as he recognized her. Dolph had yet to compromise with, surrender to, or ease into his age. He was no longer a "pretty boy," which his mother and certain Ojinaga whores called him, but he sometimes tried to maintain the image. For a while Jerri had suspected him of dying his hair, but thick grey strands were now visible on that once black mop.

Dolph's chest and legs were still powerful, so he pulled away from the two San Antonio policemen who seemed to be escorting him. Behind Dolph were Pepper, Pooter, Walter Boone, and even more police officers. Jerri wished that she had timed it so that she missed Dolph. With his friends to encourage him, he had no doubt argued with the cops. Dolph had this indignant streak due to his inability to tolerate indifference, intolerance, or ineffectiveness in officialdom.

Jerri told herself to duck her head and keep walking to avoid Dolph's pleas. But she looked up as he trotted away from the policemen and up to her. At first they just sized each other up. Then Dolph looked over his shoulder at the policemen and shook his head. Dolph said, "Jerri, Jerri, you got to do something. This just smells really bad."

Jerri looked at him and felt herself sigh. "Dolph, I knew you'd start trouble, but why so soon?"

"Come on," Dolph said. "I'm not that much trouble. And I'm right. I mean, it's just too coincidental."

"Dolph, Dolph," Jerri said. "Catch your breath. Or at least let me catch mine. I got a phone call thirty minutes ago. I don't even know what I'm supposed to know."

Jerri watched the twin domes of Walter and Pooter come up behind Dolph. From the rear, limping, but ducking under people or stepping around them, Pepper broke through the clump of police and onlookers. He stepped up to Dolph and turned to face the policemen. "I thought your job was to listen to us, not to tell us what we saw."

Dolph turned his back to the policemen. "So Oscar is dead, and . . ." As Dolph was about to finish, one of the policemen tugged at his elbow. Dolph jerked his elbow away. "Look," Dolph said to the policemen. "Until I'm arrested, charged, shot, slapped with your gat, or beaten, I'm still an innocent citizen doing the state a favor by testifying. So just give me some space." Pepper squared his shoulders, ready to start swinging. Walter and Pooter's two bald heads, swung almost in unison, to read the situation.

"Sir," the officer said. "We'd just like you to go home. Let us complete the investigation."

"If I let you take the investigation, you're going to take the easy way out and miss the bad guys." Jerri pitied the two overworked San Antonio detectives trying to keep Dolph and Pepper from doing their job for them.

Dolph turned his attention to Jerri. He puffed out his chest. It still did stick out farther than his belly. "Jerri, Jerri, when something is just so cut and dried, when it is just too easy, when fate and circumstance seemingly conspire to give a deep insight, when God talks . . ."

"Sir," the policeman said to disrupt Dolph's sentence.

"'Sir,' to you too," Pepper said.

Dolph gave the cop a quick glance, then turned to Jerri, "When all that happens, when it all seems so right and clear, we just have to know it's wrong."

"So right is wrong. Is that what you're telling me, Dolph?" Jerri asked.

"We have an investigative team," the policeman said.

"Yeah, but do they want to shovel the shit?" Dolph asked over his shoulder.

"You got a big shovel?" Pepper asked. The policeman hung his head. Other police started to close in.

Dolph stared at Jerri, and his sad eyes begged her before his words did. "Jerri, I mean holy good goddamn, Oscar mentioned his wife and the lawnboy, then poof, seconds later, Oscar's dead, the lawn boy's holding the smoking gun and admitting he did the crime, and Pepper, Pooter, Walter, and I are repeating the obvious: that when you smell a turd . . . ."

23

Jerri felt her shoulders sag. "Please, Dolph. I just got here. Coincidence is not illegal."

"When coincidence is just so obvious, then there's usually something behind it besides coincidence," Dolph said.

"So far, from what you've said, Oscar Montalvo planned a suicide just to frame another guy," Jerri said and smiled at the policeman. With his mind running away with him, Dolph was hurting the case. Jerri decided to shut him up.

Walter said from behind Dolph, "An ingenious plan, but I'm thinking that Oscar wasn't the suicidal type." Jerri could protect the case from Dolph but not from the combined smart-assed comments of Dolph, Pepper, and Walter.

Walter's and Pooter's eyes pleaded. Pepper said, "We're the good guys, Jerri."

Jerri took a step backward to put space between Dolph and her. She was rescued by young detective Jacob Simpson working on this, his first case. Jerri knew he wouldn't last. Oscar Montalvo, the doctor, and his brother Charlie were too important for rookie detection. Jerri almost heard the rip when she tore herself away from Dolph and his friends as she followed Simpson into the bowels of the police station, where he began to tell her about the trouble her friends had caused. They seemed "arrogant," Simpson said. They seemed to think that they knew more about law enforcement then the San Antonio Police Department. Jerri Johnson nodded and didn't even turn her face to the young detective as she told him, "Dolph Martinez is a highly decorated and promoted border patrol agent. He's got a master's degree in history. He's been shot and nearly killed twice. He's caught and prosecuted criminals on both sides of the border. And he once busted his friend Pepper. He probably knows about as much as the entire San Antonio Police Department." He was also responsible, in some fatalistic way, for the violence that caught him. And his fate had started to take its toll on him: he wasn't what he used to be. Dolph was content now to duck, but if he got a cause, he wouldn't let it go. She did not tell this to Jacob Simpson.

Simpson led Jerri to the door of the interrogation room. Waiting for her was one of the brightest and most ambitious young lawyers in San

Antonio, Rodney Lee. Rodney Lee grew up on the Eastside, the black area. An academic rather than an athletic star, Rodney used an athlete's determination to get through college and law school so that he could return to town as the defender and savior of his people. He played the role well and got the approval of white politicians.

"Jerri, Jerri, so glad to see you again!" Rodney Lee, in his impeccably tailored suit with the bright lavender tie, hugged Jerri. "I want you to hear this. You're my investigator, so I want you to hear my client firsthand."

"The San Antonio Police Department has an investigation ongoing," Detective Jacob Simpson said.

"And a fine job they are doing," Rodney Lee said, reached into his pocket, pulled out a card, and pressed it into Simpson's hand. "I am going to rely upon your support, but I would like to do some background checks, maybe some interviews, talk to witnesses, so that's why I always retain Ms. Johnson's expert services."

"I see," Detective Jacob Simpson said.

"And you of course know that I am on the City Council, and I support the Police Department without question. And I hope you'll remember that if I happen to run for mayor next year." Jerri tugged on Rodney Lee's jacket to stop his speech. Rodney shook Detective Simpson's hand once more, then opened the door to the interrogation room. Simpson tried to step in, but Rodney blocked his way. "Now, I'm sure that you are aware, Detective Simpson, that a client and lawyer's meetings are private."

"That's not exactly right," Simpson said.

"A little privacy, please. We all have the same interest: to get the truth and protect the innocent. Ms. Johnson," Rodney said and held the door open for Jerri. Beside him in his expensive suit, Jerri felt as if she had bought her suit at Wal-Mart. She had graduated from khakis and tennis shoes to high-heels and suits. When depositions, testimonies, and meetings with corporate and wealthy clients took over from chasing bail jumpers through windows, Jerri went to a fashion consultant specializing in inexpensive business wear for middle-aged business women. During her khaki and tennis shoe days, Jerri had lost all fashion sense. There was still money to be made from bail jumpers and petty criminals, but that's why Jerri hired Dolph Martinez (and his part-time, amateur crew—Pepper,

Pooter, and Walter) and two other operatives. But looking at Rodney Lee and feeling the ache in her arches work up her calves to her knees, she wished for khakis and tennis shoes. It had been a busy day in front of proper clients and proper legal testimony. Her hose, her suit jacket, her tight skirt were biting her.

Rodney took off his jacket and draped it around a chair. So Jerri did likewise. At the other end of the table slumped the lawn boy, Ramón Burgiaga. Rodney's grin lit up his face, but it was a lawyer's grin, not an honest one. Something was going on behind that grin. "Well, my good man, I'm your lawyer."

Ramón was a cliché, just what the romance novels said he should be. He was almost too pretty, certainly too pretty to make his living at physical labor. His hair hung down in waves, no doubt an expensive haircut. His chest and biceps muscles were taut, making his gimme T-shirt stretch against its seams. Under the sleeve of the T-shirt on his left arm was the standard barbed wire tattoo. Peering out from under the right sleeve was an Aztec chieftain in three colors. Maybe, Jerri thought, this time, coincidence was right.

"Mr. Burgiaga," Rodney began again. "I'm you're lawyer, Rodney Lee."

Rodney walked to Ramón, stuck out his hand, and even while he was shaking Rodney's hand, Ramón said, "I ain't got a lawyer."

"In this country, you have to have a lawyer. So the court will appoint you a lawyer, but you don't need the court to appoint you a lawyer because I'm representing you."

"I don't need a lawyer. I did it. I told them what I did."

"Yes, but you were probably under duress. You're probably still under duress." Rodney paced the room in his shirt sleeves while his mind worked inside his slick, coffee-colored, shaved pate. Ramón shifted his eyes from Rodney to Jerri. She knew he was trying to intimidate her with that gaze. Out of his environment, out of his league, he knew he couldn't match wits with Rodney, so he figured he could intimidate a woman. Jerri accepted his gaze and returned it. She had dealt with the intimidation, the stares, the muttered comments, the patronizing consolations—on both sides of the law—all of her career.

Jerri made herself smile at Ramón. She was tempted to wink. Jerri had started out the wife of an artist, but Royce drifted toward his art and away from her. Then as a graduate student in literature, she met the first great romantic love of her life, Vincent Fuentes. Without Fuentes in her life, she would probably have become an English teacher, say in junior high, standing in front of grape-gum-smelling kids, instead of gazing at murder suspects. Thanks to Fuentes' well-connected gangster father, Palo, Jerri put a halt to her literary ambitions and worked both sides of the law, helping illegals into the country while chasing bail jumpers, who were sometimes her former clients. Tracked down by police on both sides of the border, Vincent Fuentes, out of desperation, surrendered on the Texas side to a lone Border Patrolman: Dolph Martinez. When Dolph wouldn't arrest him for American crimes but only take him to a detention station to be sent back to Mexico, Vincent Fuentes shot himself through the head with a dainty .22.

Jerri pulled her eyes away from Ramón's gaze to see Rodney stop, put his hands on his hips, and look at Ramón with his locked gaze on Jerri. "This is my associate, Jerri Johnson. She's the finest investigator in the city. She's here to listen in. She'll do some checking into the case." Rodney pulled his hands up in front of his face. Slowly and meticulously, while looking just over his fingertips, he brought his fingertips together.

Jerri's eyes swung from Ramón to Rodney. She had sat through several criminal law classes at St. Mary's University. She had been invited back by several professors. She could probably have passed the bar without ever having completed law school. She was probably as good a lawyer as Rodney, but she was still and always would be an investigator. Jerri let the lawyer part of her take over. "Mr. Burgiaga, I'm only an observer here. But what I observe is that this state will try to inject you or send you to prison for the rest of your life in order to fill its quota of deaths and sentences—because you are basically an insignificant man who killed a significant man. And the only hope you have is Mr. Rodney Lee here." Rodney nodded at Jerri.

"I don't need a lawyer," Ramón said.

"Oh, you need a lawyer," Jerri said. "The state will give you one, but he'll be worthless and won't help. But Mr. Lee is one of the finest lawyers in the city." Jerri turned to Rodney, who again nodded his head in thanks and pressed his fingertips together. "But why he should care about you is beyond me, so the long short of it is that you're getting high-priced counsel for nothing. So you should shut up and listen."

Ramón put his elbows on his knees and leaned forward toward both of them. "Look, I know what I done. He was going to kill me. He was always talking about killing me. So I just done it first."

"How?" Rodney asked. Ramón snapped his head to look at him. Rodney was starting to sweat from all his moving and arguing. Jerri could see the sweat stains under the arms of his pastel blue silk shirt. "I mean, did you just time your peeing with his or what? How did you happen to be in that restroom?"

"It ain't so hard to figure out where Oscar Montalvo is going to be. So the night before, right before closing time, I go into the restroom, put a little pistol in a plastic baggy, and drop it in the toilet tank. Big John don't check shit. So next day, I see them old men talking shit. I go into the restroom, get my gun, stick it in the back of my pants, and wait for the beer to work through Oscar Montalvo."

"So it was self-defense. You knew he was angered. You suspected that he was a danger to you. So you thought that you'd better get his ass first," Rodney talked as Ramón stared at Jerri. "Am I going too fast for you?" Rodney said, and Ramón turned his head to Rodney. "Or were you so afraid that you couldn't think straight?"

"I'm thinking straight. I did the crime, I can do the time."

"That's original," Jerri said.

"From what you are saying, then, this was pre-meditated," Rodney said. Jerri had to suppress her chuckle. From the way he talked, from the way he stuck to his rehearsed script, Ramón could not premeditate a trip to the 7-11. "Pre-meditated means that you'll get the injection," Rodney continued.

"I figure that I can take what comes. I figure I got my defense," Ramón said.

"You got yourself on a railroad car to the jail. That's where that term railroaded comes from, you know," Rodney said. "My people know a lot about being railroaded. Don't let yourself be duped."

"Aint no dupe," Ramón said. He dropped his eyes. He knew that he was outclassed, out of his league—again.

"Then come on, you're a smart guy. Don't take this rap."

"I've signed a confession."

"I can work around that."

Rodney tried to push him, to plead with him, but Ramón told the same story three more times. He said certain words, included certain incidents, giving just enough of a defense so as to avoid death. He did not look at either of them while talking so that he did not get confused. He had rehearsed and studied for this test. Dolph, Jerri knew, was right. What Ramón didn't know was that not only was he the perfect dupe for someone behind the scene but that he was a clear open-and-shut case for the San Antonio Police Department and the Bexar County prosecutors.

Finally, Rodney gave up. Stepping up, putting on his coat, he said that he would be back. Jerri pushed herself up too, and as she walked to the door that Rodney held open for her, she felt Ramón's eyes on her. She turned toward him. For a moment, before he could drop them, she held his eyes with her gaze and saw the sudden fear. He knew he wasn't that smart, that he could be duped, that he had been duped his whole life, that this might be the worst time. "Think about it, Ramón," Jerri said and walked through the door.

Chapter 3

The police station had scared Walter, so he left as fast as he could. At least it had not been the morgue—or the hospital. The hospital would have been worse. The hospital reminded Walter of the tubes, the slapping rubber gloves, the puking, the waiting for the removal of the cancer that was eating up his ass.

Walter pulled his bug spray van into the driveway of the crumbling old house that he shared with another renter. It wouldn't be Walter's house long. Because the artists in the city had made this part of town newly fashionable after seventy-five years, the property values had increased. Before too long, Walter's old-moneyed landlord would sell the house to yuppies or artist wannabes with real jobs.

Walter made his way through his dark house, flipping on lights when he could feel for them, and went straight to his bedroom. He wished that he had not seen Oscar dead. The wish was purely selfish. So to get his mind off the image that wouldn't leave his head, Walter looked at the map of Mexico on the wall of his tiny bedroom. Chihuahua City, Hermosilla, and Campeche were all circled in red. From the red circles, red lines with arrows pointed to notes tacked to the map or even on the wall outside the map's boundary. The freshest red ink was around Cancún, and from there a red line and arrow reached down toward Playa del Carmen. Walter was honing in.

Cancún was growing and had a good hospital, or so he had heard. Playa del Carmen was filling with Americans and Europeans. Dependent on tourism and retirees, the locals dared not hurt the outsiders. At first the desert had appealed to Walter, then the Pacific coast. But now the idea of a Caribbean breeze, humidity, low jungle, and Mayan history appealed. He knew a guy, who knew a guy in Houston. He had the name of a condo complex. He had put down a payment. He had gathered his money close to him.

Walter reached out to touch the map. You can't help but die alone, he thought, as the image of dead Oscar crept around in his head. But still, you could find some comfort before you died, someone to acknowledge that you had lived, preferably on your own terms, someone to leave your last thoughts, ramblings, or screams to. He would have preferred that that someone be Sarah Boone, wife number one, the woman he gave his name to, the name she kept and that became a simple, Anglo-sounding trademark, Sarah Boone, Chainsaw Artist. Her carvings were known all through the American southwest. But Sarah was still busy in her world of scenic locales, chic decorations for the tasteless rich, publicity, and business. She wouldn't go to a Mexican Caribbean town.

Wife number two didn't speak to Walter, and he tried not even to remember her. Because of her political correctness, her polite, socially accepted, feminist endorsed radicalism, Walter had intentionally dropped down several societal rungs. While still with Claudia, he had let his technical writing business go to pot and had become a bug sprayer. Now he planned on becoming a bum on a Mexican beach. He just needed someone to go with him.

There were the starlets and secretaries in Hollywood. He especially recalled. Traci Miller, the secretary who had helped him revise his Hollywood script, *The Circles of Hell*, a screen version of Dante's Inferno, one last time before it fell finally into the hell of forgotten Hollywood scripts. Traci was probably a Hollywood executive by now. No other names came to him. He had squandered his fortune and his marriage to Sarah in Hollywood. Now all he had to show for his good times were flickering images, like an old, worn print of a thirties black and white movie, of the faces, legs, breasts, and asses of women whose names he couldn't remember. But that was something. That was a good enough accounting of his life—despite the loss of Sarah. He didn't care about the money he had lost.

Walter got up from his desk and walked to his bed. His feet caught on a pile dirty clothes. He sniffed. He needed to wash some of the bug-spraying clothes that he had shucked off when he came home really drunk two nights before. The lousy gamblers, the snake-bit losers, the people with poor teeth but rich stories, Walter's folks, were dying out. They were a generation or two behind this padded, pampered, pussified generation. Walter figured his type of folks still existed in Mexico.

So Big John's, for Walter Boone, was church. He worshiped there. He was there first. And now the city was going to destroy Big John's to make the river pretty for tourists.

Walter was making himself sad. So he walked to his kitchen, got a glass and some ice, looked for a bottle, couldn't find it, and finally located some scotch on the living room coffee table. He sniffed. His room smelled like old fast food and bug spray. With his scotch on the rocks, he went to his boom box and pushed a button to set Willie Nelson to singing "You Were Always on My Mind." Walter was lost in his memories. He couldn't shake them. Or maybe, they wouldn't let him go.

When Walter moved out of the yuppie house over in the King Williams area, he had found one-half of a small sub-divided house built in the late twenties. It was a poor neighborhood just south of downtown. But the yuppie puppies followed Walter there and turned the whole area into a cheap art and vendors' paradise. Like South Congress in Austin, South Town in San Antonio became the funky avant-garde area. The art here, appropriately Hispanic, was a notch in prestige above Sarah's chainsaw sculptors and notch below making any money.

Walter turned Willie down and walked back into his bedroom. He stared at his map. Mexico would happen. Mexico was a conviction. In a way, he was lucky. Unlike Oscar, he could see it coming. He knew it was coming. He had saved some money, uncharacteristically, just enough years to live as a Romantic until he died.

Walter hoped to go in his sleep without an exploding brain or heart. But until he did go, he wanted some company. He needed his own kind around him. The answer, obviously, whether he liked it or not, was a friend, not a lover or wife or ex-wife or ex-lover, to accompany him to Mexico. Oscar was dead. Pepper Cleburne had found him a woman that had deluded him into thinking that she would last. Pooter Elam was still listening to some sort of sonar sent out from his past. The only one who might really go with him was Dolph Martinez.

Scotch, old man sentimentality, and Willie Nelson were sending Walter into the worst kind of old man drunk. He felt like crying. The slap of the doctor's rubber glove on his wrist was what he remembered, but it was not at all the worst part, nor was the operation. The chemotherapy was the worst. Walter had endured it, but because of it, or because of something he had contracted in his youth, his heart was damaged. He could wait around in this pussified country for a new heart, or he could join some compatriots in Mexico for what time he had left. Walter patted the pacemaker tucked into the flap in his left shoulder. His liver had survived; his prostate was enlarged but safe; his ass was cancer free; but his heart had only so many ticks left.

* * *

Jerri Johnson and Rodney Lee made it through the police station and out the door before Jerri demanded Rodney's story. "What are you thinking?"

"Too many ears here," Rodney said. Both were parked in lots behind City Hall. So they walked east in the early evening haze to Military Plaza, the gulf breeze picking up, the street lights coming on down Dolorosa. They sat on a park bench behind City Hall. Across Dolorosa was Jerri's office, Sam's Investigating and Security Services. Before her building finally got bought and rebuilt according to the somewhat historically accurate building codes, it was the run down, crumbling home of Sam's Bail Bonds and Investigating Services. She had been Sam Ford's legs. He was too fat to move from behind his desk. Eventually Sam made her a partner, mostly so that she could help share the losses rather than the profits. Sam retired and left the business to Jerri, and after Joe Parr's death, she became serious about it. She got a subchapter S corporate ranking for taxes. She bought as many state-of-the-art computers and programs as she could afford, hired a web designer once a year to give her web page bells and whistles, hired three full-time investigators (including Dolph), and six part-timers. She still specialized in bail jumpers, but now she herself worked doing trial investigations for some of the most prominent attorneys in town. "Why on earth do you want to defend that poor, lost soul?" Jerri asked Rodney Lee.

"Can't you see the logic?" Tourists were making their ways to the Mexican Market or down Commerce or Market to the river and the Alamo. "Pretty night," Rodney said. The early evening light taunted Jerri. On the other side of City Hall, in Military Plaza with the old men and the pigeons, on the steps, she had re-met Vincent Fuentes. He whispered and beguiled and led her to risking her life and her career. She knew how Ramón felt. During that escapade, she had seen another poor man—a laborer, a Mexican national over his head and crossing people smarter and more powerful than he—fall when slugs from an automatic weapon knocked him backward over her balcony railing and onto the hood of her S.U.V. Later still, on those steps, Joe Parr came to her to apologize for following her and using her to catch Fuentes, and she married the tall, easy Texas Ranger. She held Joe Parr's hand and watched him die after several slugs from an automatic weapon cut across his body as he was fetching the morning newspaper. "Jerri, you're zoning out on me," Rodney said.

Jerri shook her mind without shaking her head. "No, I see no logic in what you are doing. Let some public defender take the job. Ramón is meat. He's too easy. And somebody knows that."

Rodney slid his arms out of his finely tailored jacket to begin his argument. "And that's the logic exactly. He's cooked. He's condemned goods. But Rodney Lee, son of the Eastside, promising young black city councilman, the next great black hope, puts aside career and ambition, to seek justice, to fight unfairness. It's just the thing to get me elected mayor."

"You call that logic?"

"It's got a loop or two."

"You really think that anybody will believe that you put aside career or ambition."

"Not everybody knows me as well as you do."

"I should have figured."

"And this is where you come in."

"I'm still having a little trouble following the first part."

"Just think if I can get him off."

35

"You have lost your reasoning."

"Obviously, he's rehearsed his testimony. Obviously something else is going on here. Somebody paid him. Somebody knows something. Somebody with more brains and money than shit hook Ramón cooked this up."

"Oh really. You think so? Is this where I come in?"

"So I, 'young hot shot lawyer, defender of justice, decent unambitious mayoral candidate,' quote, finds out who. That's where you come in. You find out what happened. You find the who.'"

Jerri crossed her legs, felt the pleasant April night surround her. The night air and San Antonio's water, at least, were pure. Diluted, mixed Rodney started again: "If you can find out the truth, then I can shove it in front of Ramón's nose. Then he will change his story. And I win the case."

"You don't trust the San Antonio Police to find the truth?"

"They're hampered by the legal truth, by what will hold up in court. You aren't. You just find out the truth. I don't need a conviction of the guilty people, just acquittal, or at least a good showing for Ramón. In fact, if I can just get sympathy for him if he is convicted . . ."

"Oh my," Jerri said and leaned back on the bench. "It was a lot simpler and easier when I was finding bail jumpers."

"But look at what you've made of yourself. You could try this case as good as I could. In fact, I want you with me. Be seen around me, in the courtroom. Get yourself recognized."

"In other words, do most of the work for you."

"Well, yeah, but you got help too. Get your team on it. Dolph seems to be a good sort." Rodney raised his hands and pressed his fingertips together. "Just remember my political image is in your hands. Hell, maybe my campaign theme is in our hands. Rodney Lee, integrity not politics.'"

"How about I come up with a few bumper stickers for you?"

"Why I'm just what the city needs, a black Henry Cisneros. Handsome black man, ready to defend his people by helping rich white people bring business and progress to town."

"You saw what happened to Cisneros."

"Won't happen to me," Rodney looked sternly at Jerri, as though warning her, then he smiled, "I got no mistress."

36

"So you think San Antonio is ready for its first black mayor?"

"I can be more than black. San Antonio is ready for me."

"Do you think San Antonio is ready for its first gay mayor?"

"That little fact needs to stay in the closet."

* * *

When Pooter showed up an hour late, the manager cussed, and the red-headed bartender that Pooter was supposed to relieve jutted out her bottom lip and smeared lipstick over her top lip. Normally he worked days, six days a week, but he had offered to take the night shift for Jolene. He let Jolene pout and fuss at him about the expensive baby sitter and the manager cuss him for losing money—before he told them he had witnessed the murder of a friend. That news shushed them. Pooter kept his smile to himself.

He had long since learned to hide what emotions he could. He liked to let his mind wander where it might. And a blank face, Pooter knew, hid a wandering mind. A wandering mind that stumbled across amusements and truths was why Pooter had no ambitions beyond being a bartender. Wiping Cappy's bright wooden bar that reflected the requisite brass and sunshine allowed Pooter both to talk to the few afternoon customers and let his mind wander. Boredom was not a problem for Pooter.

The job that Pepper had gotten for him was the perfect job for Pooter. Cappy's bar was never busy. The clientele was mostly interested in eating and not drinking, so Pooter rarely had to threaten anybody or cut some one off. They had interesting stories when they cared to talk to Pooter, and he in turn could weigh their stories in his wandering mind and give advice. Several folks even showed up during his shifts just so they could talk to him.

The bar was compact, neat, organized. Nothing got in the way. It was functional, just like Pooter's apartment. He never kept too many clothes or goods. He could move quickly. His apartment was a tiny one bedroom with a balcony overlooking a courtyard. On his balcony he had honey-suckle growing, and it attracted hummingbirds, butterflies, and bees. With daylight savings time coming on, Pooter, after work, could sit on his balcony in his in the old fifties-style complex on Austin Highway, an area and a complex that the bustling city had forgotten, and enjoy the last moments of daylight while he looked at the flying critters that hovered around his honeysuckle. He had once seen hummingbirds fight to the death. One gored another and left the tiny body on Pooter's balcony. Pooter held the still warm body and tried to give some comfort to the dying bird.

As he wiped down the bar, a movement that had become nearly instinctual for him, he let himself smile at the customers in the restaurant. Some actually smiled back. But guilt hit him. He should feel sorry for poor Oscar or at least think about him or remember him.

Oscar's hard face seemed sculpted by worry. The salt-and-pepper hair that hung over his forehead made his face seemed to droop. His death erased the drooping face and worry and replaced it with a blank expression. Oscar almost looked happier in his death mask. Pooter's remembering Oscar was disrupted when a man in a suit came up to the bar, and Pooter straightened to take the man's order. As he made the cosmopolitan and the man looked over his shoulder at the date he was trying to impress, Pooter recalled the image of Oscar lying in dried piss and fresh blood and the young Mexican kid trembling as he conspicuously held the gun. Oscar's seemed like a prepaid funeral, only someone other than Oscar had made the payments.

As the man took the drinks back to his date, Pooter knew that Dolph was right. The truth was deeper. Unlike Dolph, Pooter distrusted the "truth." He would leave truth to real philosophers, the kind you actually read, the kind who had been dead for awhile. Like Joan Phelan, Pepper's new girl (Pooter's old girl), Dolph thought that he could tease some truth out of all the manipulation and absurdity around them. And when he couldn't, like Joan, Dolph would slowly implode. That's when Joan turned to drink. That's when Dolph became morose—or mean. Hence, Pooter suspected that Dolph would soon be calling on him for muscle.

Pooter's mind went back to a few months before. Dolph had thought that a Taser might be a good hand weapon for Sam's Investigating Services. Pooter and Pepper helped him come up with the idea at Big John's. So Pooter was partially responsible for the Taser. After Dolph filled out the proper forms, got a package in the mail, and showed the new toy to Jerri, Rodney Lee suggested that, in order to help testimony in court as to the abilities and the non-lethal nature of the weapon, it be should tested on someone who could testify what it was like to be shot by a Taser. Dolph and his buddies distrusted Rodney's advice, but Dolph was determined to make the case for his Taser. "How bad could it be?" he asked them around the picnic table at Big John's. Pooter suspected not just that shooting Dolph with the Taser could be bad, but that the whole idea of having a Taser could be bad.

So, the next day, instead of gathering at Big John's; Pooter, Walter, Pepper, and Dolph gathered at Mission Park, drove across the dam, and stopped at two of the shaded picnic tables. Dolph begged his companions to shoot him with the Taser and to record its effect on him. They vehemently refused. What kind of person could deliberately shoot a buddy, even if it was just to stun him? Finally, Pepper agreed to shoot him.

Dolph paced some six or seven feet away from his friends, puffed out his chest like he was facing a firing squad, and gave the command to fire. Before Pepper could squeeze the trigger, Dolph started yelling for him to wait. He begged Pepper not to hit him in the face, to aim for his chest. Dolph paced back out in front of them, Pepper aimed the Taser, but Dolph again began to yell for him to wait. Pepper asked what now. Dolph said that he just had to steady himself.

Pooter couldn't stand the whole scene. He stepped in front of Pepper and volunteered to be the guinea pig. He was bigger, he said. Walter suggested that they shoot a tree and lie about the results. Dolph again stuck out his chest, ready for the barbs and the electricity, but again he hesitated. And Pooter guessed that Dolph's old memories of the backpacker's bullet tearing through his guts and the bigger bullet breaking his shoulder darted through his mind the way the Taser's jolt of electricity was about to. Pooter yelled for Pepper to stop again. Pooter walked to the car and pulled an ice chest out of the car, and each one of them drank a beer.

When Pepper finally shot Dolph, Pooter and Walter watched as Dolph writhed, twitched, and slobbered. Pepper turned his head away from his friend.

Unfortunately, a Park Ranger had watched. He called 911, and before

Dolph could stop writhing, slobbering, cramping, and sizzling from the inside out, a San Antonio cop who happened to be parked right down the drive having a sandwich and watching the river flow past was holding a pistol on Pepper, Pooter, and Walter. The lingering voltage in Dolph's brain kept him from making words. With his hands behind his head, Pooter thought that that must be the worst part. Suddenly you didn't have a mind; you were just poorly working body parts, robbed of humanness. Dolph forced himself to talk, tried to explain, but the cop had no part of it. Jerri and Rodney Lee had to come to the police station to get them from going to jail.

Pooter came back from memory to find himself wiping the bar. Dolph, Pooter knew, was just itching to use the Taser on someone else. If only Dolph could have been better at finding truth instead of pondering mysteries, he might have been able to solve the mystery or Oscar's death, and then Dolph wouldn't be aiming a Taser at people.

* * *

"Why the hell is it we attract criminal activity?" Pepper asked Dolph as they scooped scrambled eggs laced with bacon and pico de gallo into their mouths.

"I'd say it's worse than that. We seem to get involved watching friends get killed," Dolph said and rolled a warm corn tortilla in one hand, between two fingers, until it was nearly as thin as a straw, like the old Mexicans did.

"Don't get morbid," Pepper said.

"I could have said we caused several friends to get killed."

"Okay, now you're morbid," Pepper said.

Pepper had whipped up the eggs out of instinct, expectation, hunger, and skill. He micro-waved the bacon, sliced an onion and a tomato, got some butter smelling slightly burned, then dumped it all in a pan and began stirring. It was a simple recipe he had learned cooking for the prisoners while he was doing his time. After Pepper made the batch of eggs, he looked back over at his shoulder at Joan Phelan, standing in the kitchen, looking up from her drink at him.

Pepper washed down his scoop of eggs with a swallow of beer. Joan had also bought a twelve pack and a bottle of tequila to go with the eggs. They had come out of the police station, Pepper had called Joan, and they all met at Pepper's house. The eggs were one of those meals that would have tasted good if it were tire rubber and ketchup. Pepper and Dolph had missed dinner and in the anger and frustration, hadn't even noticed, so now, with calm, the matters of the stomach returned, and they shoveled the eggs like long timers, like some of the guys Pepper met in prison, guys wanting some real food to cure the constant constipation. Pepper stopped himself from remembering. "I wish things would just stop happening," he said.

"It's a blessing to live in exciting times," Dolph said

"I'd think it'd be more blessed in times when nothing happens. You got yours and nothing happens to it," Pepper said. "But I guess those times don't happen too often. . . . At least not to the likes of us."

Joan Phelan walked in from the kitchen with her shot of expensive sipping tequila poised just below her lips. She looked at Pepper and Dolph, shifted her eyes to her drink, and downed it. She had had a drinking problem. Pooter had helped pull her out of it. Pepper hoped that he wasn't kick-starting it.

She was an attractive woman, especially for Pepper, who knew he was ugly. Joan was the best he could ever hope for. But Pepper figured she was with him because she had some hurt that you could see once in a while when she just let her shoulders slump. Sure she had a past, had a history. Who at their age didn't? But, though Pepper saw no fault in her that he couldn't excuse or accommodate, he sometimes thought that she looked like she itched under her own skin. "You two may not live like normal human beings, but I have to go to work," Joan said.

"Hell, don't kid me," Pepper said, chewing on eggs. "You—like ol' Dolph here was—are on the state teat. Don't give us that working shit."

Pepper watched Joan as she advanced toward him, ignoring Dolph. To Pepper she had that look that certain women get that make you just want to know more. Call it pheromones. Dolph could resist. Pepper, to his credit, couldn't. Joan made his teeth itch.

Joan got to Pepper and kissed him, his mouth full of eggs. "You two reprobates eat your eggs and clean up after yourselves. Though I have this

41

tickle in my mind and a little lower that makes me want to stay, I'm going home to get some sleep and to be responsible. Responsibility is something that we all need to work on—especially you two." She kissed Pepper again, and blew Dolph a kiss. "You know your friend Oscar. Does he have a brother named Charlie?"

They both answered "yes" in unison. "Yeah, Charlie Montalvo. I dated him," she said. Both Dolph and Pepper swung their heads toward her. "Of course he was well before you," she winked at Pepper. "And no match for you." Pepper was particularly glad that she added that part. "Charming guy, but peculiar," she added.

"So what did you think of him?" Dolph asked.

"I think I did him because I felt sorry for him. But that can only take you so far."

"Don't you just got to love her?" Pepper said. He was beginning to feel that tickle too.

Smiling, turning her back to them, shaking her hips under her blue denim skirt, she walked out the front door and left them to their eggs and liquor. "Goddamn, now you tell me why I shouldn't go charging out that door and grab her and pull her back in here," Pepper said.

"Cause you're old, and she might kick your ass."

"Dolph, maybe I was meant to fuck up with that whole litter of previous wives and lovers just so I could get this one."

"And how many times, for both of us, did the one who made us forget the previous litter leave us with our hands shaking the bourbon out of our glasses?"

"But this one is different."

"I wouldn't ask too much of her—or yourself."

Pepper was tired of listening to Dolph, "Why do you always have to sprinkle mouse turds on my cake?"

"To protect myself from having to rescue your sorry ass."

"Eat your eggs. We're supposed to be in mourning over Oscar."

"Well, first off, we go see his daughter and straighten her out."

Pepper downed a shot of tequila, chased it with beer, then with eggs. "Oh shit, Dolph, I can hear it in your voice. You're getting that Dolph crusader tone. Crying children, hurt old ladies, crazy people with grand causes—all those things twist you up." A Dolph crusade had sent Pepper to prison. He had done the crime, but crusader Dolph just had to right wrongs. Then a pretty lady, Jerri Johnson, sent Dolph on another crusade, and Pepper, just out of prison, got most of his knee shot off. Then to protect all of them, because he was the only one who had the nerve and the will to do it, he shot Reynaldo Luna in the head, execution style. Pepper thought that he might have nightmares after that little adventure. But it was dark; he couldn't see much blood; so he just tucked the image in the back of his mind and didn't think about it too often—except when Dolph got his crusade look.

"I'm just saying . . ." Dolph said.

"Maybe, your just saying is what gives us a propensity toward criminal activity."

"I wasn't the one smuggled those weird-ass drugs into the country."

Pepper swallowed hard. Dolph's ducking eyes did the apologizing. Pepper pointed his fork at Dolph. "That's not what I'm talking about. Don't bring that up. That was for a good noble cause."

"The cause was fixing your swimming pool so you could make your old hot springs cabins into your wet dream idea of a resort." Dolph just couldn't leave any point alone.

"That was a noble cause, and it turns out I was right. Look at what the billionaire fuckers and the state are doing out in Big Bend. There's parks and resorts and art galleries." Bits of scrambled eggs were flying off of Pepper's fork as he slashed it through the air.

"Well, I'm just saying that I work out of moral imperative, so I think that we need to straighten out Oscar's daughter so as to honor his last desires. His wife is another case. She's probably somehow responsible for killing him and will probably get away with it."

There it was, moral. Pepper was getting scared. He didn't want to lose anymore body parts because of Dolph's moral whims. "I sense an indignant tone. I got a rebuilt knee, you got wounds in your gut and your shoulder that all resulted from that indignant tone. You got to let things lie."

"You gonna let poor Oscar lie?"

"No."

43

"Well, then, what do you intend to do?"

"I guess I plan to listen to your goddamn crazy scheme because some fucking kitty is stuck in a tree. And then I'm gonnna hope it don't come back to bite one or both of us in the ass." Pepper smiled. And Dolph poured each of them a shot of tequila. "But do me a favor. Don't listen to all them voices in your head. Shut 'em off and down. Then see what you decide. Make this crusade a little more reasonable. Don't let dead people's voices advise you."

"I won't bring up certain of your past errors, so don't you remind me of my quirks."

"Your quirks have gotten me shot and arrested and imprisoned. Let it go." Dolph could not look at Pepper, could not let go. "Don't turn into spooky Dolph. Don't turn into Sister Quinn."

"Live with it, huh?"

"Injustice is just the natural order of things."

"Maybe so, but we can fix some things."

"Or fuck 'em up."

They both stared at their drinks. "Does that crazy nun Sister Quinn, Vincent Fuentes, or poor ol' dead Joe Parr still whisper sweet nothings inside your head?"

"They're usually laughing at me." Dolph downed his tequila. "You're a lucky man to have found a real woman you can adjust to."

"I know the odds ain't good, given my nature. But I plan to follow this one through."

"You think you can stand it if it turns out bad?"

"I'm hoping I had enough practice to have gotten used to it."

Dolph walked out of Pepper's 50s—style—modern house a little after midnight, leaving the bottle of tequila about half full. After Pooter shut the door, he went back to his tequila. He had just enough tequila to make him nostalgic. Yet he still wanted to make sense of where he was and how he got there.

When Dolph and Pepper first came to San Antonio from the wilds of the Big Bend area, they were both spooked. It was too big, too modern, too Anglo. So both of them rented apartments and drifted around the city, learning its layout and history. They both drifted to the underdeveloped, forgotten, largely Mexican Southside. On the Southside, time had stopped somewhere around the time Pepper and Dolph had stopped changing. On the Southside, they could hear Spanish, eat barbacoa made at mom and pop diners, make deals with people who didn't worry about city ordinances or improvements. It was as close as they could come to what they had run away from.

Pepper bought this house on an island that the San Antonio River makes just before it gets to Southeast Military Highway. If he had to, Pepper could walk to Big John's. That is how they found Big John's Ice house walking and looking around. They kept going back to Big John's because the patrons seemed like the folks they had left. And now Oscar Montalvo was dead.

Pepper peered into his shot glass and smiled to himself. Danger lurked there in that glass. He gulped it down anyway and remembered Dolph's Taser. When he shot Dolph with it, just for practice, he felt really bad for himself and Dolph, but then shooting Dolph felt kind of good too.

* * *

After talking with Rodney Lee, Jerri stopped at the Nix Hosptial just before visitor hours ended. She found Palo asleep. She opened the blinds and let in a beam of light. Palo's eyes flickered like the monitor to his side. He smiled from his half consciousness. "Jerri?" he muttered before he could even see her.

"It's me, Palo," Jerri said.

"I get mixed up now if I am dreaming or really waking up. It don't really matter, I guess."

"I just dropped by to say good-night," Jerri said.

"You don't have to," Palo said with a low growl accompanying the words out of his throat.

"I have another case, Palo," Jerri said and bent over her old friend, who should have been her father-in-law or yes, more appropriately, her spiritual father. His corruption and his will had tainted Jerri. He had made her more than her real parents.

"Tell me about the case," Palo said. When he got the words out, he started breathing heavily. "Old people like to talk about weather, about

45

their sicknesses, about the times they shit. I like to hear about your cases."

"A yard boy killed his employer because the employer threatened to kill him. Evidently he and the doctor employer's wife were sleeping together."

"They sound stupid," Palo said.

"They don't seem to be," Jerri said.

"Then somebody is lying," Palo said. He breathed in, tried to cough.

Jerri leaned back over him, "Don't worry about the case."

Palo nodded. With his eyes shut, he said, "Thank you for watching me like this. It's good to have someone watch you when you have to die."

Jerri fought herself. She wanted to cry yet cuss him. Before she was through pining and holding down her indignation and sorrow, he was back asleep.

From the Nix Hospital, Jerri drove to the San Antonio Country Club just off of North New Braunfels. The San Antonio Country Club was what an old-style country club should be: snooty, tasteful and sophisticated, old rich, old people. The color barriers were legally gone, but membership was still mostly by invitation only. Jerri herself wasn't a member, but Sandra Beeson was. When Sandra Beeson joined the Country Club and began to associate with people who lived in a genteel world that no longer existed, she and her son, Dolph Martinez, became even more distant from each other. So, Jerri accepted the job of watching over Dolph's mother, just as she accepted the job of watching over Palo.

For a while, Dolph had even lived with his mother out in Alpine. Pepper, newly out of prison, with more delusions about resorts bubbling in his head but with more care and financial responsibility this time, started building a bed and breakfast. Sandra Beeson showed up to take care of her estranged son but ended up taking care of Pepper's bed and breakfast. She followed Dolph and Pepper to San Antonio. But she ran with the Country Club crowd, not Dolph's crowd.

Jerri pulled in under the awning, behind a Rolls Royce: a lawyer, old money, real estate. San Antonio, with a million people pushing into its metropolitan area, still did not have that many rich people. San Antonians enjoyed comfort, not wealth. Leisure was more important to them than money. Let Dallas and Houston make the big money; San Antonians would drink beer, eat Mexican food, and have their fiestas and celebrations. So not too many people had a Rolls.

Sandra Beeson appeared at the door and waved to Jerri. She turned to wave at some men who had escorted her out. Sandra Beeson had plenty of men waiting to escort her. She pulled open the passenger door to Jerri's BMW. What could Jerri say? She had some money. Her son worked with a computer firm in Dallas that survived the dot com fiasco. He had his family and life. What was she to do, save hers, Joe Parr's, and Sam's Investigating Services' money for her grandson?

Sandra curled her gown around to one side of her butt and plopped into the seat beside Jerri. "Hi, dear," Sandra said.

"How was the party?"

"A bit staid. Sometimes they intimidate themselves. Everyone was stiff."

"Why do you go to these things?"

"Why, Jerri, as you should know, as you should start to do for yourself —for the gentlemen."

"There's more to life than parties and gentlemen."

"There is?" Sandra said.

Jerri pulled around the Rolls and whisked down the long driveway to New Braunfels. "What else am I to do in my advancing years? I have time and some money, you know. . . Same as you," Sandra said.

"I wish I could take the delight that you do in these soirees."

"Oh, you could. And you should. What are you waiting for? I did that for too long. You and poor Dolph are getting old too fast."

"Well, thank you," Jerri chuckled.

"No, think about it, Jerri. You need to get out. Meet some gentleman. Why, he might not be your type, but Dolph might give up drinking beer with criminals, ex-cons, and social misfits if you would go out with him."

"You're right, he's not my type. And he works for me."

"He should be your type." Jerri didn't answer, and this conversation hung in the air between them just as it always did. "You've become a mother for him and all his misfit friends."

"Stop," Jerri said.

"No, you have. You rescue people. You rescued me. Look at what you've done for me. You've made me society. And you've rescued Dolph and all his friends. Made them solvent. Given them a purpose. But you could give Dolph back what he should have become." Sandra thought for a moment. "What I made him turn against."

"If we keep talking about this. I'm going to say something mean like I did last time."

"My lips are sealed."

Jerri went down Hildebrandt to Broadway. She glanced down the road to see Cappy's Restaurant, where Pepper or Pooter were closing down and reading receipts. She passed Incarnate Word University (the very secular Catholic school), drove uphill toward Trinity University (the very secular Presbyterian school) neither of which could Jerri or her parents ever afford when she was growing up in San Antonio. She turned into the old high-rise condominiums, among the first condos in the city, where she and Sandra lived: on the border to Alamo Heights and Olmos Park, among the San Antonio old rich.

When she pulled into her parking place, Sandra, who had remained as quiet as she could for as long as she could, said, "Thank you so much. I'll go back to driving myself once my vision becomes just a little clearer." Sandra had just had cataract surgery. When Jerri had asked why she wouldn't be coming home with the gentleman who had driven her to club, Sandra said that he couldn't stay up that late.

On the way up on the elevator, Sandra pulled a bottle of perfume out of her purse and handed it to Jerri. "It's a blend, specially made. You go to this place, and they make it special for you. Only I made this with you in mind. It's registered under your name. Thank you for taking care of me."

Jerri, the tough investigator who dealt with scum and slick lawyers, almost cried.

Sandra got out first, and Jerri continued to her top floor suite. Jerri entered, slipped out of her shoes, unzipped her skirt, let it fall, hiked up her slip, uncurled her hose, and pulled her feet out of them. She unbuttoned her blouse, shrugged, and let it fall as she went into the kitchen. All she found in the refrigerator was a pitcher of mixed margaritas and some pico de gallo in a jar. She pulled out both, grabbed a glass and a package of chips, opened her sliding glass door, and walked out onto her high balcony in her slip and bra.

She piled her late dinner onto a small table and sat down in her lawn chair. Joe Parr had liked to go out to his back yards, first his and Melba's back yard, and then his and Jerri's in his underwear and sip a beer while he felt the late night breeze, listened to late night sounds, and smelled flowers or freshly watered lawns in the night air. This was for him.

When she met him, Joe was haunted by Melba. She had died before he could make their marriage good in their old house in Alamo Heights. When he married Jerri, he made sure that he made their marriage good. When he was shot down and murdered on the driveway of their suburban house perched high up by itself way northwest of town, in the hill country, he started to haunt Jerri, and then real estate developers started moving subdivisions around Jerri. So she sold at a very good price and moved in among the old rich.

Jerri hiked her feet on her balcony railing, not caring if from way down below someone could peek up her slip at her butt, and stared at the lights of San Antonio spreading out beneath her bare feet.

* * *

On his way home, out South Presa, on to 281, then over toward Elmendorf, Dolph pondered his move from the border. The Big Bend was haunted. Jerri Johnson was a new world, a modern world, a sanctuary, the escape that Dolph had thought he had wanted the whole time he was in the Chihuahuan Desert. So he followed her. And then Pepper came, then Pooter, then his mother. They were all misfits, losers, gamblers, stuck in their ways. If they didn't watch out for each other, who would?

Dolph followed the street lights until they disappeard. Then they picked up again. Land on this side of town was relatively cheap compared to the Hill Country views and vistas on the northside. So some of the former Southsiders who had made good through their mostly blue collar jobs moved into spacious acreages in the old farming territories south of town, close to some of the original Spanish ranches and properties. Dolph's neighbors lived in old sandhills that couldn't support crops or cows but could hold a foundation for a house and grow bluebonnets in March and April. Dolph's neighbors had grown up in the city, and they wanted suburban vistas, but they knew their places were not north of town but farther south. Dolph lived here because of Jerri.

Dolph pulled his Nissan up to the gate to Jerri's property. No more trucks or SUVs for Dolph. He had sweated in one far too long during his years with the Border Patrol. He pulled the gate open and felt the tequila starting to make his head swell. Jerri wanted to be a gentlewoman rancher or farmer. She hired someone to bulldoze her property twice yearly and plant grazing grass. She did it mostly for aesthetic reasons. She wanted: cows grazing on short grass under old live oaks.

But she needed a ranch foreman, and that was where Dolph came in. He lived in the portable home that was mostly like a trailer, and he supervised the ranch. Neither Dolph nor Jerri knew anything about ranching or farming. So some of Jerri's Herefords had interbred and created deformed or retarded cows. Most of the crops failed. As foreman, Dolph took note of the retarded calves, the sickly looking cows, the limping cows and called a vet. He checked the corn and the alfalfa, and if it looked sickly or ripe, he called a neighbor to plow it under or harvest it. He read some books, talked to the Bexar County agricultural agent. Mostly he was content to watch the fat cows grazing under the live oaks. When he thought about it, it was a world that he had created, that he had come to, so he had no right to bitch about it.

Going through his home that was mostly a trailer, Dolph pulled a beer out of his refrigerator and went out the back door to the deck. He patted the pair of reading glasses bouncing off his chest. He sat in his plastic outdoor chair and watched his sleeping cows under the oaks. The foamy spray hit him in the face when he opened beer. From his years as a border patrolman, from his years living at Pepper's failed resort out in Big Bend, Dolph didn't sleep much. He thought that once he got out of the Chihuahuan Desert, he could start sleeping. But still, in this kinder, gentler, nearly urban environment, there was too much to think about. Too much to remember.

Guilt was almost automatic with memory. Like the owls whom the locals along El Camino del Rio believed were really the souls of the dead, dead souls whispered to Dolph during the nights: Vincent Fuentes, whom Dolph saw blow his brains out because he, Dolph, would not arrest him on the American side of the border; Sister Quinn, his conscience, the poor misguided nun, whom the locals believed was a curandera, who let herself get duped into smuggling guns and prescription medicine, whom Dolph arrested and then let get beaten to death by Reynaldo Luna; and Reynaldo Luna too, whom Dolph tracked down and Pepper shot in the head, Mexican execution style, while Dolph had second thoughts. It is a moral imperative to tease the logic out of seeming coincidence. God wants justice, but laws and trials and private investigators are not smooth-running machines. They are clogged by bureaucracy and social do-gooding. Logic, salvation, and justice need to be seized. But the price is high, and it's easy to fuck up. Dolph had exhausted himself trying to seize God's will out in the desert and had fucked up. He had thought San Antonio would allow him to ease himself into ease. But now Oscar Montalvo was dead. And though it was not his job to make Oscar's death as right as it could be, if not him then who?

Oscar's death was a part of the big picture, the long view. Dolph figured that he had spent so much time tracking the signs, staring at the small stuff, dust on a rock, that he had made himself myopic and thus unable to see the panorama, the big picture. Before he had even left Big Bend, he had trouble seeing the tufts of dust in a desert vista. So a couple of years back, he got laser surgery. He could see into the distance again, but he needed readers to see up close, so he kept a pair bound to a cord hanging around his neck and bouncing off his chest. Sometimes he even shared his glasses with Pepper when Pepper forgot his. Sipping his beer, Dolph hung his readers off the tip of his nose so that he could read the label on his beer bottle and then shift his eyes to peer into the dark at the shapes of cows floating through the mysterious airs of the spring night.

Chapter 4

If Jerri were to start a private investigation business from scratch, she'd buy a good computer, subscribe to every online data base that she could find, and hire a techno geek to help her with the computer. Then she'd hang out at the San Antonio Public Library and the Bexar County Courthouse, make friends, and bring coffee, candy, and gifts to all the secretaries and minor clerks. A private investigator could make a decent salary just doing computer, library, and courthouse searches for people who were too lazy, computer or bureaucratically illiterate, or too busy. Six or seven searches a day, $150-$250 a pop: Jerri did the math. But she had started prior to the big computerized databases. If she had it all to start over, she would not hire Dolph Martinez and his crew.

Dolph could run a computer, knew the library and the courthouse, was smart. But he was bored by routine. He needed a mission. He needed someone to save. Jerri and Dolph shared an intellectual bent. Both had graduate degrees. This penchant that both thought they had left behind qualified them to investigate crimes, atrocities, deceptions, adulteries, fakery, and forgeries that were real instead of literary or historical. So Jerri understood that Dolph wanted something besides the ordinary research, wanted to go beyond it to stretch and strengthen his intellectual muscles. For Dolph these were sometimes spiritual or moral muscles, which Jerri could never completely understand.

Unlike Dolph, had Jerri stayed in academics, she would have been a good administrator. She understood greater social good, appreciated the smoothly running machine, gradually came to value profit. Crusades, for Jerri, while admirable, were dangerous. So on one side of her was Rodney

53

Lee explaining how he would manipulate the judicial system to his political advantage, and on the other side was Dolph, begging her to let him find out the truth about Oscar Montalvo's murder.

Dolph was always the more complicated problem. Jerri's dealings with him were like trying to pull chewing gum from her fingers. She and Dolph had their tightly raveled pasts wrapped around them, and so they appreciated each other. No, as Dolph's mother knew, it was more than appreciation. Jerri knew that she contributed to Dolph's stickiness. So she swiveled her chair toward him. He sat across from her desk, his fingers laced, hands behind his back. Rodney Lee stared at him. Dolph's eyes shifted quickly from Rodney Lee to Jerri then back and then again, as though still tracking the signs. Dolph began slowly and succinctly: "Let me look into this."

"It's never a wise idea to have someone involved doing the investigation," Jerri answered. "Please, Dolph, don't put me in this position."

"You'll probably be called as a witness. Your testimony would be discounted," Rodney Lee interrupted. Rodney stood up from his chair. Along with Dolph, Jerri scolded Rodney with her eyes. "How can he be objective?" Rodney turned to Jerri and asked.

Dolph answered: "I put my best friend in prison. That's how I can be objective."

Dolph had what Pepper called his "spooky Dolph" look in his eyes. When Dolph listened to the voices of Sister Quinn and Vincent Fuentes that rolled around in his head, he could get dangerous. From the way his eyes slid toward Rodney without his head moving, Jerri knew that Rodney might be in danger.

"I'm fully aware . . . ," Jerri started.

"Don't blow this," Rodney said.

"Don't interrupt," Dolph said.

Joe Parr, just before he married Jerri, had listened to his dead wife Melba talking. He even let himself see her, he told Jerri. She both tormented him and comforted him, and she suggested that he pursue Jerri. After he was killed, Jerri stayed up late in their large suburban home listening for Joe's voice. But she never heard him, or he never talked. With Dolph now grown spooky, Jerri entertained the thought that perhaps those who can hear the dead know more than other people. Jerri looked across her desk at Dolph. Behind him was a replica of an 1840 map of the Republic of Texas, the one with a finger sticking up out of present-day New Mexico up the Rio Grande and into Colorado. She had bought it from Texas Parks and Wildlife as a connection to a past that she sometimes feared she might lose. "Jerri," Dolph said. "You know I can find out what happened. I already have my suspicions."

"The least it is is unethical," Jerri said. "*Foolish* is another word that comes to mind."

"Exactly," Rodney Lee said.

"That's *exactly* what I thought when Joe Parr was killed." Now Dolph was using the trump card: guilt. Everyone knew that Reynaldo Luna had gunned down Joe Parr. But no one was willing to pull him out of Mexico, and the Mexicans were not willing to extradite him. Jerri thought that seeing Reynaldo die would even things, would ease her guilt over not hearing voices in her head. So Dolph, Pepper, Jerri, Pooter, and Dolph's Mexican compatriot and her once nemesis, Henri Trujillo, tracked him down to a desert bar outside Ojinaga. Out in the desert, next to a kiln lighting their faces, Dolph had pleaded for mercy for Reynaldo. Pooter agreed. Knowing that they were already committed too far, Pepper put an end to the debate by shooting Reynaldo through the temple. Revenge didn't help much. But it made the tight knit among Jerri and Dolph and Pooter and Pepper tighter.

Jerri swung her swivel chair toward Rodney. He was haloed by sun streaming in from the window behind him. The view of the courthouse out that window reminded her where she and Sam's Investigating and Security Services had come from, "Rodney, what do you want? I mean, do you want to find out who is really behind this? Then, second, do you want them prosecuted?"

Dolph too turned to listen to the potential future mayor of San Antonio. "I want to defend my client. I want to find the truth." Rodney dropped his customary smile. "I don't care whether that truth holds up in court or not."

Dolph leaned back in his chair and crossed his arms, looking smugly at Jerri, "Then I'm your man."

"This just smells bad, like you yourself said," Rodney said to Dolph.

"Let's just call it coincidence," Dolph said.

"Do you know Mrs. Montalvo?" Jerri asked.

"Never met her."

"Then I'll interview her, and you find out what you can about her."

"I already know that Oscar created her from nothing."

"What the hell does that mean?"

"He made her body, face, and mind. Plastic surgery and state education. Cleaned her up, passed her off for decent."

"No, wait, maybe I don't want to know the truth. This is all just a bit weird," Rodney said. Jerri raised her eyes to Rodney to remind him of his own dips into the weirdness pool.

"You want to drop the case?" Jerri asked.

"No," Dolph answered.

"Is that okay with you, Rodney?" Jerri asked.

"Just build me an argument," Rodney said.

Jerri clapped her hands together and said, "Let's get started."

"Let's give Oscar's relatives a little respect and give them some time to get him in the ground," Dolph said.

"Some," Jerri said.

When they left, Dolph pausing in the doorway to thank her, she gazed back out the window to the courthouse. Below her was Sam's Investigation Services original office. Gutted and restored, it now housed a secretary and Jerry's computers and surveillance equipment. She chose to put her office above the original office, with the federal offices, the lawyers, and county employees. "Yes, Dolph?" Jerri swivelled to him.

"We need to do this."

"You take this too seriously. You can't fix everyone's personal problems. Why don't you broaden your interests? Get a cause. Donate to some political group. Become an activist. Start a blog."

"Those causes seem so impersonal."

"Don't get shot again. Find out, but don't charge into anything."

"I'm too old for that."

"Good."

"Okay, now don't overreact. Mrs. Montalvo probated Oscar's will when the courthouse opened."

"I guess she aims to get the sticky business out of the way before she deals with her grief."

Dolph lingered while they asked with their eyes if they could somehow help each other.

* * *

Dolph had his Taser stuffed in the back of his pants as he rang the door to Oscar Montalvo's daughter's apartment. Renee lived off of McCullough, just before the San Antonio College area, in an area that was a mixture of genuine poverty, student poverty, and gentrification.

Renee lived on the bottom floor of an old mansion that had been divided into apartments. A bald head with a pale face, droopy eyes, and nose and ear rings appeared in the crack of the door. "Renee Montalvo?" Dolph asked.

"No, man. No, I'm Izzy. Renee ain't awake yet."

Before Izzy could shut it in his face, Dolph got a foot in the crack the door made, leaned into the door, and kept Izzy from closing the it. "Wake her up," Dolph said, then forced himself to smile just as he forced the door a little farther open. He eyed the space, then kept a shoulder to the door as he squeezed into the first floor of the mansion. Izzy was bare-chested and wore only a pair of jeans sliding down his skinny hips to reveal striped boxers pulled up above his navel. He had the ubiquitous barbed wire tattoo circling the outside half of his left arm. He couldn't keep his eyes still. He had not smeared the sleep from his eyes or slobber off the side of his chin.

"She's in no shape," Izzy said.

"Izzy, right? Short for Israel?"

"Israel Gutierrez," the kid said. Dolph made a note in his brain.

"You ought to go by your given name," Adolph Martinez said.

"Dude, who are you?"

Dolph tried to keep smiling. "I'm a friend."

"You look cop-like to me."

"I used to work for the Border Patrol. It made me look this way. Believe me, if I had a choice I'd look different. Maybe even like you."

"You making fun of me?" Izzy said. He seemed to be asking a real question, as though he really didn't know.

"I think you're a good looking kid."

"You a faggot?"

"You a drug dealer?"

"Hey, maybe you better go outside."

Dolph stepped past Izzy and crossed the living room to head for the hall. It was a long hall with two doors. He chose one, opened it, stepped in, as Izzy shouted behind him, "Dude, man, you don't live here." Inside, in a king-sized bed with the one broken foot so that it slanted toward one side, was Renee Montalvo. Her hair was crushed on the side that she had been sleeping on. The other side of her head puffed out as though it had been teased but not combed. Her eyes were wide open, and she cocked her head to one side to look at Dolph.

She looked at Dolph with those baby seal eyes, begging for protection because she was helpless. She reminded Dolph of some of the wets that he caught and dropped off at the holding areas or drove back across the bridge to Ojinaga. Dolph begged his mind not to go back there. Of course, as Dolph well knew, her beatific expression could have been left on her face from the drugs she got from Izzy.

"Look, man," Izzy started. "Do I come to your house and rip you outta bed?"

Dolph glanced over his shoulder at Izzy, then returned his gaze to Renee. "Renee, you don't know me, but your father was a friend of mine." Renee dutifully nodded her head, making her curls of black coiled hair bob in front of her face. "Things need to be done."

"Dude, would you quit bothering her. Like, can't you see she's in grief, man?"

Dolph stepped closer, then closer still as Renee's view followed him. He sat on the edge of the bed. "Oh shit, now come on dude, I mean like holy shit. You're getting to be impossible to deal with," Izzy said. Renee stared at Dolph.

"Your mother is taking care of arrangements, but she hasn't gotten here from Dallas. Your stepmother is paying. But we need some help, some advice. If you could pick out a suit for him to be buried in."

Renee reached up and put her hands on both sides of her head. She started to shake it. "No, no. This is just too much. Let me get used to things. This is too much." Dolph scooted closer, and Renee started kicking the sheet and bedspread off her.

Dolph pushed himself off the bed. "See there, you scared her," Izzy said.

"Renee, you need to help bury your father."

"No, no," Renee said and pulled her palms down her cheeks. She was not crying, but she looked as though she was trying, as though her head was too dry to make tears. "Can't you leave me alone? Let me get used to this."

"How well do you know your stepmother?" Dolph asked.

"I don't even know Lee Ann, not really. She's just this money-grabbing whore as far as I'm concerned."

"How much has she grabbed?"

"You've seen her, talked to her."

"I've never met her," Dolph said.

"Hey, wait, wait, wait, wait." Izzy shook his hands out in front of him in order to help himself think. "You're asking questions. You really even know Renee's daddy, or are you just another cop?"

"How many cops have been here?"

"You know, you look a little old to be a cop."

"You look a little young to be threatening me."

"Whoa, come on, dude! Let's not get ugly."

"What are you talking about?" Renee asked.

"I'm talking about you doing the right and proper thing and helping your Dad get buried. You could see to it that his will is executed. You could stand in the back of the funeral home after the viewing. You could go to the service, ride in the family's limo to the burial plot. See him off."

"No, no, no. I just want to be left alone."

"Now see what was I telling you?" Izzy said.

"He was your father."

"What's this 'was'?"

"Unless you missed something, death means that *is* becomes *was*, and you owe it to your family to help your father stop being *is* and becoming a *was*, a memory."

"Slow the fuck down," Izzy said.

"He was terrible to my mother, not abusive, just indifferent." The snow seal eyes were back—watery, wide-open, pleading—and boring right through Dolph's long scar from his gut wound. "Women just confused him. He liked them too much."

"It's a Hispanic thing," Izzy said.

"Hell, I'm half Hispanic," Dolph said.

"You got it too?" Izzy said.

"But he was my father." Renee said.

"That's right, and unless you want dreams haunting you, unless you want voices talking to you at night, you need to help now to send him off."

Renee pulled her legs up and rested her chin on her knees. She had not had time to really wake up from a debauched night and get cleaned and dressed: she wore only her panties and a tank top. "My father. My father," she said as though disgusted with him.

"Get cleaned up."

"I'll get dressed," she said.

"I mean more than that." Dolph squared off and looked at Izzy. "I was there when he was shot. The last thing on his mind, the last thing he talked about was you."

Dolph heard a sniffle from Renee. He saw Izzy stiffen. "He wanted you cleaned up, off the drugs." Renee caught her breath.

"Whoa now, gramps, you coming in here all John Wayne like, and now you're talking drugs? Uh, uh, oh no. Ain't gonna be happening. Not in our house."

"Your house?"

"We share it, me and Renee," Izzy said.

"I'm not on drugs," Renee said.

"Then it'll be easy to quit," Dolph said.

"You're just like so way out of bounds," Izzy said.

"Why don't we go outside and talk about it?"

"Oh no," Renee said. "You stay here, Izzy. You go away, Mister. Nothing nasty. I'll clean up.'"

"See?" Izzy said.

Dolph walked toward the door, reached to grab Izzy's arm, and pulled him out after him. "Hey, hey, hey," Izzy said as Dolph dragged him.

"You have a back yard?" Dolph asked. Dolph pushed and dragged Izzy into the kitchen, then shoved him against a door. Dolph unlocked the door, pushed it open, and then swung open the screen door.

"Wait, wait, wait," Renee said as she ran into the kitchen, barefooted, bare-butted except for the bikini panties, breasts bouncing underneath her tank top.

"Go back to bed," Izzy said.

"Take a shower. We're having a discussion," Dolph said. Renee's eyes were pleading with Dolph not to hurt Izzy.

"Don't worry, honey," Izzy said. "I can handle this old man."

"Exactly," Dolph said, felt himself smile, felt himself want to cry. "Take a shower. Drink some coffee. Go down to the funeral home."

Tears were forming in Renee's eyes. She dropped her head, turned her back to Dolph, and walked out of the kitchen. Dolph shoved Izzy out of the door.

Izzy stumbled down the steps, nearly falling, but churned his feet to catch himself. When he hit the bottom step, before he could turn himself around, fast draw style, Dolph pulled the Taser out of the back of his pants, and pulled the trigger.

His remembering was slowing down time. Dolph was able to see the two barbs hit Izzy just under his shoulder blades. Those barbs had to hurt just on their own. Within the slow moments of Dolph's eyeblinks, Izzy, like Dolph had been, was squirming and wriggling on his stomach while his body writhed and shook without his permission, without his control. He slobbered. "Hurts like a son of a bitch, doesn't it?" Dolph said and sat on the porch to watch Izzy hurt.

Time speeded up again for Dolph. Izzy was through with the first burst of electricity and was trying to figure out how to work his body. The second burst hit him, and he started writhing again. "Now what I did is really illegal. And you could report me to the police. In fact, any honest, decent citizen should report me to the police for what I just did." Dolph hesitated as Izzy coped with the next blast through his body.

"You old fucking . . ." Izzy was learning how to talk again.

61

"Now don't forget I can control how many jolts you get."

Izzy rolled over and went contorted, trying to pull the darts out of his shoulders. "Now, as I was saying, any decent, honest citizen ought turn me in. But see that's the catch, once you give up decency and honesty, you no longer have the police to protect you. Most criminals don't think of that. See, besides your tax money, acting right buys you police protection. Now criminal activity can be lucrative, but you give up police protection, and private protection is really expensive."

"Fuck you." Izzy slobered out of the side of his mouth.

"Like I was saying, I can control how many times you get zapped. You want to try again?"

"Stay away from me, you crazy old fucker."

"You seem to be missing my point, Izzy. So let me explain. When you go to report me to the cops, you're going to have to tell them why I shot you. And even if you don't, I will when they arrest me. You pegged me as a cop. I am of sorts. So I'm used to police stations and talking to cops. So I'll tell them why I shot you. And since you're just a piss ant criminal who can't afford his own protection and who the cops don't really give a shit about, you're going to have a whole lot more problems than me. So you see, what I'm saying is that I got your balls in a vice. No, let me try again. I got an electrode attached to your balls, and I get to choose when to turn on the juice."

"You better hope I don't fucking get up."

"You seem to be entirely missing my point, let alone the fact that you still have some conduits of electricity sticking out of your shoulder blades."

"What do you want, you crazy old fucker?"

"Now you're catching on. But I'd appreciate it if you'd drop the 'old' part. I'm okay with 'fucker.'"

"Fucker, fucker, fucker."

"You're getting better. But what I want you to do is to get Renee to the funeral. And then I want you to keep her from taking anything, and then I want you to stay away from her. If I catch you around and she looks all Bambi-eyed, then I figure I get to play with my gun again."

Izzy started shaking his head. "I live here."

"I'll give you some time to find another place and move out. But the drugs leave this afternoon."

Dolph, even though he hadn't really promised to take care of Oscar's daughter, had taken care of the promise he made to himself to take care of Oscar's daughter. Now he'd look into taking care of Oscar's wife.

* * *

"Who are we seeing?" Sandra Beeson asked Jerri as she pulled her lips back from her teeth, giving herself a wide smile and held the long nail of her pinky finger up to her teeth as she checked in the mirror for food. Sandra had relaxed that much around Jerri. When they had first met, Sandra was nothing but proper. She did no primping in front of Jerri.

"Her name is Lee Ann Montalvo. She lives in Alamo Heights."

"Old rich?"

"She isn't. Her husband Oscar Montalvo was new rich, but he bought the former house of old rich who were just new rich when they bought the house in 1951." Jerri was impressed with how the world in San Antonio had progressed. A third generation Mexican, in San Antonio, Oscar could remain Mexican but live within the tree-shaded, formerly all-white, most exclusive old rich enclave in the city. There were richer areas, but this one inside the loop was old, refined money. Oscar and Jerri had both progressed.

"And why are we trying to see her?" Sandra asked.

"Her husband, Oscar Montalvo, remember, was killed yesterday." Lately, Jerri found that she had to repeat things for Dolph's mother.

"Oh, no, no, this isn't another case, is it?" Sandra shriveled in her seat and tugged at the hem of her skirt.

"You have a way of putting people at ease. People at ease say more."

"You should put me on your payroll."

"Your son is already on my payroll. I don't want to be accused of nepotism."

Jerri knew that Sandra would busy herself with snooping, conversing, or distracting a witness, someone being questioned, or a criminal. As the suspect watched Sandra flittering about, they usually got distracted from their story. That distraction might allow Jerri to catch a lie.

"You and Dolph make such a good team. You should finally become a

63

team and then hire me."

"Sandra, I could probably get along better with you than Dolph."

"He has his moments, though."

Jerri pulled into the driveway of the older house. It had the folding, crank-closed windows of the late forties. It stretched for nearly half a block, behind oaks and pecans that made a shady front lawn with bare patches that couldn't get enough sun. Clearly, the landscapers kept the plants and flowers growing. Perenials lined the length of the house, interspersed with hedges and colorful grasses, and large pots on stone pavers were spaced throughout the yard. Jerri got out of her BMW and planted her flat-heeled, rubber-soled shoes on the pavers. Sandra stepped out her side of the BMW, and she when got off the driveway and on the pavers, she tottered on her heels as they stuck in the seams between the stones. Jerri waited as Sandra walked ahead of her, balancing and swaying on her heels.

"This is nice," Sandra said as they walked up the new sidewalk. Yes, Oscar must have ripped out the old split, chipped, jagged sidewalk left over from a time when cities still built sidewalks in their neighborhoods and put in the more fashionable stones. The expense of keeping this woman, Jerri thought.

"Who are we interrogating?" Sandra asked.

"Interviewing. We're interviewing. And her name is Lee Ann Montalvo."

"Is she Hispanic too?"

"Wait and see," Jerri said.

Lee Ann Montalvo answered the door in a robe and house shoes. As she opened the door to let Jerri and Sandra into her mansion, her knee and then her thigh slipped out of the gap in her robe to reveal a short negligee. She wore makeup, her hair was in place. "The police have been here. They've called. I've nothing left to say. I'm said out." Lee Ann said. Lee Ann looked down at her dress. "I was taking a nap. I'm worn out. The police woke me first."

"We're not police," Jerri said. "We're investigating for the accused."

"And I'm nothing," Sandra said. Sandra flowed around the living room, designed for entertaining, and then into the dining room so that she had to raise her voice for Lee Ann to hear, "You have an absolutely lovely house

"It'll do," Lee Ann said.

"We're sorry if we woke you up," Jerri said. "But I have a few questions."

"The police have all my answers. I'm tired of giving them. My husband has just been killed, for God's sakes."

"That dusty, textured baby blue how did you create that?" Sandra said as she stared at the dining room wall.

"Are you cops or interior designers?"

Sandra frowned and took long steps to join Jerri in the living room. "You have a lovely house. I've noticed it from walks and drives through the neighborhood. I've always wanted to see inside."

Jerri was suppressing a smile. Sandra was working her magic, disorienting Lee Ann so that she couldn't keep up her pretense of the grieving widow. Jerri made an excuse for Sandra: "We're sorry, Sandra and I are friends. Sandra can't drive right now because she had cataract surgery, so she's hitching a ride with me."

"We live right down from you on Hildebrandt, next to Trinity, in that high rise."

"Fine, fine, fine," Lee Ann said, noticeably sucking in some air. "But see, my husband's dead." Her eyes were moist.

"My, my, my," Sandra stepped up to her, produced a tissue from her purse, and held it in front of Lee Ann. Lee Ann took the tissue, blew her nose, "It ain't right." She halted. The women exchanged a few glances, smiled. "It's not right. Not right that I should have to keep answering questions at the same time I'm seeing to burying my husband."

"What about Ramón Burgiaga?" Jerri asked.

"He don't. He doesn't matter."

"He's in jail and could get the death penalty. This state just loves to sentence poor people to the needle." Jerri let her eyes roam to find Sandra, just to keep in her in sight, to watch out for her. "It's another matter for rich people," Jerri added to Lee Ann.

"Jerri!" Sandra scolded Jerri. "What are you implying?"

Jerri said quickly before Sandra could switch sides, "From what I understand, you lost a husband but no love was lost."

"Oh my God! Jerri!" Sandra said, stepped up to Lee Ann and put an arm around her. Lee Ann looked at Sandra as though she smelled bad. She pulled away from Sandra. "Dear?" Sandra said. "I'm only trying to give what little comfort I can."

"Stay away from me, both of you." Lee Ann said. "I got nothing to say."

"I'm sorry. Excuse me. I apologize." Jerri said.

"As well you should," Lee Ann said.

"I'll start over. Your husband knew of the affair. Your affair was the last thing on his mind."

"Oh my, God," Lee Ann said, put her hands up to her face, and when she pulled them down, she was indeed crying. Sandra now stepped up to her, circled her arm around Lee Ann, and hugged her. Lee Ann, this time, let her.

"Just one question then. Do you believe that Ramón Burgiaga could have killed your husband?"

"Well it sure as hell looks like he did, don't it? Doesn't it? I mean, he had the smoking gun in his hand."

"How do you know that?"

"It's, it's what they say is all."

"A figure of speech, dear," Sandra added, her arm still around Lee Ann. "During your affair. . ."

Sandra and Lee Ann gasped.

"That's rather indelicate," Sandra said.

"You obviously knew him. Did he seem like the type of guy who would murder a man?"

"Right, right, I obviously knew him. He was scared. Oscar had threatened him." Her crying had stopped. "So what do you want me to say? What is it you think you know?"

"I would like to be sitting down. I would like to have been invited in and offered a seat and discussed this . . . instead of standing up, bracing ourselves and shouting," Jerri said.

Sandra said, "But, Jerri, you are being a bit rude."

"I was fucking him. Okay. So last's I heard that ain't no crime. Immoral but legal, okay. So write me off as a bitch, but I done nothing illegal, and you can't make it stick." Lee Ann ducked out from under Sandra's arm, and one bare knee and thigh, then the next slashed out from the robe as Lee Ann stepped closer and closer to Jerri. Jerri backed up, letting Lee Ann talk as she stepped toward Jerri. "Maybe you didn't notice that Oscar Montalvo's sorry ass was some twenty years older than me. Maybe what you don't know is that he got this big jealous streak and wants me locked up away from all the young men he thinks is chasing my still trim and well-kept up, not middle-aged and sagging, ass. And so he makes himself crazy watching me." She stopped walking to catch her breath and some composure.

"Maybe he thought he had reason to keep you locked up." Jerri said. Sandra scowled. Lee Ann fought against getting even madder.

"Maybe he did. So I was fucking Ramón because I was lonely and wanted someone besides this old man."

"And so Ramón, of his own free will and volition, killed your huband?"

"Jerri, Jerri, dear," Sandra scolded. "This conversation has gotten ugly." Sandra and Jerri's eyes stuck in a gaze on each other.

"Ramón's got as much volition as he gots balls," Lee Ann said, squared her shoulders, stuck one shapely leg out of her robe, and dared Jerri to bring it on.

"Thank you, Mrs. Montalvo," Jerri said. "I'm quite satisfied that Ramón lost his head. Enjoy the rest of the day."

"Well, that's better," Sandra said and hugged Lee Ann.

After they had made their way across the shaded, landscaped yard to the long driveway, and comfortably buckled into Jerri's BMW, Sandra said, "I guess you know that woman was lying. She couldn't even figure out if she wanted to talk old rich sophistication or West Texas white trash."

"I think she wants to brag about getting her husband killed and living here."

"And to think she lives less than a mile from us." Sandra said.

On the way to Palo and the Nix hospital, Jerri realized once more how fully she appreciated Sandra Beeson. If she were to let Dolph have the favors she suspected he wanted, she would do so in part to make his mother happy. And Jerri realized she could use Sandra yet some more. Sandra could help her deal with Palo.

67

* * *

Palo had the shades pulled and the lights low because the brightness had started to bother him. He lay on his back because, as he had complained, his sides seemed less sturdy, unable to support his frail body. His uneaten breakfast sat next to his lunch, which he would not eat in spite of the nurses' entreaties.

After their eyes adjusted to the dark room, Jerri and Sandra leaned over Palo and studied his face. "He looks almost like a skeleton," Sandra whispered.

"No es muerto," Palo said. Sandra's eyes looked shocked, but Palo smiled. "Maybe a day, two days. You count more at the end. And the start too. But I can't remember the start. I'm counting minutes now. Pretty soon, I count the seconds."

"Stop counting," Jerri said.

"You already made me lose the count."

"You still tease everybody."

Palo let his eyes shift from Jerri to Sandra. "The good thing about dying is that you get so many women around you."

"You could still get better."

"This room is the last place I will live. I will not see my house again."

Sandra slowly lowered her hand and placed it on Palo's forehead. She gently massaged it. "This is a pretty lady," Palo said.

"How are they treating you?" Jerri asked.

"They make me comfortable. Or as comfortable as they can or I can be."

"What did you do before you got here?" Sandra asked.

Palo slowly rolled his head toward Jerri to ask if it was okay to talk to this woman, more important, to ask if he could tell her the truth. Jerri noded. Palo tried to smile. "I was a criminal." Sandra patted his forehead. "Not a really big one. Not one of the narcoticos. I came before them. But in Saltillo, in Chihuahua, I got to say things and have my way. Then I came to this country. And I made Mexicans Americans."

"I know all about this," Jerri said.

Sandra walked to one side of the room, grabbed the back of the chair and pulled it closer to Palo to listen to him for as long as he had the breath.

"I have some time."

Jerri pushed the guilt into the back of her mind. She no longer knew what to say, how to treat Palo. Sandra, just as she had helped with Lee Ann, could help comfort Palo. Sandra would be a refreshing, new audience for Palo, someone who could delightfully fill the seconds that he counted. Jerri opened the door, stepped through it, and left Palo and Sandra in the room. From Dolph and Sandra's memories, Jerri guessed that Sandra had not been a very good mother. Jerri herself had not really been a good mother. But now, Sandra could become anyone's mother, even Palo's.

Jerri walked to the Nix cafeteria for a doughnut and a cup of coffee. She was trying to eat healthier than a mid-morning donut, but she felt the need to eat what was bad for her. Jerri felt like ingesting doughnuts, liquor, chocolate, cigarettes, pots of coffee, greasy burgers, fries, chips, refried beans. She sat her coffee down, stared at the swirl of coffee as she stirred sugar into it, and held her donut in her other hand. She took a bite out of her donut. It was at least a day old. She felt like crying or cussing. Why couldn't they do something with a hospital's decor other than the ubiquitous fake-cheery utility?

How do you wait and watch while someone dies? Do you acknowledge the death, at least give the dying dignity by not lying? They know they are dying. Or do you deny it to them, reach for some hope when there is none? Do you discuss the pending unknown, or do you just find the last bits of earthly news, of minor errands to ease them into that unknown place? Or do you just let them talk?

After Jerri's third cup of coffee, when she could feel her nerves twist about and taunt her, Sandra joined her. "So did I do what you expected?" Sandra asked. "I just listened."

"Thank you. I don't think I could have made it through another session."

"Is he asleep?"

"I think so. He just sort of drifts off. One of these times he won't come to. Maybe he won't come out of this."

"What's he dying of?"

"He's just old."

Sandra deliberately dropped her head and bobbed it as though looking

69

for a coin she had dropped on the floor. "I had Dolph too young. He's nearly as old as me now. As they age, our children get closer to us in age." Sandra looked down at her toes, pulled her head up, and tried to smile. "Look at us here in this hospital you, me, and Palo. Three stages of agedness. We wait after him to take our turns."

"You know, I hardly ever see my son and his family. They live in Dallas. I have grandbabies."

"And I'm supposed to tell you to go see them, to take advantage of them, because I'm grandmotherly, but the truth is you should do just what you are doing." What good was Sandra, Jerri thought, if this old woman couldn't confirm the clichés.

After leaving Palo to his suffering, Jerri drove Sandra to her club. After she had met again with Rodney Lee, telling him that Lee Ann Montalvo was both more and less than the act she was putting on, she drove by Charlie Montalvo's unassuming, quiet, even poor-looking law office on Military Drive. Like brother Oscar, Charlie remembered his roots on the Southside, just as Oscar used medicine to help the poor and the forgotten, so Charlie used law. Like Oscar, he got rich appearing to be a man of the people.

Charlie had taken off work early, and with a little prodding, she traced him to happy hour at the Cadillac Bar in the south part of downtown.

* * *

Charlie was careful to keep the cuffs of his suit jacket off the bar. He could afford the cleaning, but sometimes the spilled beer and ashes stained them. His suits were expensive, more expensive than his brother's, but then a lawyer needed to look better than a doctor. Poor Oscar, Charlie reminded himself to think. Then he stopped his mind from drifting to consider all the probate matters connected with a brother's death. Lee Ann would get everything. Charlie was there when Oscar signed it over, including the money he had stashed and constantly bragged about to Charlie. Charlie spent his money on women so Oscar claimed. So Oscar built himself the perfect woman. Now Oscar was dead, and Charlie planned to see the widow later that night.

As he thought about the way Lee Ann looked when the light in an otherwise dark house wandered to her body and lit those molded breasts, buns, and thighs, Charlie saw a petite but muscular woman making her way toward the bar. She was older than Lee Ann, but with some work, with some attention to herself, she could be attractive. Despite Charlie's image of Lee Ann lit in a dark house, he let himself imagine what he could do to make this small woman realize her full potential. Charlie found himself guessing about what he could do for a lot of women.

The woman planted her elbows on the bar and glanced at him. He nodded and complimented himself that, with yards of bar to lean against, she had chosen a section next to him. Closer to her, he saw that she was even older than he had expected. Her age was thrilling. Charlie liked young women, but the right older woman, looking the right way, a woman like Lee Ann, for instance, a woman like Joan Phelan, for instance, and perhaps this woman standing in front of him offered a roughened but healthy and honest sexuality. "Charlie Montalvo?" the woman asked.

Charlie smiled and raised his glass to sip from his margarita made with a premium tequila. "I'm Jerri Johnson," the woman said when Charlie pulled his glass from his lips. "I'm representing the man representing Ramón Burgiaga."

Charlie felt his face and his mind grow slack. Charlie said, "Ms. Johnson, do I need an attorney?"

"You are an attorney."

Charlie took a long sip from his margarita. "He who represents himself represents a fool."

"This has nothing to do with you. And I'm sure that you want the truth of your brother's murder known."

Charlie turned away from the woman to face the mirror in the back of the bar. Looking at his face, he begged himself not to give himself away. In the mirror, Charlie saw the panic in his eyes. He hoped that he wasn't going to see tears. "Can't you leave me with my grief?" he asked the woman.

"I see that you are alone with a glass or two of your grief."

"We mourn in our own ways." Charlie saw himself smile in the mirror. He also caught the reflection of the woman. The reflection, at a distance, made her younger, and more attractive. He forced a smile in the mirror, forced her to smile in the mirror at him.

"How well do you know your brother's wife?"

Charlie concentrated on the reflections in the mirror and talked to those reflections, not just hers, but his. "I know he married her."

"Mr. Montalvo, could you face me?" Jerri Johnson asked. "My eyes are really straining trying to look at you in the mirror."

Charlie turned. "Why of course. It's always a pleasure to chat with a pretty lady at a bar."

The pretty lady frowned. "So you've met her?"

"Of course, I've met her. She's my sister-in-law."

"But can you say that you know her?"

"How can you really know anybody? What do you want me to say? What are you looking for?" Charlie felt his voice catch. "Look, you have the guy. You have the evidence. Why make more of this case?"

"What would you do if you were defending Ramón Burgiaga?"

"I'd plead my ass off, over and over, until I got something he could live with."

"He might get the needle."

"Bullshit. Passion, a jealous husband, open threats. No way. This is Texas."

Charlie leaned on his elbows and looked back into the mirror. The worried look was back. He saw fear in his face. Then he saw Jerri's reflection again. "Very well, let's talk to reflections. So what do you think of Lee Ann?"

"Lee Ann is," he stopped, hung his head, seemed to search the air in front of him for an answer. "Lee Ann is loving, but she made a mistake when she married my brother."

"She got plenty of money."

"And plenty of heartache. My brother was demanding. He was practically molding her." Charlie thought about what he had said. Who is to say, that, in his own way, Oscar hadn't been abusive?

"Like Pygmalion."

"And she turned out different than he thought."

"So he was stuck with her."

"If there were a judge here, I could object to your leading questions."

Charlie dropped his head and stared down at a wet spot on the bar so that he wouldn't have to look at the reflections in the mirror.

"Who are you defending? Oscar or Lee Ann?"

"Who are you accusing?" She didn't say anything. And to think that when she walked in, Charlie thought she was attractive. Obviously she had come in prepared, and to his credit, though he was not prepared, Charlie had forced her to a dead end.

"Look, all I want is information. You know what I am. I'm just gathering data. I don't know how Rodney Lee is going to play the defense."

Charlie stiffened. He had heard of Rodney Lee, knew that he got what he went after, had heard the rumors. "Rodney Lee is taking the case?"

"Pro bono."

"Holy shit," Charlie said. It slipped out before he knew what he had said, knew he looked guilty. So he drank a margarita.

"Lee just wants justice. Things just seemed so packed and tight against Ramón. Rodney just wants to even the playing field."

"Bullshit. Can't I just let my brother die? Rodney Lee will turn that trial into a circus with him as the ringmaster. And then he'll run for mayor. My brother should have watched his mouth. What was this poor ignorant son of bitch to do? What was he to believe?" Well played, Charlie thought to himself. Lee Ann would applaud. He wanted to call and tell her.

"Then you don't want revenge for you brother's death?"

"I want to be left alone."

"Very well, then." Jerri Johnson stuck out her hand to shake. They shook. No sooner was she out the door than Charlie was on his cell phone to Lee Ann.

She greeted him as "darling," but when Charlie told her about Jerri Johnson, Lee Ann said, "Damn, hang up. Talk to me from your home."

When Charlie pulled into the garage and banged on Lee Ann's back door, she said, "No, your home, stupid."

"My home is with you now."

"Not yet."

"I need you now."

When she let him in through the backdoor, Charlie saw that, since she wasn't expecting him, she hadn't made herself up. He was expecting. She wasn't.

"You have to leave."

"Oh, baby, nobody knows I'm here."

"How will it look to that lawyer?"

"A brother comforting his brother's widow. This is all normal, even for the nineteenth century."

"We live in the twenty-first."

"And God bless it," Charlie said and grabbed for his brother's widow.

Chapter 5

Besides the grime on his back, the sweat soaking his clothes—making them bunch up around him and making mud underneath him—the rancid, mildewy, musky smell bothered Dolph. "You just learn to put up with it," Walter had told him on a previous case. But after so long under a house, Dolph would start coughing. So he had his mouth full of cough drops. He had an amplifier pressed to the floor above him, ear phones in his ears, and several small battery operated bugs in his pockets. His readers hung on the end of his nose.

"Is this legal?" Walter asked as he went about his business, spraying for real bugs. The spray was working. When they got to Oscar's house, just at the break of dawn, they backed out when they stirred up a hive of wasps. Then, they encountered daddy-long-leg spiders and then roaches leaving the house. Later still, Dolph swallowed his scream as a roach made its way down his face. That is why he kept his readers on the end of his nose: to see them coming.

Dolph pulled the stethoscope's plugs out of his ears. "I just happen to have this new amplifier here and thought I'd try it out. Nothing says an exterminator can't have hobbies."

"What about those little things in your pockets? Those are wiretaps, aren't they?"

"No, wiretaps go through phone lines. These are radio listening devices."

"So I got the wrong terminology. Are they legal?"

"I don't think they're going to work through the floor. So it's a moot question. But look, Walter, we're in the business of finding information.

That's our job. We don't necessarily need to worry too much about legal and that is a great comfort to me after working for the U.S. government."

"Just like my job is to get rid of bugs. Whether it's environmentally safe or not is another thing." Walter squirted some kind of juice into a corner.

"So what are you spraying?"

"You can breathe it. Just don't ingest it."

On his elbows and knees, Walter crawled closer to Dolph. As he looked up at Walter, Dolph noticed a smear of grime across both lenses of Walter's glasses. "How do you see?"

"I squint a lot."

"Jesus, when's the last time Oscar had his house sprayed? He's got an insect apartment complex down here." Dolph looked around him, then picked his hands up to inspect his palms. When he tried to push himself up, he hit his back on the floor above him. Walter took off his baseball cap and ran his palm over his bald head, leaving a greenish-brown smear across his dome. He put his cap back on his head. "God all mighty, why don't they give you some more room in here?"

"The idea is to support the house, not give you room." Walter scurried along to another corner like he was Gregor Samsa and doused it with spray. "New houses have slabs. This will eventually become a thing of the past."

"Shhh," Dolph hissed. "The idea is not to let them know we're here." One of Oscar's last wishes, at Walter's prodded, was to have his house sprayed. So Walter was honoring that. It just so happened that Dolph was helping out and that Pepper was sitting in the van full of dated surveillance equipment and watching the front door.

Walter backed up toward Dolph. "See, in Mexico, an old man, a retired man with American money, can live like a king."

"Walter, now's not the time."

"I know it's corrupt. I know it's abuse of a Third World country. But think of it. Like this case, if somebody wants money, instead of murdering some poor ol' guy, why not just go to Mexico? You want something, you buy it. It's simple. Here they put you in prison if you don't have money. There you don't have money, you work for Americans with money, or sneak into America."

"Walter, you don't need to tell me about Mexico."

"In this country, the worst crime is a crime against wealth. In Mexico, the worst crime is a crime against the state. So we just sit there with our money, someplace nice. Another stash of money in an American bank in case the whole place implodes, and we watch the world forget us. What do you say, Dolph? No more crawling under foul-smelling old houses breathing in bug spray."

Walter's wooing had started again, as it usually did when Walter got distracted or bored. Even though he knew Walter was full of shit and distrusted his plans, schemes, and sermons, Dolph still listened. And after awhile, Walter always started to make sense to Dolph.

"You know the Chihuahuan desert," Walter went on. "I'm thinking Chihuahua City. You speak Spanish. We'd be invincible. We could crawl out of here and crawl out of the indignities that this used-to-be-grand country forces on the aged, the poor, and the infirm."

"Walter, later."

"I've got what, ten, twelve years on you? I don't have time. I want some life left to enjoy."

"Walter, you do okay by yourself right here."

Dolph heard taps on the floor above him. He pressed the plugs in his ears and the stethoscope against the bottom side of the floor. "I can hear em without that," Walter said.

In a moment, Dolph could hear talking. Did Lee Ann talk to herself? Then there was an answer: a male voice. Through the stethoscope, Dolph heard a kiss. He looked over his shoulder and pressed his lips together to imitate a kiss. "You shouldn't have come here, and you should have gone before now," Lee Ann said. More kissing, and though he couldn't have heard, fondling, Dolph guessed. "The cops. The cops." Lee Ann said. "And these strange people. This woman lawyer, detective something, something, or something."

"I talked to her," the male voice said. Dolph strained to recognize the voice. He went through a Rolodex of voices in his memory. Nothing came from his memory to his mind. Walter lifted his head up to press an ear against the floor.

"Did she have that funky old lady with her? Bitch wandering through the house poo-pooing this and that?"

"I've met her before. I think."

"The old lady?"

"The lady detective."

"Get dressed. Get out of here before the neighborhood starts waking up."

Who, who, who is it? Dolph's mind begged him. "Where did you know that lady detective from?" Lee Ann asked.

"I think that I met her at some party at my brother's." Dolph dropped his stethoscope and bumped his head when he reached to get it. He fumbled it back up against the floor. Walter strained to keep his ear on the floor.

"Oh god, get your ass out of here. We don't need to give them no can of worms to open up on us. Jesus."

"I'm stressed."

"Sorry." More kissing.

They heard footfalls crossing the house. On elbows and knees, they crawled toward the opening. Pepper was outside in the van with binoculars and a camera with a zoom lens, but Dolph wanted a look in case the man went out the back door. Dolph squeezed through the opening, jumped up, and motioned to Walter to stay where he was. Dolph stepped out of the flower bed and looked around him. He saw a spray can, swung its strap over his shoulder, and made his way through and around the landscaping to the backyard fence, a six-foot-high hurricane, overgrown with ivy. He tried to climb the fence, but the weight of the spray can pulled him down. He pulled his arms out of the straps, went clawing at the fence, and got over it just in time to see the back door opening. He halted and peered both ways. He breathed in, decided to take his chances, stepped around the corner, and proceeded toward the back of his house. Charlie Montalvo stepped out of the back door and spotted him. He jumped. "Whoa, you scared me. Can I help you?" Charlie asked.

"Exterminator," Dolph said and tugged on his baseball cap to pull it lower onto his head so that he could barely see out from under the brim. "I'm looking for another entrance from the backyard. We may have to

78

fumigate."

Charlie looked back toward the door, then came down the steps from the house. Dolph took a step up, then back. He looked toward the garage, which was separate from the house. Charlie wove his way through lawn furniture and tapped his shoes against the stone pavers that made trails among the backyard gardens, fountains, and ponds. Charlie's suit was rumpled. He was unshaven.

He stopped in front of Dolph and cocked his head to see under the brim of Dolph's cap. Dolph went through images in his mind to try to remember if he had ever met Charlie. "I'm Walter Boone," Dolph said and stuck out his hand. "I got a contract from Oscar Montalvo to spray this place. And let me tell you what. It really needs it." Charlie started backing away from Dolph. The back door opened, and Lee Ann, in a short negligee that showed off her toned thighs below its hem and some cleavage above it, stepped on to the porch and swung her eyes toward Dolph. She remembered propriety, said "You wait" and dashed into the house. Charlie shook his hand from side to side to wave good bye to Dolph.

Lee Ann appeared back on the porch in a thin robe. "What are you doing in my yard?"

"Exterminator."

"Exterminate yourself out of here."

"But I have an order from Oscar Montalvo."

"He's dead."

"Oh my, I'm sorry miss. I'm sorry," Dolph said and backed toward the fence.

"There's a gate over there," Lee Ann pointed at a gate on the other side of the house, closer to the garage. "What are you doing climbing the fence?"

Dolph slowly followed Charlie. He opened the gate just as the garage door opened, and Charlie backed his Lexus out of the garage. "Get out of here. We don't need exterminators," he heard Lee Ann say.

Dolph let Charlie get out of the driveway. He all but forgot about Walter under the house and hurried to the exterminator van parked across the street. The back door of the van opened to meet him. After opening the door, Pepper leaned back into a folding lawn chair, his binoculars and

79

camera dangling from his neck, and smiled while he pulled at the diamond stud in his ear. "Damn, if you'd a told me that Lexus was parked in her garage, maybe I could have snuck in there and put one of those magnet beepy things up under the car."

"We don't need one. We know where he works."

"So you know who parked his Lexus in Lee Ann's garage so to speak?"

"Charlie Montalvo."

Pepper's smile disappeared, and he blew through his lips. He turned his head to see the Lexus driving down the shaded, exclusive Alamo Heights Drive. "You're gonna have to help me figure this one out, chief."

"We should have been watching last night to see when he showed up."

"So Oscar ain't even in the ground, and his daughter camps out with drugs and her loser boyfriend and his brother is—I guess—banging his widow?"

Dolph unfolded another chair beside Pepper. Pepper reached into an ice chest beside him and pulled out two cold beers. "It's too early," Dolph said.

"Nothing like a morning beer. I didn't bring any coffee." The tops of the beer cans popped in unison. Dolph was glad for the coppery taste against the back of his throat. "Where's Walter?"

"Doing his job."

"So, how sleazy is this?"

Dolph held out his index finger. "A. Charlie could be consoling the widow, but he's probably fucking her." Pepper held out his finger to help keep count. "B. Charlie could have helped set up poor ol' Ramón."

"Oh Jesus. You got that spooky Dolph look in your eye."

"C. Charlie plotted his own brother's death. D. Lee Ann is using Charlie like she used Ramón."

"Oh Christ, am I gonna get another part of my body shot off?" Pepper sipped at his beer.

"Mostly, though, I was right. This just stinks to high heaven."

"So you're going to fix it." Pepper sipped his beer. "And I guess I'm going help."

"You work part time for me now."

"Shit," Pepper frowned, but his eyes smiled.

"Don't you want to see Oscar get some justice?"

"How's justice going fix him being dead?"

"Well then, a little justice would sure as hell make me feel better."

"What are we going to do now?"

"Talk to Jerri." Before he pulled his cell phone out of his pocket, Dolph asked Pepper one more question. "You ever thought of retiring in Mexico?"

"Used to, but now I got this sweetie."

* * *

As Walter maneuvered his bug spray van out of Alamo Heights, he checked to his right on Pepper and then in his rearview mirror on Dolph. Dolph sat in the back in the folding chair next to the bug spray and the surveillance equipment and pushed the buttons on his cell phone. When he could get no reception, he cussed and banged his phone on the arm of the folding chair. Pepper slumped in the passenger seat and watched Dolph, as though his patience could help Dolph and the wireless signal. Walter was beyond such worry. He helped Dolph out strictly for amusement, not because he wanted any part of Dolph's concerns with justice or protection.

"I usually get a little mid-morning pick-me-up about now," Walter said to Pepper as the first few rain drops hit the windshield.

"I don't see anything wrong with a morning beer, but don't it get just a little embarrassing buying it that early and then drinking it in a bug van?" Pepper asked he finished off his can of beer.

"It's non-alcoholic," Walter said.

"Well what the hell is the use of even making the effort then?" Pepper asked. Dolph continued banging his cell phone and cussing.

Walter tilted his head back, let his thick glasses slide to the end of his nose, and checked over them to the backseat. "It's the hills. They block out reception. We'll clear them soon." More rain beat harder on the windshield.

Within a few minutes, they had cleared the northern edge of Alamo Heights and were pulling into the traffic at Nacogdoches into the new Quarry area. The April shower had picked up and was making a mess of the dust on Walter's windshield. Walter spotted his pick-me-up spot: the

Quarry Smoothie Shack. As he steered the van into the Smoothie Shop, Pepper said, "They sell nothing here can pick you up."

"I like vanilla, guava, and pineapple. Reminds me of the malts I drank as a kid. You can't get malts anymore. You know the ones they served in those steel two-pint containers, mixed while you're at the counter."

"Is this your second or third childhood?"

"Growing up can be tough," Walter said. Dolph still cussed from the chair in the back.

Walter pulled up under the tin awning over the front of the Quarry Smoothie Shack. The owners had bought an old gas station, pulled out the filling tanks, but left the cement islands. Walter left his passengers in the car, shrugged his shoulders to the cool rain beating on the tin awning, walked into the gaudy bright green, yellow, pink, and white store (decorated in the color of fruits), said hello to the pretty teenager who waited on him, ordered his smoothie, and guessed at what Pepper and Dolph might like. Walter was deliberately trying to enter his third childhood. The enemy of human existence was that old son of a bitch time. No matter what you did, it just came and got your ass. And most adults conducted themselves so as to insulate themselves from time. If they ever thought of it, they saw it as some cyclical thing to fill. Take out the trash, pick up the kids, make the calls, make love to the wife, get up for work, etc., etc., etc. Walter was taking delight in the time he had to fill.

The pert teenager with dimples and pig tails handed the smoothies to Walter. Walter seemed to remember that her name was Miranda. She was so homely she was cute. She was alluring because she was still too young for the self-loathing that afflicted the less attractive in late adolescence. Walter liked getting a smoothie from her as much as he enjoyed slurping it down. For the very young, without experience, time provided newness. Miranda was on the verge of experiencing cyclic adult time.

At the door, Walter held and balanced the three styrofoam cups in his hands and shoved his shoulder into the door. Outside, he waited just a minute to listen to the rain battering on tin, wishing he had a tin roof so that he could listen to the rain splash on it. Mexico probably had lots of tin roofs, but not much rain, except in the more tropical areas. Maybe the Yucatan area was the place to go: Carribean breezes blowing summer rain on a tin roof.

When Walter returned to the van, Pepper leaned across the seat and opened the door for him. When Pepper took one one of the smoothies from Walter and straightened back up, Walter saw that Pepper had another beer. "What the hell are we doing?" Dolph yelled. "Charlie Montalvo may be banging his dead brother's ex-old lady, and we're drinking beer and shopping for shakes."

"Yours and Pepper's are strawberry and banana. Try it and then call it a mere shake," Walter said.

"It'll ruin my beer," Pepper said.

"Try it," Walter said.

Putting his beer to one side, Pepper tentatively sucked some of his smoothie up the straw, tasted it, and then nodded his approval.

"Okay, so I'll let the beer get hot," Pepper said.

"Walter, Walter," Dolph yelled from the backseat. "I still can't get reception. I got to call Jerri."

"You know, just how important is it that she knows now instead of two minutes from now?"

"You know," Pepper said between his gulps. "I think Walter's got you on this one."

"I can't get reception," Dolph yelled.

Walter, balancing his smoothie between his thighs, started the van and backed up just bit in the parking lot. "Now try." Dolph looked at his cell phone and began pressing buttons. "That tin awning."

"Hell, with trees, valleys, and tin; what good are the damn things?" Pepper asked.

"Exactly," Walter said. But Dolph was busy yelling the big news into the phone.

Walter directed Pepper to reach into the glove compartment. There Pepper found a stash of very good cigars. Pepper took one and handed one to Walter. "Dolph's conversation looks like it's gonna be a long one. Might as well add to our pleasure."

"Or kill ourselves," Pepper said. "Ice-creamy-like stuff, a cigar, and three beers just don't seem like a good combination in my gullet."

Walter lit, puffed, and blew smoke at Pepper to answer him. "What in the hell?" Dolph asked from the backseat. "Just what the hell are y'all doing?"

While Dolph cussed, Pepper lit his cigar. "Say, this is good."

"Rolled on the thighs of pubescent Jamaican girls, I understand," Walter said.

"We gotta get started," Dolph said.

"You got a smoothie," Walter said.

"Jesus Christ, you two. Our buddy Oscar Montalvo just got killed. Don't you want his killer caught?

"Seems like his killer is beyond Oscar's worry now," Walter said.

Pepper shrugged. "I think Walter's right again. He's got you beat all over on this one."

"Dolph, seems like your mind is tying your guts and liver in knots," Walter said. "Try to relax."

"Got you again," Pepper said.

"Roll your windows down," Walter said. "Let a little of that April rain spritz your face. In a city as hot as this one, it's a crime not to get a little natural coolness when you can."

Pepper cracked his window, but Walter rolled his halfway down and enjoyed the splatter of rain on his face as well as the icy smoothie sliding down his throat. As Dolph sucked at his smoothie and sulked in his Dolph way over the wasted minutes, the van filled with the smoke from Walter and Pepper's cigars and the early morning breeze. And the back of Walter's throat burned slightly from the chill of the smoothie.

"So Walter," Pepper asked. "What made you decide to become a bug killer? When you were a famous writer and then a college teacher?"

"I was a failure as a famous writer. I had a screenplay that made me a lot of money for a number of years, and I had a real good time pissing that money away and never wrote another sellable anything. And I had subsistence-level money teaching, but then I got fired for fucking and drinking amongst the strict Baptists of the community. And you forgot to add that I was a technical writer here in this very town, writing the legalese lawyers got bored writing. And they gave me enough money to afford a classy wife, a step teenager, and a wet dream gentrified house in the King Williams area. And I fucked that up too."

"So why can't you keep a steady job?"

"The first two I had, bosses didn't want me being me. The last one, I was my own boss and, along with my wife, I started wanting me to stop being me. Spraying for bugs, I'm not important enough to have to stop being me."

"I got you beat on wives, lost jobs, and fuck ups," Pepper said. "You make it sound like there's hope for us yet."

"I hope so." Walter tried but couldn't quite explain to Pepper and Dolph that the secret for an aging man was to get to the far end of adulthood and return to a childlike appreciation with the caution of an adult. For on the other side of birth, nearing death, fully realizing the indignity and linearity of his own existence, an old person can slow time, can pick out moments from the cycles of time that we use to fill up our lives, and make some of those moments seem to last. And by buying a smoothie from a pert young girl, having a cigar with friends in a bug van, an old person, conscious of the end of his time, can even repeat elongated moments. Walter didn't have many times left.

* * *

Once again Ramón Burgiaga sat on one end of the long table in the police station while Rodney Lee strutted and waved his arms at the other end. Sweat stains grew down the back and under the arms of Rodney Lee's jacket as he gestured. Jerri wondered if Rodney Lee sweated because he grew nervous or because he was excited when he performed. She sat quietly to one side, anticipating Rodney Lee's arguments and constructing his new ones. "Now, you may wonder," Rodney said, "just why it is that I get to talk to you in this nice, cozy room instead of through a thick, smeared, scratched piece of Plexiglass."

Ramón hung his head again as though he was tired of hearing these sermons or as though the sermons were finally wearing him down. "That's cause I am somebody important around the PO-lice station. I am well known. And here I am, pro bono, here I am delivering you my reputation and abilities and the detailed investigative work of Ms. Johnson. And look what you got to say. . . which is nothing."

Jerri began fidgeting because of her conscience. From a moral perspective, not a legal one, and certainly not Rodney Lee's political perspective, perhaps Ramón ought to be allowed to accept the fate he had been coerced into choosing. Rodney Lee brought his finger tips together and stared over them at Ramón. "My good man, as my people say in our vernacular, Lee Ann Montalvo be fucking her husband's brother." Ramón raised his head, looked at Jerri. Jerri nodded. "That right, that the truth. You let that sink in. You think about what that could mean as to why you did what you done. You thinking?" Ramón dropped his head. " Cause you better think. Cause I don't know what it mean. Ms. Johnson don't know what it mean. Only Charlie Montalvo and the grieving widow lady know what it mean. But you, you, I bet you got some guesses as to what it mean."

"I shot him. He threatened me, man. He said it. Oscar told his wife, man. He told her. He say he kill me. So I kill him. I don't think. I kill him."

"My man, my client. I got some more news for you. See, Mrs. Johnson, there, she been to the courthouse. Probate court, will reading. See, Oscar Montalvo got these accounts—Cayman Islands, Mexico, Venuzuela—and they got gold, deeds, diamonds in them. See, Oscar Montalvo should never have been no doctor. He should have been an investor. He tripled his doctor money. He is one rich motherfucker. Your mind working better now?"

Jerri had the urge to run out of the room. Ramón was illegal. He had been ducking the authorities his entire time in this country. Because he was illegal, he was outside the law, but because he was not a criminal, he was outside of the protection afforded to criminals. Palo had taught her that. Afraid, resorting only to a tight-lipped Mexican macho he only half-trusted, Ramón would fake stoicism and shut up, which made him a perfect target for Lee Ann and maybe Charlie. That macho stoicism also made him a perfect malleable tool for Rodney. An image from years before came to Jerri, another Mexican innocent faking toughness: Angel, several bullets from an automatic pistol pushing him into a gainer off her balcony and landing him on the hood of her Suburban. She never got the imprint of his body out of the hood of that Suburban. The image, like this instance, repeated itself.

"I killed him. Self-defense. That's what it says. American law says."

Rodney ran around the table to the side of Ramón's chair. Even Jerri found herself rising and moving toward him. "Who told you that?"

"Everybody knows that."

"You're illegal. You got no rights. You the perfect chump. You know what chump is."

"Wait!" Jerri yelled. "Leave him alone for just a second, Rodney."

She walked up to Ramón. She pulled a chair up to him. "Go ahead and admit that you're scared. You don't need to tell us that you're scared, but admit it to yourself. You've been pushed and shoved around ever since you came to this country. Now it seems like you're finally doing something about all the pushing around you've suffered. But you're just being used again. Maybe we're pushing you too. But right now, Rodney Lee and I are the lesser of a lot of evils."

Ramón stood and backed toward the door. Rodney braced himself, ready to call for a cop to help. Jerri could see confusion in Ramón's eyes. "Lee Ann said only five or ten years, probably less."

Rodney practically jumped up and down. "My man, my man. Now tell me, how did she know that?"

"I don't know. I think she just knows."

Jerri stood, grabbed the chair, and scooted it toward Ramón. He sat down, defeated, she guessed. "Did Charlie tell her how many years you could get?"

"I don't know. I don't know Charlie. I never see him."

"Wait, wait, wait, wait!" Rodney said. He held his palms out in front him waving them back and forth. "Did you ever actually fuck Lee Ann Montalvo?"

Ramón looked at Rodney like he didn't understand the question. "Yes."

"How often? How many times?"

"Do we have to go here?" Jerri asked.

"Don't you see? You were set up."

"I fucked her a lot," Ramón said. "After working on that place."

"The landscaping you did was beautiful. Quite well done." Jerri said. "You're an artist. You have a future in this county."

Ramón smiled, probably the first time in a really long time. "I'm good at it. I chipped some of those stones myself to get them to fit."

"Sounds like Lee Ann, and maybe good ol' Charlie, chipped you some to get you to fit the crime," Rodney said.

"I ain't talking."

"You could own your own business." Jerri said. "I know people who would hire you. You don't want to go to prison."

"No matter what Lee Ann promised you," Rodney added.

* * *

Dolph needed some advice to help him twist his mind around what he saw, so he drove to Cappy's. Pooter was opening the bar at Cappy's for the nooners, those businessmen who needed a slight bump to get on with their day. For a good bar, a classy bar, like the one at Cappy's, Pooter was indispensable. He was quiet and discreet, and his study of philosophy made him a good advisor. He was a lineman, always a lineman. He executed without anyone observing him, for the good of the team, and if needed, he could throw or take someone out. Which was why Dolph hired him and liked him around. The drinks at Cappy's were expensive, but for their price, a customer got not just a clean, handsome quiet place to drink with other well-to-do patrons, but, if he or she so desired, an intelligent conversation or commentary from a Ph.D. in philosophy. Which was why Dolph wanted to talk to him now.

"So just how sleazy is it?" Pooter asked as he dipped beer glasses that the night crew had failed to clean in a soapy sink.

"Charlie Montalvo spent the night with Lee Ann Montalvo," Dolph said.

"Big deal. So?"

Dolph's second beer of the morning was as good as the first one he had had with Pepper. "So is he fucking her? I mean is it like that?" Dolph raised his readers from his chest to the tip of his nose to watch the bubbles in his mug of beer, as though seeing details, closely, would help him think.

Pooter started debating. "He was comforting her. She was lonely. No reason to be suspicious. Can't a man simply spend the night with his sister-in-law? That's not necessarily sleazy. Maybe he's not fucking her." The debate was the reason Dolph had come by. Pooter's objections and deliberations helped Dolph come to his convictions about cases and people. Walter was too full of shit to offer much objectivity. A conversation with Pepper had no order.

Dolph started detailing what he was starting to believe. "Come on. She's hot. She's fucking the lawn boy, or so she claims, but she could really be fucking Charlie. And then they, the two of them, could be fucking the lawn boy over, setting him up to knock off Oscar, so they could get his money, of which he has got a lot, because, as Jerri told me, he has all kinds of funds stashed all over the Spanish-speaking Americas."

"I thought Heidegger was hard to understand." Pooter walked up to Dolph and set a beer and some French fries on the bar. "Want some of my breakfast?" Pooter's bald head caught some of the light beams sifting in from the front window and making soft and comforting tans, yellows, and browns in the polished wood. Dolph envied Pooter his job. Dolph had just crawled through the muck under a rich guy's house; Pooter's work was surrounded by softly lighted wood and beer. Walter's romantic view of Mexico might be a place where Dolph could buy a calm life like Pooter's.

"Or she's an evil bitch, the Frankenstein monster that Oscar created but that got out of his control, and now that she has gotten rid of Oscar and the lawn boy, she's going after Charlie. Or. . ."

Pooter interrupted. "Or he is not fucking her."

"You really think?"

"Are you fucking Jerri?"

"What the hell even makes you say that?"

"You work with her. You see her more than anyone else?"

"Hell, were you ever fucking Joan?"

Pooter hesitated. He sipped his beer and chewed a French fry. "I did, for a while, when she was desperate and drunk." Pooter chuckled.

"And now she's fucking Pepper." Dolph was immediately sorry, but Pooter had asked for it with that Jerri comment. "And I'm not fucking Jerri because she won't let me."

"And she won't let you because she's snakebit. Worse than you or Pepper. Every time she finds somebody she likes, he dies."

"Come on."

"You come on."

They both halted. Dolph had lost his concentration on the case. He couldn't solve anything now because his mind was whirring in a whole other direction. Maybe a beer more and he could let it whir out. Since he was now lost in big thinking, not detailed, close up thinking, he took his readers off the tip of his nose. Dolph asked gingerly, now not being mean, not trying to make a point, but just asking, "Okay, so Jerri is snakebit. And I guess what we could do to each other scares me too. What about you and Joan?"

Pooter rubbed the top of his head with one hand and sipped from his mug of imported beer with the other hand. "I'm ugly, slow, not the star. When her political career fell apart and she fell into the bottle, I helped pull her out. I got better looking." Pooter smiled, and Dolph, with his smile, urged him to go on. "I'm content to be where I am and think, not to torture myself with what ifs, but just to amuse myself with thinking. Joan can't do that. She always needs somebody to help."

"So that's Pepper, for now." Dolph didn't let his mind skip ahead a year or two to forecast Pepper's mind and body when Joan left him.

Pooter nodded. "When she came in here to see me and met Pepper, she flowed as only she can do, the charmer, the lady holding her age well despite the liquor and the hard luck, the politician and socialite, the dynamic community college teacher. She lit up the room more than the morning sunshine coming through the windows. And Pepper, for all his shortness and ugliness, always has had a way with women. He had to have her."

"So you watched her go to him?"

"She's happy."

"So is he. For now. But his hand will start shaking the whiskey out of his glass when she leaves him."

"But he's got something for now. All we get are little pieces. And what we are, in some sense, is how we think about the little pieces in our pasts."

Pooter turned his back to Dolph and walked to the end of the bar. Dolph craned his neck to see more than Pooter's back and the back of his domed head. "This isn't upsetting you, is it?"

With his back still to Dolph, Pooter said, "If we could know all that influences a person, all the reasons that go into his perceived self, then we could perfectly understand why he does what he does. We shouldn't constantly simplify people."

Dolph said, "Sometimes it is simple," but had no conviction in his reactionary statement.

"Just like Charlie, Oscar, and the lawn boy."

"So I should just forget what it looks like?"

"Maybe you should just wonder if you can leave alone what you don't know. Maybe you should leave things as they are. Maybe you should just leave Charlie alone."

Pooter turned around. He didn't look sad, but he looked like his mind had temporarily gone someplace else, like he was in trance. Dolph asked him, "You mean just let Oscar die? Just let Oscar's death be a mystery? Just let him go. Just like that?" Dolph snapped his fingers.

"Just let Charlie out of it."

"What about Lee Ann?"

Pooter snorted, "She sounds evil."

"God damn it. You and Walter try my soul."

Pooter walked back to Dolph and leaned over his French fries. "You know, that's why I'm just muscle for you, Dolph. I'm the philosopher, but I don't need to know the whole story. You want too much out of the story. You want too much from truth."

Dolph ground his teeth. "I just want them to know that I know. I want to make what happened stand still just a little so I can wrap my mind around it. Jesus, you and Walter."

Pooter shrugged. "You and Jerri. If you could just keep your minds from thinking so much, you just might eventually get together."

Dolph turned to look at the side of Pooter's big head. "So what time do you get off work? You think you could cruise by the Cadillac Bar and check to see if Charlie's Lexus is sitting in the parking lot? Jerri says he's prone to visit the place for happy hour."

"I have simple desires, but I do find ways to enjoy what you pay me."

* * *

Charlie stared into the frozen foam inside the circle of salt. It was his third margarita, and this new one was loosening his thoughts. He was thinking that Lee Ann was getting more and more difficult. She jumped from one consideration to the next and seemed to scold him when he couldn't keep up with her. But who could?

As he sipped the ice, he looked around the Cadillac Bar, and he couldn't help imagining Oscar lying dead and bleeding in a disgusting, urine-soaked bathroom. Charlie could guess why his brother liked to sit out in the heat, drinking lukewarm beer with the blue collar sorts of people Charlie usually ended up representing when they hurt themselves. Though it was an imitation of and named for the famous old bar in Nuevo Laredo, the Cadillac Bar off Flores was clean and well kept. There was air conditioning and even some misting fans out on the porch. And the bathroom was clean. Even if the bar had let in some gunman, in the Cadillac Bar Oscar would not have died soaking in strangers' piss.

Charlie caught himself. He was not responsible for the idea of killing his brother. But he was responsible for the legalistic details. He had had a long talk with Ramón about what he could and could not do. Charlie had suggested that their conversations were just hypothetical. Ramón was certainly too dumb to have figured out what Lee Ann and Charlie were pushing him into. Charlie's brain switched to the cool swallow of flavored ice and tequila. But tracking back to capture his thoughts, he couldn't believe that Ramón could possibly believe that Lee Ann would wait for him while he was in prison. He wondered what sorts of ego and delusion could have convinced Ramón that Lee Ann would find him attractive, would stick with him. For Oscar had nursed and nurtured not just her body but her mind. She had two degrees—well, one was an associates degree from a community college. Ramón, however, was hiding from immigration.

Brotherly love, Charlie thought and looked out the back door at the mist floating through the outdoor patio of the Cadillac Bar. But how could he have loved a brother who went to a dilapidated old ice house with that band of rag tag brothers instead of joining his real brother? Especially when Charlie had invited him countless times. Oscar was absent when Charlie got his degree. He was absent at Charlie's wedding. And he was absent when Charlie tried to go to him with his marital problems. But he sure took Charlie's money when Charlie contributed to his charities or investments.

How could Lee Ann possibly have stayed with a man like Oscar? He had made her, but she had grown beyond him. "Pygmalion," the attractive but aging lady detective had said. Naturally, Lee Ann would find Charlie more attractive, in every way, more of a mesh for her wants and needs, than Charlie's successful but still insensitive and uncouth brother. But now Lee Ann was acting insensitive and uncouth.

The lady detective was aging, but she was pretty. He thought about how it might feel pushing himself into the lady detective's short, compact body. That thought led him to another. He sipped the margarita for help remembering. Joan Phelan was aging and pretty. She was taller than the lady detective, maybe prettier. And Charlie liked the way Joan Phelan always stood up to him, told him how to conduct himself, but then let him into her arms, her bed, and her good graces. Thinking of Joan Phelan, Charlie left the Cadillac Bar.

When Charlie pulled into Joan Phelan's driveway, he opened the glove compartment of his Lexus and saw four garage door openers. One was his, the other was Lee Ann's. The other two he wasn't sure about. He tried one, and no doors opened. He tried the other, and Joan Phelan's garage door allowed him to enter. He pulled his car up alongside Joan's, closed the garage door behind him, got out and knocked at the door that opened into living room.

When Joan opened the door, he felt himself relax and smile. Joan started cussing: "You can't call? You just pull into the garage? Who do you think you are?" She sounded like Lee Ann.

"I'm sorry," Charlie said.

"Give me my garage door opener back. Go to your goddamn car, get my opener, and give it back to me." Charlie did as he was told, though when he grabbed the garage door opener, he wasn't sure that the had gotten the right one. When he got back into the house, he handed the opener to Joan. "Now back out of my garage door."

Charlie turned to look at it. "It's still closed." Before Joan could click the opener to get the door open, Charlie reached for her and took her hand. "I miss you. I was thinking about you. Do you still have a tequila shot and a margarita after work?

"Charlie, Charlie, Charlie. Like a bad penny, your name just came up."

Charlie caught his breath. "What? My name?"

"The man I see now. He's a friend of your brother's. I suppose you've heard your brother was killed?"

Charlie, quick as he could, slid past Joan and into the living room. "My God, what does he think? What's he saying?"

"I'm saying to go home."

Charlie tried hard to smile. He begged with his eyes. Joan began to wilt. "Got a drink for me?"

She started to melt, but not the pitcher of maragaritas she had just made. She poured one for each of them. As they sipped, they moved toward the sofa. And Charlie asked, "So who is the new guy you're seeing?"

"He's a rough, but deep down, he has an old soul." Joan chuckled, "And that soul's been beat up a little." They sipped in unison. "He reminds me of Pooter."

"So is this a serious relationship?"

"Serious enough that you should leave."

"So where is he?"

"He's working. I think he's trying to find out what really happened to your brother."

Charlie froze. He stood. Maybe he had better leave. Instead, he accepted another drink.

They drank on through the sitcoms and then the nine p.m. drama shows. They even started to laugh. When Charlie rolled into Joan and started to kiss her, she pushed him away. They backed away from each other. "I'm seeing a man," Joan said. Charlie, remembering Lee Ann's cussing and his brother lying in a urine. All the pressure squeezing him pushed him toward Joan. This time she did not push him away.

All his life, the one area where he excelled more than his brother was in getting women—not in keeping them. Instead of growing morose, instead of drinking, Charlie liked to fall into the arms of a woman. He knew that they may not have really cared for him, but the feel of their cool skin against his always made him think that at least they were faking care for him very well. And in physicalness with a woman, he felt closer to being human and closer to other humans than he did in law, education, knowledge, or family.

Sometime, after they both fell asleep, Joan's gasp awakened him. She pushed him out of her bed. And he gathered up his wrinkled suit and made his way to her couch. As he lay down, he saw her sleek body outlined a bit with some lost light coming from outside. Her body was not as good as Lee Ann's. She was not as enthusiastic. But he had felt something more honest and secure with her. "Get out of here as early as possible. As soon as you sober up," she said.

Chapter 6

With Pooter directing them from his cell phone, Walter, Dolph, and Pepper manuevered the exterminating van through the traffic on 281 north of town. They had entered the land of sprawling suburbs gobbling up views from the hills above Balcones fault. Jerri Johnson and Dolph's mother lived right on the very edge of Balcones fault. From their balconies they could see it below them: Trinity University and the San Antonio zoo. From their old rich area, the city pushed north in successive waves of real estate expansion, past the first loop, 410, and then up to and past the second loop, 1604, and onward, looking for isolation, those views, and leaving declining, deteriorating neighborhoods behind them. Dolph, Pepper, and Walter all lived south of downtown to avoid the views and the northern expansion.

"Jesus, take it easy," Walter said. Dolph tried zipping in and out of the stalling and starting traffic.

"I think I see a Lexus up ahead," Pepper said from the backseat.

"Look, this is no Orkin or some major exterminating firm. Any dents you put in my van, I pay for," Walter said.

"Just like driving in Mexico," Dolph said and turned to smile at Walter, one hand on the wheel, the other holding the cell phone to his ear, listening to Pooter calling off the landmarks and the mile markers of 281 North. Dolph had yet to get used to the gasoline-like smell of the bug spray stacked in the very back of the van. Walter had gotten used to breathing poisons.

"I get nervous out here," Pepper said from the back of the van. "I come out here to visit Joan, and I nearly panic. Just too many goddamn people."

97

"This is America," Walter said. "Take whatever distinction attracts you in the first place, then fill it with people, build some McDonalds and Wal-Mart super centers."

"Same thing is happening in Mexico." Dolph said.

Through and around two more cars, and Dolph saw Pooter, crammed into his small Toyota hybrid, waving his hand from side to side. Pooter returned his hand to the wheel, an earpiece from the cell phone hooked over his ear, always safe, watchful, a good lineman, a good bouncer and muscleman. Immediately ahead of them, Dolph saw Charlie Montalvo's tan Lexus. "I didn't know Charlie lived out here." Pepper said from the back.

"Do we know Charlie? Do you know Charlie?" Dolph asked.

"Yeah, Joan knows him. He was at a party Joan took me to. And, remember, he was at that party Oscar threw for his daughter, a real handsome guy."

"So he's met me?"

"I think," Pepper said.

"Shit," Dolph said. "He's seen me."

"Maybe he thinks you're just moonlighting for me," Walter said.

"Let's hope."

A few miles farther north, as the suburbs started to thin out, more cedar and rocks between the gated entrances, Charlie turned left into a subdivision. "God, he lives in the same place as Joan," Pepper said. The roads curved and rolled to show off some scenery. There were some of the cedars, at one time thought to be intruding trash trees, but now recognized as an endemic part of the Hill Country, but the developers had mowed down most everything else. Most of the yards were bare except for sprouting squares of St. Augustine grass; the suburban ornamental trees had yet to grow. Dolph turned as Charlie turned down another curving street. "Geez, he's going down the street to her house."

"How the hell can you tell?" Walter asked. "Why can't they build straight, grid streets anymore? I'd be lost forever in this place."

They turned again. "He can't live that close to her," Pepper said.

When Charlie pulled into Joan's driveway, Dolph checked in the rear view mirror. Pepper said nothing. He gulped hard, pressed his butt into the floor of the van and his back into the side of the van. When the garage door folded up and opened, like Joan was expecting Charlie, or even worse, like Charlie had a garage door opener, Pepper's face went blank. His lips worked but the cuss words did not filter out of his mouth. Dolph passed Joan's house, but Pepper's head swung back to look out the back windshield at Charlie's car in Joan's driveway.

Pooter stopped some way down the long block and around a curve from Joan's house. Dolph pulled up behind him. Dolph and Walter tried to get out curse words of encouragement, but nothing came out of their mouths. Words could not keep up with their fears and their runaway imaginations. Pooter got out of his hybrid and ran to Dolph's window. "Holy shit. What's he doing at Joan's?" Pooter said. The side door of the van slid open.

"You fucker. Did you know about this?" Pepper asked.

"Pepper, calm down. Get in the car with Pooter and get out of here."

"I ain't going nowhere. I'm here for the duration."

"I don't want you here."

"You ain't got a choice." Pepper left Dolph alone and turned his attention to Pooter. "So tell me you fucker, what do you know?"

"Nothing. I know she may have dated him once. He's kind of a smooth guy." Pepper pushed himself toward the door. Pooter pushed him back into the van. Dolph grabbed Pepper's shoulder over the console between the two front seats. Walter leaned back for a better view of the fight that looked to be starting.

"Where you going?" Dolph asked.

"Let me go, I'm stretching my legs," Pepper said.

"Get in the car with Pooter."

"I thought I was going home," Walter said.

"You all go. I'll stay," Dolph said.

Pepper pushed himself backwards, away from Pooter, into Dolph's hands. "I'm staying."

"We're damn good at this surveillance stuff," Walter said. "I wonder if anybody still hasn't seen or heard us?"

Pooter pushed himself into the van. Walter and Dolph straightened themselves in the front bucket seats. Pepper curled his arms, pressed his face against the window on his side of the van and stared at the driveway in front of Joan's house. "I always thought Joan would want an apartment downtown or near downtown, like me," Pooter said. "I never figured she'd commit the money to moving way the hell out here."

"What the fuck is she doing with him?" asked Pepper.

"All I'll do is wait until he leaves," Dolph said. "Everybody else go home with Pooter."

Pepper crouched with his hands on his knees. One knee was artificial, rebuilt because it was all but shot off helping Dolph. Without forcing more words out of his mouth, Pepper was reminding Dolph of the past so that Dolph could not possibly kick him out.

Pepper sat with his back against the wall of the van while Walter and Pooter got out and crammed into the Prius, Walter saying, with the way he tilted his head back to see out of the top of his thick bifocals, for Dolph to protect the van at all costs; Pooter, in his typical style, resigned himself to his backup role. They drove away.

After splitting a can of beans with Pepper, washed down with a can of beer apiece, Dolph moved the van across the street from Joan's. Then he joined Pepper. Dolph sat in the folding chair next to all the odds and ends of surveillance equipment. Inhaling the bug spray scent made the beer and the beans roll around in his stomach. Pepper, butt on the floor, back against the van wall, asked until well into the night, "So is he still there? Ain't he left yet?" And so it went, throughout the night, Dolph catching a few winks, Pepper getting none.

At first light, when Dolph was fully conscious but slightly drugged and nauseous from smelling bug spray throughout the night, he uncurled, pushed against the knots of his body, and groaned as he got eye level to the van's window and looked at Joan's house. In front of the house in scattered groups were deer. He remembered seeing them roaming through the neighborhood when he woke up during the night. These does were timid and skittish, yet they pillaged the suburban lawns and flowerbeds like an arrogant inner-city street gang. Dolph looked from the does to Pepper, whose whole face seemed to droop. "You haven't slept have you?"

"You still can't shake that government job, can you? Still think you're on the state teat. Always worried about sleep."

Dolph rubbed at his face, feeling its weariness and slack. He knew he must look as bad as Pepper. "I gotta quit this kind of shit."

"That fucker. So he's fucking Oscar's widow. Now he's fucking or trying to fuck my lady. Let's go kick his ass."

"How do you know he's still there?"

"Nothing's moved."

"So you have been up all night?"

"What else am I gonna do besides worry?"

Dolph tried straightening himself but felt stiff knots in every one of his joints, even his fingers. "God damn, I'm getting old."

Pepper straightened. "What?" Twisting against the pressure in his joints, Dolph turned to the van's window. What he saw must have been running a hot ice pick through Pepper's groggy but now seared mind: the garage door curling open and the back end of Charlie's Lexus moving slowly into the driveway. The deer scattered.

As the Lexus got into the driveway, the door folded all the way open, and standing in the frame of the open garage door was Joan Phelan, smiling, hugging herself, and waving to her friend, lover, confidant, co-conspirator. Before he thought, Dolph said, "Pepper, relax. This doesn't mean anything."

But instead of an argument or a "fuck you nicely," Dolph was answered by the whoosh of Pepper pushing past him to the back door of the van. The door of the van was gaping open before Dolph could move. Pepper was out the door as Dolph got to it and grabbed.

Dolph lowered himself out of the van to see Pepper hobbling toward the Lexus. Dolph was slow because of too many nights squatting in cacti and looking for illegals, but he was still faster than the hobbled Pepper. As he dashed toward Pepper, he saw Charlie look out the side window of the Lexus and mouth, "Dolph," and he saw Joan running toward Pepper.

Before he got to Pepper, Dolph saw Charlie jump out of his Lexus, run to Joan, and hold her, just enough to slow her down on her way run to Pepper. Pepper no longer had a filter for his words. They were coming out of his mouth quite well. Dolph got to him as he was cussing in the general direction of Charlie. Dolph caught the heel of a shoe as he dived for Pepper's thighs. His tackle was good. Pepper went down cussing.

Joan stopped and stood in front of the curled Pepper and Dolph and braced herself. Charlie moved toward them. Yesterday's suit was crumpled and his tie was slung over his shoulder. "So who the fuck are you?" Charlie yelled.

"If my former buddy would get up off my ass, I'd show you who the fuck I am."

"Everybody just stop! Or just leave!" Joan yelled.

Dolph tried to push himself up, first knees, then hands on thighs to a full standing position. Joan sniffed: the bug spray. "I can explain," Dolph said, chuckled at the cliché. As he well knew, his mind was not working fast enough to explain a thing.

He didn't have to. Charlie's eyes drifted to the van, the open door. Dolph saw the clunky gears of Charlie's supposedly quick lawyer's mind slowly churning: Dolph, the exterminator van, Lee Ann's house the day before. "Dolph," Joan said. "You smell like rancid chemicals."

"Dolph," Charlie's lisps registered as the situation registered in his mind. "How long have you been watching? Do you have a warrant? Why the hell are you watching?"

"Dolph's watching who?" Joan asked. Cylinders clicked in her mind, which was much faster than Charlie's. "Oh shit. Dolph, you're spying on us."

"Not you, honey," Pepper said.

Charlie started backing toward his Lexus.

Dolph looked at Joan, then at Pepper. He bent to help Pepper up. Then he stepped in front of him to keep him from advancing toward Charlie. "Run, Charlie. Go. Get out of here. Everybody here is just screwed. You stick around, everything's just gonna get worse. Go think about it."

Charlie did as Dolph ordered. He backed his Lexus away. And when the Lexus got partially down the rolling, curving suburban street, Joan walked to Pepper, threw her arms around him, and kissed him. Lucky Pepper, Dolph thought, and all but forgave him for totally fucking up everything. Then Pepper starting yelling.

* * *

The screaming and the accusations started in the front yard, scattering the deer and attracting the good suburban neighbors. It never occurred to either Pepper or Joan to step closer together so that they could talk in quieter tones. Dolph even tried pushing Pepper toward her. But still they yelled.

They moved their hollering into the house. Pepper yelled to ask why Joan so conveniently left Charlie Montalvo out of her stories to him. Joan yelled her answer back by asking Pepper what right he had to determine her friends. "Just look at your friends," she yelled back. "I'm not fucking my friends," Pepper responded. Like two fighters, hesitant to get too close before the match really started, they faced each other while one stood still and the other circled, both yelling, then the other stood and the other circled. Pepper made a swipe and grab at a vase in the orderly living room. Joan's response—"Okay, let's go all the way white trash on this if you want. Go ahead, throw the fucking vase"—kept Pepper from throwing the vase.

Joan turned her back to Pepper, made her way into the kitchen, and poured a cup of the coffee that she had just made for her and Charlie. Pepper followed her to the kitchen. Remembering his big grand kitchen in the failing resort he tried to build in Big Bend; remembering the kitchen he constructed with Dolph's mother for the bed and breakfast in Alpine; remembering the large, shiny, clean industrial-strength kitchen he cooked at in prison; remembering the warm feel and smells garlic and onion and cumin in the kitchen where he now worked massaged Pepper's mind. Kitchens were for reconciliation, retreats, alliances. Before he was arrested, he talked to Dolph and made chili for the arresting officers in his Big Bend kitchen. He realized that women had treated him worse than Joan. This was no great matter. He stepped toward Joan, knowing that he was smiling, and that smile must have made her stand still instead of back away. They hugged, took their first sips of coffee, and simultaneously realized that they had left Dolph outside with the tame deer and the gawking neighbors. When Pepper opened the door, Dolph was concluding his call to Jerri. Pepper jerked his head to steer Dolph inside.

"So what does Jerri say?" Pepper asked.

"Jerri says, 'Oh shit,'" Dolph hung his head. "Jesus, Pepper, you could have screwed the whole case here."

"Hell, Dolph, you know how I get when it comes to women."

103

"That's a hell of a defense. You were working for me, on a case. This is serious, this is not just fucking around. You don't let a woman interfere."

"Like you ain't never let a woman interfere. Need I remind you of a little incident in Mexico when I held a gun to a fucker's head because Jerri Johnson gives you the say so. Just like she is now giving you the say so."

"That's two different cases."

"So where the hell do I fit in?" Joan asked and stalked into the room, looking like a tiger, ready to resume her fight with Pepper if necessary. Seeing her anger directed toward someone other than him made Pepper want her, made him happy he had charged Charlie. "So I'm in my own house, entertaining a guest, and I find out you two are watching. And then my lover comes charging in here accusing me of God knows what."

"We were watching Charlie, like I said, honey," Pepper said stoking the argument that had just worn them out. "You gotta admit," Pepper started to say, but Joan cut him off.

"I gotta admit that a friend—a *friend*, notice I said *friend*, someone I've got no reason to tell you about—comes over here, and because of that I'm indicted in some sort of half-concocted case."

Pepper's eyes felt like they were going to pop out of his head from his lack of sleep, his anger, and his frustration at his inability to just let the argument simmer down and then finally turn cool. "He must be some kind of a special friend."

"Jesus, so was the brother."

"So you were fucking Oscar too!"

Dolph screamed, sort of like the low growl from a hurt dog. Pepper turned to look at his buddy. Dolph hung his head and his shoulders. He looked around himself. He dropped himself on the couch and let his head fall back onto the edge of the couch. "Ain't you even tired, Pepper? I got hardly any sleep, and I know you probably got none."

"All you people on the government teat worry about is sleep."

Joan actually smiled, turned, went into the kitchen, and came out with three cups of coffee and some plastic-wrapped Danishes on a plate. She placed the tray in front of Dolph. Pepper took this as a peace sign. He lowered himself into a recliner and grabbed a cup of coffee. "I'm wide awake," she said to Dolph. "I got a good night of sleep." She turned to glare at Pepper. "I wasn't watching anyone. And I wasn't fucking anyone." She hesitated and looked straight at Pepper, "Even though Charlie Montalvo tried. But he always tries."

Before Pepper could make his tired mind and frayed nerves forgive and forget or fight some more, Dolph asked, "What did Charlie want? What did he do?"

With her leg, Joan slid a footstool over her laminate wood floor. She sat on it, in front of the coffee table in front of Dolph, her knees pointed toward Dolph, her coffee resting in her lap. God, she was beautiful, Pepper thought. "I'm a lawyer," Joan said, "but should I call one? Whom am I talking to?"

"You could be talking to the police."

"Fuck you, then, Dolph."

"You want to fucking lighten up?" Pepper said, looking at Dolph. He reached for Joan, but she would have nothing to do with his outstretched hand. She was tough, smart, wasn't taking shit, was not about to crack. Dolph could be annoying, but she would have none of it. She was more than a match for Dolph. Pepper knew why he loved her, why he wouldn't at all mind if she were the last woman he ever truly came to love hard and deep.

"Jerri will tell her lawyer what happened. He will tell the police because he wants to cooperate with them because he needs them. He's very political."

"I should understand political," Joan said.

"The long and the short: the police will come question you."

"Is that all?"

"Depends on what Charlie has to say."

Joan looked at Pepper, held his stare. His heart leapt to his throat. "Honey," he uttered. "Tell Dolph."

"Both Montalvo brothers are political. I met Oscar. I slept with him." She stopped and reflected Pepper's stare right back at him. Well, of course she did, Pepper told himself. Why shouldn't she. She has a right. Fuck her.

"Then I slept with Charlie." Joan turned to look at Dolph.

"Oh well, that explains fucking everything," Pepper said, nearly knocking his coffee off his lap as he straightened up.

Dolph calmly sipped his coffee. "She's at least being honest, Pepper," Dolph said.

"Whooppee shit for honesty."

"You're forgetting how you met me. I was in that restaurant with both of them. That's how we met."

"Well, who haven't you fucked?" Pepper said. Immediately, he regretted what he said, hung his head, brought it up to see Joan now hang her head.

"They're quite a pair. They compete over everything. That's why I dropped Charlie. I expect now he's gone right to the source, right to his brother's wife."

Dolph pushed himself to the edge of the sofa and set his coffee down on the table. "So what did he say?"

"He said he wanted to sleep with me again. He said he wanted to get together. He cried. He said he was involved with things he couldn't handle."

Dolph stood. The coffee table shook and his coffee splashed when his shins hit the edge of the coffee table. "So did he say who he was involved with? He mention Lee Ann? Is he truly indeed fucking her? Did he fucking help kill his brother?"

Joan looked up at him wearily. Pepper felt left out. "He's scared. So he figured he'd get a piece of the old girlfriend. That's how I figure it. That's all I know," Joan said.

"And you're sure he didn't get a piece?" Pepper asked.

"And you're sure that's all he said?" Dolph asked.

"It's the story I'm telling you. It's the story I'm telling the police. I'm a lawyer. But it's also the story I'm telling my new lover, Pepper. So you two can sit here and debate all you want on whether you think it's the truth or not. Me, I'm tired of having to defend myself."

Pepper was in love all over. He took it that she had said all that she had said for him alone. He turned to Dolph, "So why does Jerri even have to know about this?"

"She already knows," Dolph said.

"So why does she have to do anything? You know me." Pepper said to Dolph, then he looked at Joan so she would know that he was talking to

106

her too. Pepper was at a point where he had to choose between his past with Dolph and the promise of some kind of future with Joan. Even when he made his most fucked-up decisions, he had thought them through. And even after he had seen that they were gigantic fuckups, he knew that he had had to make the decisions he had because he just couldn't bear not knowing how the choice would play out. "I'm going to have to choose, ain't I?"

"No, you don't," Dolph said.

"Joan is worth more to me than setting Oscar's death right. Here, right now, I quit. I'm sticking with Joan. I got this new lady and having her is giving me back some years I wasted. I'm not with you on this."

Dolph's face twisted up. Pepper knew that he was calling in markers for past deeds. But he and Dolph didn't work that way. They didn't keep tabs but just a little. He had always told Dolph what he had done or what he would do. Or he just did it, then told Dolph. Dolph might not have approved. Hell, Dolph even busted him. Though they had cussed each other plenty, they had never fussed at each other. They let each other fuck up. Dolph said, "Pepper, we have to go to a funeral. You better get some sleep. I'll get Walter's van back to him. I'll talk to Jerri."

Pepper looked at Joan and said to Dolph, "I guess I need to say 'thank you, buddy.'" He said to Joan, "You'll see, baby. Doph'll come through."

When Dolph left, Joan came to Pepper and kneeled in front of him. He bent forward, and she leaned back and tilted her head to kiss him in such a way that, even if she had kissed or fondled Charlie the night before, Charlie's favors were not like the kiss Pepper was getting now.

* * *

As Charlie steered his way out of the low hills that guarded Joan's suburb, his mind rewound the movie of the bullet-headed man with the diamond earring charging toward him. His lawyer training told him that this man was not important. What he believed to be important, what stuck in in his mind was Dolph Martinez's face. He had seen that face the day before at Lee Ann's house. A year or so before, he had seen the face at one of his brother's parties. Dolph—strange name for the Mexican-looking man—was one of Oscar's drinking buddies, from that crumbling old ice house where Oscar liked to lord it over his social and financial lessers. Dolph Martinez was an exterminator? So why was he following Charlie? He had an assignment to spray Lee Ann's house and then Joan's. Pondering these questions, Charlie nearly hit a deer.

No, no, no. Dolph was a cop—no, a private detective. No, Dolph worked for a woman private detective. A woman private detective had just talked to Charlie at the Cadillac Bar. Jerri Johnson was her name. The deer watched as Charlie all but missed a curve in the road and took out some tall grass, some prickly pear, and nearly a cedar tree.

As he jerked his car back into the curve, he felt his thighs for the cell phone in his slacks pocket. More twisting and convolutions, more curves, more staring deer, and he was on the cell phone to Lee Ann. "Get off the phone," she said succinctly. So Charlie drove down 281 to Alamo Heights and pulled into his brother's mansion.

"So you've got a private detective following you around, and you drive to my house in broad daylight on the day of your brother's fucking funeral. You numb nuts, stupid, son of a bitch," Lee Ann screamed when she met him in the dark living room.

"He's your husband," Charlie stated. And the cussing started again, but because he was growing used to Lee Ann cussing at him, Charlie's attention and his eyesight roamed around the dark living room. Some of the paintings were gone. The drapes in back were gone. The main sofa was gone. The living room was dark because the blinds, still up, not sold or stashed, were closed. Lee Ann, Charlie decided, was sealing herself in.

Lee Ann wore herself out cussing and settled on one question, "Are you absolutely sure that it is Dolph Martinez and that he works for a private detective firm?"

"Mostly."

"Good goddamn. What was I thinking to ever even let you in my house, not now, but the first time. You know what's at stake here?"

"Why don't we open the blinds?"

"Are you fucking nuts? Get out of my house. Go on, get out. It stops now. Don't come over here. Stay at your own house. Just leave. Go away."

Charlie backed toward the door and raised his hands and shook them in front of him. He looked at her face. It seemed to be cracking. Oscar had

had his doctor friends pull it too tight. Steam, or whatever her anger was building in her head, was about to rupture her face. Then his gazed dropped down. She had on the black slip for her funeral dress. Her cleavage rose up over the slip. "Honey," Charlie said. "Let me stay here."

"Sit down." Charlie sat on the floor. Lee Ann paced in front of him. "So what do they know?"

"I'd say they know nothing."

"So why were you at this Joan Phelan's place?"

Charlie jolted himself upright. He tried pushing his mind to work faster. "I couldn't see you. I was scared, that was all. And she's an old friend."

"Good Lord, you are scum!" Lee Ann brushed a strand of hair out of her face. "Your brother is just dead and now you're abandoning me, his wife."

"No, no, it's not like that. She's just a friend."

"You spent the night."

"My house is being renovated. There's stuff all over. She invited me."

"So how can I trust you?"

"Baby, what can I say? I'm here. I'm coming to you."

"You're running to me." Lee Ann turned her back to Charlie and asked softly as though to herself, "How can I trust you?"

Charlie pushed himself up and embraced her from behind, his arms wrapped around her as he pressed his chest into her shoulder blades, felt her nice buns on his thighs. "Baby, baby."

Lee Ann stepped away from Charlie. "This guy chasing you. This guy is the jealous boyfriend. What? Think!" Charlie tried to answer, but Lee Ann interrupted. "Shut the fuck up. I told you to think first. Don't just answer with your crotch but think. Remember."

Charlie tried to answer again. But Lee Ann shushed him. The short man running toward him, the ruddy face, the buzz-cut head, the diamond stud earring, the waxed moustache, how could he forget a face like that? Pepper. Pepper. Pepper. Dolph Martinez's buddy, another friend of Oscar's. "Pepper something or other. Pepper somebody."

"Why was he chasing you?"

"He was jealous, I guess."

"What do they know? What do they think they know?"

"They know I was here night before last. They know I was there last night."

"Let's hope they think you're a horny toad, can't keep it in your pants, and are waving it around like you had a flag on it."

"Honey, I'm with you, baby. This whole thing ought to show I'm with you."

Lee Ann's face scrunched up, and that pang of worry communicated itself to Charlie without her saying anything. "Ramón will shut up, right?"

"That Jerri Johnson woman works for the lawyer representing him, Rodney Lee."

"Oh shit."

"He won't talk. You told me he won't talk. You told me to explain it all to him."

Charlie pulled his mind away from Lee Ann's artificial body. "That still doesn't indict me."

Both of them froze. "You son of a bitch. You backstabbing fucker."

"No, I didn't mean that."

"They saw you leaving my house. They're probably outside right now watching as your sorry ass pulled in here. So don't you think they're doing a little guessing? And don't you think they're telling poor, ignorant, clueless fucking Ramón what they're guessing?"

Charlie stepped back from Lee Ann. "Oh shit."

"What's wrong now, cocksman? Gone a little limp?"

Chapter 7

Pooter, Dolph, Walter, and Pepper sat in the first pew on one side of the church aisle while the family sat in the first pew on the other side. The priest had already praised Oscar's worth to the community; now he was lying about how he knew and appreciated Oscar who hadn't been in a church in twenty years.

Pooter had a way to put his mind elsewhere yet keep it focused. Doing so got him through four years as a pulling guard at the University of Texas. His body knew the plays and the techniques; his mind yearned for more. So Pooter let his mind sum up Oscar.

None of them—Dolph, Pepper, Walter, or Pooter—really knew Oscar. They had stumbled upon him at Big John's. He was simply a guy they drank with. Pooter was sure that deep down Oscar cared for some hazy notion of "his" people. His people didn't include his family. And in that way, Oscar was a part of their crowd—his pallbearer bar buddies and himself. None of them really had a family. Dolph, Pepper, Walter, and Pooter had all lost a real traditional family somewhere, and they all had replaced it with those like them.

Pooter knew himself, knew what he was good at. Even with his mind roaming to where it wished to go or Pooter let it go or desired it to go, Pooter was good at watching over people. He had tried an actual sexual style affair with Joan Phelan years ago in Austin when she was in a downward, alcoholic skid from her failed attempt at running for political office, but when she went to Big Bend to escape her failure and to start anew in isolation, and even then started a series of affairs with men bad for her, Pooter watched over her. That satisfaction ultimately felt better than the sexual affair. So when she ran from Big Bend to San Antonio, Pooter eventually followed her. But by the time he came to San Antonio, he also had Dolph and Pepper to watch over. And here, to watch over all of them, was Jerri Johnson.

Pooter had tried to explain to Jerri that her role, as fate or circumstance had prescribed for her, was watching over people. It had not given her a family or a husband. In fact, the gods deliberately seemed to take those things from her. So he urged her to find her happiness in watching over people. As far as he knew, she could not.

Pooter's mind got so far beyond the church where he was sitting that he had to order it back while the priest droned on about Oscar's nobility. He looked over at the pew across the aisle, the one with the family, the place from which the attack was likely to come, the one against which, he would protect his friends.

One of his jobs was to keep Dolph awake. He looked to his left. Dolph's chin was hitting his chest. To Dolph's left was Pepper, who had caught some sleep at Joan's house. Given the situation, only some of which Pooter had heard, Joan had decided to stay home. Pepper showed up cranky, mumbling, cussing, looking sideways at Dolph. As Pooter well knew, that kind of crankiness in Pepper, as with most men, was surely due to a woman. "Be nice to have a beer," Pepper whispered to Dolph, loud enough for Pooter to hear. Pepper must have been getting happier if he was thinking about beer. Pooter elbowed Dolph. Dolph pulled his head up right and then shook it and turned his attention to the pew across the aisle and to the family.

Pooter followed Dolph's gaze. Pooter knew that he was to watch, to pay attention. He could, but since he could also let his mind go elsewhere, he sometimes missed details. Dolph was much better at watching and noticing. In fact, in one discussion he had with Pooter, one of those intellectual debates that the two had fueled with alcohol, where the enjoyment came from the way the argument spun all around some central idea, and never quite stood still, Dolph had said that the real world moral imperative was just to notice. Dolph won that debate.

Dolph elbowed Pooter. Pooter looked to the family pew and saw Lee Ann crying. Her emotions were as fake as her face. Pooter could not imagine men murdering and betraying each other for her. He couldn't see the attraction, not even in her man-designed body. Seeing her sob, her lawyer, Charlie Montalvo, offered her a handkerchief. She accepted, and with her other hand, she reached to hold his hand. With one hand in hers, Charlie then wrapped his other arm around her. "See," Dolph said. And Pooter wondered just what he was seeing. Dolph whispered, "The hand-holding is just a little too long for comforting." Pooter looked. It wasn't the hand holding he noticed. It was the desperate way Charlie looked at her, like he had already lost her.

Farther down the aisle sat Oscar's daughter, Renee. Her chin trembled, but she tried to fight against it. She must have also been trying to turn her attention away from the service by staring down at her skirt, then running her flat palms against it to straighten out the wrinkles.

To the other side of Renee was the most mysterious woman: Renee's mother, Oscar's first attempt at marital bliss. She watched the others. She smiled at her daughter, but her mouth pulled tight when she looked at Lee Ann deliberately trying to make her chin tremble, just as hard as Renee was trying to keep her chin from shaking.

"Touching, ain't it," Pooter heard Pepper say.

At Mission Park Cemetery, right across Military Drive from Big John's Ice House, Dolph's gang and two unknown men hoisted Oscar's casket on to the scaffolding that would lower it into the grave. They stood, the hot sun at their backs, the mourners under the canopy while the priest droned on some more. They just kept coming into the world and leaving, you couldn't stop the cycle, Pooter thought, though we all deserve just a bit more acknowledgment that we were here at all.

As the eulogy ended, people rose and made their ways back to their cars. Without the priest's sanctimonious droning, and after his short nap during the droning, Dolph was now fully awake and wired. He looked all around. He was someone to fear again. Since he had come east from Big Bend, he had lost all of his administrative and legal caution. Now that he no longer had the Border Patrol to protect, only his reputation or safety were at stake. So Dolph had turned impatient. Jerri could control him, sometimes. Pooter watched Dolph too, for Dolph's own safety.

With Pooter following behind him, Dolph made his way through the departing people. He pulled up in front of Lee Ann and Charlie. Pooter was too far behind to hear the first words, but he shoved and pushed his way closer to hear Dolph say, "So Charlie, things could be getting sticky. We've got some evidence and a lot of suspicions."

"Oh, Dolph," Pooter heard from behind him. He turned to see Pepper. "He's gotten worse. He just can't leave well enough alone. Now we're going do something illegal or end up getting in some kind of fight."

"So what's he doing?"

"He learned that from ol' Joe Parr, Jerri's ex, the Texas Ranger. Charge, always fucking charge. Well, hell. Hell, goddamn it," Pepper said. Pooter could see that Pepper was fighting himself as well as Dolph. Soon they might all be swinging fists.

Lee Ann had an index finger out and was poking Dolph in the chest, "This is my husband's funeral. Can't you let me even grieve before you come barking at my heels?"

"Oh shit," Pooter heard Pepper say from behind him.

"I'll get a restraining order if I have to," Charlie said.

Dolph stepped back. "Ramón Burgiaga has a new version of what happened." Dolph waited. Charlie looked at Lee Ann. Dolph continued, "And Oscar Montalvo was a friend of mine. Going out like he did, I want people to know what happened to him."

Lee Ann pulled Charlie away from Dolph. Pooter loosened his tie and unbuttoned his collar now that the public burial was all over, the actual burying, the shoveling would be done by some illegal aliens working for below minimum wage. Dolph stepped up to Pooter and Pepper.

Pepper started: "Dolph, can't you just let shit alone. How do you know Oscar wants you to bust his wife and brother? Look, look over there," Pepper gestured toward the casket on the scaffolding. "You hear or see the casket bumping and scratching from Oscar rolling around inside of it?"

"Maybe I want to know," Dolph said.

"You told Jerri what you done?"

Dolph looked away from Pepper and toward Pooter. "No."

"So what are you thinking?"

"I'm thinking that, if you push, the guilty party will push back." Dolph looked at Pooter. "Ain't that right, Pooter. Ain't that what history tells us?"

"You talking about U.S. history, world history, or our history?"

"It's the pushing part scares me," Pepper said. "Ain't we been pushed enough?"

"I thought you were out of it?"

Pepper tugged at his earlobe with the diamond earring in it. "I don't want to be, but I am. I got to be." Pepper turned his back to them and walked toward the car.

"You're probably going to need a body guard," Pooter said. Pooter welcomed the opportunity. It was what he was good at—that and putting his mind where he wanted it to be.

* * *

Instead of going to Oscar's funeral, Jerri went to Palo's hospital room because she wanted to prepare for Palo's funeral. She knew that it was not far away. This might be his last day. She found him on his side in the dark room. To brighten the room for herself as well as for him, she opened a blind, and the sun streamed into the room. She circled the bed to look at his face. Palo didn't budge. His eyes were clenched shut. She saw no sign of breathing no heaving, no rustling sound from his nose. She looked up at the monitor and saw a steady beep. Fearing the machine was not doing its job, Jerri stuck her finger under Palo's nose and felt just a tiny sensation of his breathing. Palo did not even notice the finger.

Jerri sat in a chair directly across from his gaze, as though his closed eyes had pushed her there. She wondered if he could hear, "Palo, Palo, are you awake?" She asked. She saw no movement and got no response. Jerri leaned back in her chair and let her head fall back over her shoulders and against the wall. "Oh, Palo, you and Dolph were right. There is more to the case with the murdered doctor. There's always more. And I'm so tired of the more."

She knew she had to defend Ramón, but she wanted to prosecute Lee Ann. Rodney Lee, though, wanted nothing more than to give Ramón a good day in court. Because of Dolph's and his crew's work, Ramón was not going to be railroaded into a death sentence. "He was duped," she said to Palo.

Jerri pulled her head up to look again at the motionless Palo. She had spent far too much time with this man. "I'm tired of it all, Palo. I feel like letting it go. I've seen it. I can live with it. It's nothing new. I want to forget about this lawn boy."

Jerri knew that she wasn't really speaking to Palo. She wasn't really speaking to herself. She was cursing the dark, so to speak, and the light too. "I feel worse about my family. I've let myself become a grandmother without ever really knowing my son, his wife, or even my grandchild. Instead, I was seeing to the likes of people like Ramón."

"J. J. practically grew up without me. Now his son will grow up without knowing that he even has a grandmother. I have to force myself even to remember my daughter-in-law's name. *Naomi*. There it is. Dumb name." Jerri put her elbows to her knees and said in Palo's direction. "See there? See what I'm saying? What right have I to criticize?"

"You got a family," Palo said almost inaudibly and made Jerri pull her elbows off her knees to sit erect in her chair.

"You're awake?"

"I think, but just for a little while. You think I would have got enough sleep in my life. Now I spent what little, tiny bits of my life I got doing nothing but sleep. Don't go like this, Jerri. It's stupid. Better I got blown up back when than to sleep through death."

"Palo, please. Let's not think like that."

"I think maybe I can think what I want. Who to tell me 'no' now?"

"So you were listening to me?"

"I think. I'm not sure. But I woke up to tell you that you are wrong. You do have a family."

"They're in Dallas." Jerri shifted in her chair to look into the sun coming into the room. "And I should be too."

Palo's eyes struggled open. "Your family is Dolph and his friends. What they going to do without you? You are their mama. You got a job here."

"I'm their boss."

"We don't get to choose our families. They happen. Just like you happened to me. And you took the place of my son. And you are here, no one else, watching me die, like a good daughter."

"Palo, that's different."

"No different." His voice had gained some strength. Jerri didn't have to cock her head and nearly squint her ears. As she listened, she grew sad. He was dying, yet she had never known Palo as other than an old man. She couldn't even imagine him young. "You were with Vincent. You were with Joe Parr. That is all, no choice."

"And I lost them," Jerri said. And still, she knew that she could not say that without bitterness and indignation.

Palo's mouth moved again, but no sounds came out. Jerri stood and bent over him and put her ear next to his lips. When he said nothing, she straightened up. His eyes closed. She looked quickly at the monitor, still a steady beep.

Jerri sat back down, and when she caught her chin hitting her chest, she thought she should go. Pulling her purse to her, Jerri stepped out of the hospital room door and walked down the long hall toward the elevator. In a metal and plastic chair near the elevator sat Sandra Beeson. When Sandra saw Jerri, she rose and stepped to greet her. "What are you doing here?" Jerri asked.

"I thought you might like to see somebody," Sandra said. "I thought you might like to get a cup of coffee or a nice tall drink of some sort."

"But how did you drive?"

"My cataracts bother me at night. It's still daylight outside. It's our time of day. We're ladies of independent means with time on our hands."

Jerri gave a backward glance at Palo's. "I'll treat," Sandra said.

"You're not even supposed to drive," Jerri said.

"What's more remarkable than my driving here is that I almost knew you'd be here." Sandra tapped her head, "Intuition, huh?"

When they got to the hospital lobby, Jerri's cell rang. Her secretary informed her that Lee Ann Montalvo had called and urgently needed a call back. Not wanting to give her cell phone number up to the likes of Lee Ann Montalvo, Jerri called Lee Ann from a pay phone. Lee Ann wanted to know if they could meet, if something could be worked out, if Dolph and his crew could just leave her alone. Smiling at Sandra, who beamed back, Jerri said that of course they could work something out.

* * *

After the funeral, Dolph threw his sportcoat in the back seat of his car, pushed his sleeves up, and drove to Renee's first floor apartment in the old mansion off McCullough. He parked down the street, walked to the wide front porch, and planted himself in a chair looking over the porch railing. His nodded off a couple of times as he waited, but he shook his head to keep himself awake. Then his head fell backward as he leaned the other way.

In the old days, when he lived with Pepper at Cleburne Hot Springs Resort, he could stay up all night and then track wets the next day. Age, Dolph figured, was the culprit. He needed to get out of this business. But he always got some little tingle way down inside him, the one that Pepper always cautioned him about, that made him want to set just a little chunk of his world a little straighter. He didn't like people fucking with the chunks in his world.

Oscar was dead. Now Pepper was retreating out of the world he and Dolph had started and into a closed world with Joan Phelan partly because of the two figures walking up the sidewalk to the front porch: Renee and Izzy.

When Izzy recognized Dolph, he spun in a circle to look at Dolph. "You again, man?"

"I came unarmed." Dolph turned to Renee, "I saw you at the funeral. That was good of you. Thank you for helping thus far. Your Dad would be happy."

"Did you see? I cried," she said. "I didn't think I would." Renee stepped onto the porch, and Izzy tentatively followed. Dolph leaned in close to get a view of Renee's eyes, to smell her breath. She pulled away from him, "Mr. Martinez, please. I'm sober. I'm not high."

Dolph turned to look at Izzy. "I'm proud of you," not specifying if he was talking to Renee or Izzy.

"Are you going to make your home here or, like, what?" Izzy said. The jewelry that hung from the piercings in his head jingled when he talked.

Dolph turned to Renee. "Your father tried to make things better. That's more than you can say for most people."

"He never really tried too hard for his family."

"So what about your step-mother? What do you think of her? Better yet, what did she think of your father."

"Look, Gramps," Izzy spoke from behind Dolph. Dolph hung his head to listen. "You ain't got your toy gun now. So why don't you just get the hell outa here?"

"You really zapped him with the gun?" Renee said and giggled.

"Whoa, yeah, I told you he did," Izzy said and stepped around Dolph. As he stepped around him, Dolph caught Izzy with his fist right beneath the sternum. Izzy doubled up and then hit the ground coughing. Dolph looked around to see if anybody had seen him.

"I really did, Renee. And he deserved it. And I think that you really ought to think hard about the company you keep."

Dolph dug in his pocket to pull out a tiny police gat. He bent over and lightly bounced it off of Izzy's head. "If I remember correctly, I thought I told you to move on," Dolph said. Izzy groaned.

Renee dropped to a knee and cradled Izzy's head. "Get out of here, you crazy fucker," she said looking up to Dolph.

"You know I'm right," Dolph said. "And by the way, I wasn't about to let him get an advantage on me. I'm twice his age. The point is that he would have tried something. You got to know that about him."

Renee did not look angry or indignant. She was not about to defend Izzy. Dolph figured that she was actually listening to him. That was good enough for now. Getting Renee straightened out might be a nice monument for Oscar, and a nice chunk in Dolph's world.

* * *

Charlie Montalvo's office had been a kid's bedroom back in the early forties, spacious back then, by those standards, but today, hardly big enough for a lawyer even of his meager stature. What used to be someone's house was now surrounded by concrete instead of grass, so Charlie looked out onto a parking lot. He wished for more. He was a partner, but he wanted a partnership with a high profile firm and an office in a gleaming glass building. Instead, with two other lawyers, he primarily handled workers' claims against bosses.

He drummed his fingers and looked out into the parking lot. He was waiting for the results of his animosity over his situation: two musclemen, two enforcers, one a wired kid of his choosing and the other some borderline low-class criminal of Lee Ann's choosing.

This morning, as he cinched his tie, he noticed that it made several bunches in the collar of his shirt. He also notched his belt a hole tighter. He was losing weight, and after only a week of this stress.

Money had certainly been a motive. As much as money seemed to gravitate toward and stay within Oscar's hands, so Charlie's fingers just couldn't hold onto money. His schemes failed. His investments turned sour. His cases went the wrong way. So he stayed with the two local-boy lawyers in the once-residential house on the Southside. He had walked away from one condo so now his credit rating was a mess. He could barely make the payments on his Lexus.

People always wanted to give Oscar money and help. Charlie always seemed desperate. When Charlie's father was killed in a construction accident when Charlie was not quite three years old, Charlie's mother determined to marry up. So she found Oscar's father, not some Mexican construction worker, but an appliance salesman at the old Southside Sears who wore a tie to work. Oscar even looked like Charlie. And soon Oscar's father and Charlie's mother had a girl of their own, Gina. In college, during Charlie's junior year, after Oscar's first year in medical school, and Gina's freshman year, money got really tight for the family. So his mother and Oscar's father made Charlie drop out a year, and Gina voluntarily dropped out a year in order to funnel the money to the potential doctor, to the promising kid. Gina got married and never returned; in fact, she dropped out of Charlie and Oscar's lives. Charlie hardly ever saw her. Eventually, Charlie saw his parents retire to the nice suburban northside home that Oscar had bought for them.

His phone rang; his secretary said that his clients had arrived, and two men walked in. Izzy twitched, always in motion, used his hands to talk, that is, used his hands instead of talking. The tattoos as well as the jewelry hanging from the piercings seemed to jingle. Izzy had a fresh blue and yellow bump in the middle of his shaved head. The other man had thick blonde hair curling all around his head and a large nose and high forehead that seemed permanently sun damaged. "Have a seat, Izzy." Charlie had once defended Izzy. He had no idea how Izzy ended up with Oscar's daughter.

"I appreciate this, man," Izzy said. Charlie waited for more from Izzy, nothing came. He had contacted Izzy earlier in the morning, and once Charlie mentioned Dolph's name and said the word *intimidate*, Izzy grew quiet, yet Charlie knew that he was excited.

The big blonde man extended his hand. "Bo," he said as though he could not physically say anymore syllables.

"Bo what?" Charlie asked.

"That's all for right now," Bo said.

"So you know Lee Ann?" Charlie asked.

"Me and her go back," Bo said.

"Who is this guy?" Izzy asked.

"Sit down," Charlie said.

They both sat down, and each nervously eyed the other. "Now, Bo," Charlie started, then stopped because of Bo's hard gaze. Charlie didn't know whether there was malice or confusion behind that gaze. Again, his mind wandered to his needs. He regretted that his needs led these two into his office. "Bo, how do you know Lee Ann?"

"I known her since we was in Odessa as kids."

"And do you know why she called you?"

"To kick Dolph Martinez's ass," Izzy interrupted.

"Izzy, please. Hold on," Charlie said. "I'm talking to Bo, and you should listen because you'll be working with Bo."

"We go up to him, hold a fucking pistol to his head, make him beg, then pop him in the knee or something, cripple him, make him beg some more," Izzy said. Charlie saw that he had made a mistake in choosing Izzy. But what was he to do on short notice? He and Lee Ann had decided that she would supply one thug, and he would supply one thug. Charlie, of course, wasn't even agreeable to the thug choosing in the first place. He didn't think that things had come to this. Lee Ann had reminded him that Dolph Martinez was "living up his ass and staked a claim on it." She said that, as far as they knew, the police knew nothing, that Jerri Johnson was willing to let things stand at that, but that Dolph Martinez and his crew of ruffians were "playing who's got the big dick." So she and Charlie needed bigger dicks. So Bo and Izzy were sitting in front of him.

"I ain't gonna work with this little shit," Bo said.

121

"Well then fuck you. Little shit!" Izzy said.

"You're too wild. You gonna get us both fucked."

"Who made you fucking King bad-ass fucker?"

Charlie held up his hands to quiet both of them. "Please," he said. Please indeed. Izzy had been easy to get. He had his cell phone number in a file. Izzy had a grudge against Dolph, who was butting his nose into everybody's business. So in the dare and shove challenge with Lee Ann, Charlie had said that he could get just as bad an ass as Lee Ann could. Now here Lee Ann's bad ass was about to whip the shit out of Charlie's bad ass.

"Look, the purpose here is to remain behind the scenes, don't do shit until provoked or absolutely needed," Bo said. "And look at you, fucking cutting donuts with your asshole to play cowboy bullshit. I got a record smooth as a ten-year-old-oriental boy's ass." Bo looked at Izzy. "This Dolph guy, however old he is, could probably shoot, skin, eat, and shit you out, you tattooed, shiny metal display for ignorance."

"You mother fucker," Izzy stood up to say.

"Look at you," Bo said. "You're a walking fucking target."

Izzy reached toward his back pocket. Charlie stood. Bo was up and caught Izzy with a quick left up under his jaw and knocked him against the window, rattling the blind as he slid down the wall.

The door to Charlie's office opened, and his secretary stuck her head in. Charlie said that everything was okay and shooed her back out. He and Bo sat back down. Izzy shook again, drooled, and then came to half-consciousness. Bo opened his palm and let a roll of quarters drop into his other hand. He flexed his fist, put the quarters in his jeans pocket, and rubbed his knuckles. "This is your first time at this rodeo, ain't it, Charlie?"

"I didn't even know I was entered in the rodeo."

"Fuck, this don't look good for me. Looks like the biggest balls belong to Lee Ann."

"And who's the smartest?" Charlie asked.

"Lee Ann again," Izzy said, groaned, and rubbed his chin.

"I don't think I broke his jaw. But it would be good if I did."

"My understanding is that you are going to talk to Dolph and his friends just to scare them a little," Charlie said.

"That's my specialty. Things ain't got shitty enough for real nastiness."

"So you know how to find them."

"Like I said, I competed in this event before."

"When he gets coherent," Charlie motioned toward Izzy. "Teach him how to compete."

When Izzy started to babble coherently, Charlie helped Bo drag him out. His secretary watched idly. She had seen Charlie's clients dragged out of his office before. Charlie returned to his office, stared out at the parking lot, and wondered how all this had come to pass.

* * *

Pooter knew that his job was to look tough and watch, but he was having trouble with both because he was at Big John's. He came to Big John's to drink and bullshit with his friends; out of habit, he watched only what attracted his attention. He particularly liked the white egrets that had started coming to the dirty San Antonio River to fish. So he knew he wasn't looking tough.

Dolph preached that observing the right detail, "tracking the signs," as he and the Border Patrol did, was the secret of succes. That certainly was true, Pooter agreed, but he added that the signs you tracked were dependent upon your disposition. And as Emerson said, "A foolish consistency is the hobgoblin of little minds." So you ought to able to switch signs. Whenever he said such things, Dolph begged Pooter to please concentrate, or he would put everyone in danger. When Dolph stepped out from Big John's Ice House with a beer in either hand and handed one to Pooter, Pooter let Dolph take the lead and followed behind him toward the picnic table under the tree. There, waiting for them, were Jerri, Lee Ann, and Charlie.

As he walked, Pooter took a long swallow of his beer and glanced out to his left across the river. The sun was starting to set, and he saw a lone white egret. A breeze was blowing from the south, catching a bit of the vapor from the river, and blowing moist coolness into their faces. Pooter wished that he could just sit and talk to Dolph and maybe Jerri. But he looked straight ahead, tried to look mean, but could tell that he was smiling.

Dolph nodded to everyone around him. Jerri said, "I take it that everyone knows everyone else."

"This is my associate, Pooter," Dolph said emphatically.

Charlie eyed Pooter, and as he nodded, he asked Dolph more than Pooter, as though to mock Dolph's choice of a tough guy, "So how do you get a name like Pooter?" That was a cue for Pooter to do all but growl at Charlie; instead, he smiled and let Dolph do the growling. Dolph's eyes demanded that Charlie take his eyes off Pooter and look at Dolph.

"Got that name when I hit this guy a whole bunch of times in the face and pulling my fist out of his face sounded like 'poot,' 'poot,' like a dainty girl's fart." Pooter could tell by his smile that Dolph liked that comment. Pooter knew that, despite his size, he couldn't really look very mean. At five-six, Dolph appeared a whole lot meaner than Pooter did at six-four and two eighty. In truth, in a tangle, Dolph would be more dangerous. Pooter's job was to scare people, and then, if someone started some shit, Pooter was just to grab them and hold on. He was no longer the pulling guard. He no longer had the speed or the moves, but in close quarters, like a bulldog, he could bite and hold on. But Pooter knew that eventually, he would release his grip, let it go; Dolph wouldn't. Dolph would keep fighting after the fight had finished and the fighters had gone home. Pepper could be like that too.

Jerri, but not Lee Ann, eyed Pooter. She was probably trying to keep from rolling her eyes and scolding them both for the gonad-clanging macho act. Pooter smiled at her and himself and said, "Hello, Jerri," and nodded his head toward Lee Ann, "hello, to you too, Mrs. Molntalvo." Pooter had just seen the two women. Jerri and Lee Ann met in a neutral area, Cappy's, just to say hello, just to "sniff" each other once more, to see if there were some sort of truce, to see, as Walter might say, if they wanted to "fuck or fight." Pooter had watched them from the bar, so he could be ready if they fucked or fought. Now, thanks no doubt to Jerri, his presence seemed redundant, and probably irrelevant. Pooter knew that, in a fuck or fight, either Jerri or Lee Ann might be as dangerous as Dolph. In this company, Pooter knew that he was the sissy.

Dolph lowered himself onto the bench on one side of the table. Pooter sat on one side of him, and Jerri walked around them to sit on the other side of Dolph. Lee Ann and Charlie sat across from them. They were two camps, and they appeared as though they were bartering for the wooden planks in between them. Lee Ann started, "I want Dolph and his ugly goon there out of my life. And I want them to leave Charlie alone."

"So what have you got to hide?" Dolph whispered.

Jerri said Dolph's name just loud enough to scold him. Jerri said to Lee Ann, "I have to defend my client. But his defense is all I want."

Charlie spoke up, "So defend him, but leave us out of it."

"That's hard to do when you sound so defensive," Dolph said.

Pooter saw Jerri squeeze Dolph's thigh under the table. They should have rehearsed, gotten their cues down, decided who would play what role. But their lack of preparation didn't affect Pooter. He was just ornamentation anyway.

"You have nothing on us. There is nothing to prove."

Dolph was about to speak, but he halted himself. Probably Jerri was still gripping his thigh. "We have circumstantial evidence," Jerri said. "We have a whole lot of suspicions. They cast doubt on Ramón's whole story. But right now, you are right. We don't have conclusive evidence."

"But things sure smell bad," Dolph said.

Jerri cut him off, "So we could just stop where we are if we were sure that you two would cooperate."

"And how could we do that?" Charlie asked.

"By not interfering anymore."

"Then you gotta call off popcorn fart there," Lee Ann said and pointed toward Dolph, "and all his little friends."

"You gotta give up on Joan. Leave her alone," Dolph said directly to Charlie, and Pooter could see the meanness in Lee Ann when her gaze berated first Dolph, then Charlie

Her meanness made Pooter's attention started to drift toward history. The Indians, the Spaniards, the Anglos, and the Mexicans had all bartered their way through their histories, maybe at this very spot. Three cultures Indian, Hispanic, and Anglo saw no reason to compromise; each sought domination. Yet the history of the city showed an uneasy resignation to power, chance, and history. The Spanish Missionaries tried to convert the Couilteheticans, but let them practice their own brand of Catholicism that kept a lot of Indian religion. Before San Antonians got used to being

Mexican, they had become Texans, and then Americans, and then, most peculiar, Confederates. But even as Anglos tried to dominate the city, they let the Mexicans, and other ethnicities, have their place and sometimes a say. The city slowly allowed its frontier Texanness to be compromised into nineteenth-century urban progressiveness, and then the twentieth-century free-for-all that produced a variety of images of the city. Today over million people compromised their various images of San Antonio with other peoples just as Dolph's and Lee Ann's two groups were bargaining for an agreed-upon interpretation of a murder.

Pooter forced himself to return his attention to the bargainers. "There ain't no police yet. Is there going to be?" Lee Ann asked.

"That is their affair," Jerri said.

"Then you can live with just letting things lie as they is?" Lee Ann asked. Jerri nodded. "What about your partner there?"

"He's my employee," Jerri said. But instead of agreeing, Dolph's head jerked upright. He stared back at the porch behind Big John's. Pooter followed Dolph's stare. Two men stepped out onto the porch. Each held a beer and stared toward the table. One was a tall, well-built blonde guy. The other was a short bald kid wearing those "shorts" that came down below the knees, black combat boots, and jewelry dangling from his ears and nose.

Dolph stood up and bounced his fist off the table. "Have you no respect, Charlie?" he asked.

"What are you talking about?"

"Are those your guys?"

"I don't know what you are talking about?"

"Dolph, sit down," Jerri said. Dolph looked down at Jerri and grimaced because he knew he was going to have to piss her off.

"That little shit dancing with himself over there." Dolph hesitated and looked at Lee Ann. "Is he selling drugs to your niece? Don't you have any respect? You may have killed Oscar for whatever reasons. . ."

Jerri stood and yelled, "Whoa. Hold on."

Charlie was up and quickly saying, "So that's what you think?"

Pooter pushed himself up and saw the two strangers moving toward them.

"As I was saying," Dolph continued. "I could even work my way to understanding why you might have set your brother up. But hiring that little fucker is indecent."

Jerri hung her head. The little fucker and the bigger one started walking to the table. Pooter got ready to grab and hold. He might have to grab and hold Dolph, if Jerri gave an order first. Or Jerri, if Dolph gave the order first.

The two thugs got to the table and stood behind Charlie and Lee Ann. Pooter readied himself while Dolph pointed, "Go away, Izzy," he said. "You haven't got the stomach for this. You don't know what he's asking you to do."

"Fuck you, old man."

Pooter stiffened. He thought of the Council House fight. The Texans had invited the Comanches into parley in the middle of Main Square downtown. But the Comanche had brought their families and their captives. And when the shooting stopped, most of the Comanche chiefs were dead and both sides lost a lot of innocent women and children.

Lee Ann was quickly up and pulling Charlie behind her. The two goons stood to one side as she dragged Charlie away. After a few moments, they turned their backs to Jerri, Dolph, and Pooter and followed behind Lee Ann and Charlie. Jerri slumped back into the seat with her head in her hands, "Oh, Dolph, Dolph, Dolph, Dolph," she said.

"Don't, 'Dolph' me," was Dolph's reply. "I remember another time when you insisted on right and vengeance, and we killed a guy."

Pooter remembered that time too. He had grabbed and held. Dolph shot a really bad guy in the chest. And later Pepper put a bullet into another really bad guy's head. They had all agreed to the act, but they had all struggled with living with what they hand done. The causes and the peoples change but not the actions, not in San Antonio de Béxar.

"At least you rolled the dice. And I figure we all know one thing for sure," Pooter said.

Both Dolph and Jerri looked up at him. "We know they're guilty as hell," he went on. "Why else would they have hired those guys? Now, just like in our pasts, just like in this state's past, what we got to ask ourselves is, what are we going to do about it?"

Jim Sanderson

Jerri was too stunned to speak. Dolph said, "Holy shit, Pooter, you want my job?"

128

Chapter 8

Walter had seen the fist coming but knew he could do nothing about it. Instead of his ribs or chin, Walter curled to protect his pacemaker. So the first fist caught him in his left ribs. The second fist got his other side. And from somewhere, a third fist caught him in the temple, and his glasses flew away from his face. On his way down, he saw a blurry fourth fist come toward him and then miss him. When he was on the ground, he felt the squared toe of a boot and then another, knew that a couple more landed. He tried to see who was pummeling him, but all he could make out were shapes and flesh colored blurs. At least the grass was soft. His mind simply wandered to a better place, to Mexico, and he lost count of the blows.

Sitting in his dark bedroom in the back of his side of the house, Walter followed several wayward spots of light, not even shining in beams, dance around his map of Mexico. His eyes, as though the beating had untrained them, searched above and below the line in his bi-focals for the proper position and settled on the red circles around the Mexican cities. He switched his sight from one red circle to the next. But Playa del Carmen held his gaze. It was time to commit. He took another shot from the bottle of tequila.

He had seen two of the ass kickers turn from him and leave. He felt indignant that there were only two. There should have been far more. As though he were still a young man in a bar room fight, he thought. He had gotten home just as the sun was setting and had gone for a walk among the drinkers, artists, and gawkers of South Town. And then a short young man with a shaved head and piercings in his face was in front of Walter. Next to him was a stout man, well built but, like the short shaved-head young man, not nearly so dangerous looking as to warrant the damage that they did to Walter. When the blows started, Walter didn't fight back, didn't want to fight back, only wanted to protect what kept him in this world, his pacemaker. But he felt that it was not becoming that he just ducked and covered.

When they left him, humiliated as well as beaten, he spread his fingers out and pushed them through the grass until he felt the arm of his glasses. Luckily, his glasses were still intact, but they made a dull ache when he hung them on the bridge of his nose, so he pushed them farther down to the bulbous cartilage of his nose. He dragged himself with his elbows toward his house, but that was such a humiliating way to travel that he pushed himself up and felt the tug of muscle on his sides, which told him that ribs were hurt. His legs got him inside. He looked in the mirror and saw mostly knots and blood. But he didn't notice any missing teeth. His jaws worked. He had had an old fashioned ass kicking. They didn't used to hurt this much.

This ass kicking was a pronouncement. It would be his last one. He would never again be able to defend himself in another fist fight. The next one would kill him.

He had veered toward his phone in order to call the hospital but decided that the hospital would be worse than the ass kicking. The hospital wouldn't be able to help much with ribs. And he would be depressed in a hospital. The indignity of a hospital was more than he wanted to bear. He was almost glad that he would die of his heart rather than another round of cancer. During his chemotherapy, the sickness, the sterility, the shininess, the smell of the hospital made him feel like a specimen, just like his urine. The pain drugs were good, but they too added to the depression. Human suffering was real and demanded attention. A hospital tried to hide that suffering through its bureaucracy, its sterile smell, its shiny aluminum, its utilitarian furniture, the mentality and cheery voices of the nurses, the brusqueness of the doctors. The hospital, despite its mission, gave the impression that it had forbidden pain. The ache in his ribs at each breath was real, earned, honest pain. He suffered. He was human. If he was to die of his failing heart, he wanted to test himself with the pain and the surprise and die somewhere other than a hospital. He thought that he might like, just for spite, if he had the balls, to die on the steps of a hospital.

But he still wanted medicine, so he veered toward the cabinet to one side of the kitchen sink where he kept his liquor. In the dark, unable to see, his fingers skipped over the tops of bottles and settled on the cork in the tequila bottle's neck. Tequila would be the quickest transport to the place he wanted to be.

Now, in the darkening room, the spots of light faded and so did the map of Mexico. But then a green light blinked. With his tequila bottle in his left hand, Walter pushed himself to a standing position and groaned to reach for his answering machine. When he hit the button, Sarah Boone, his first wife, spoke to him from out of place and time. She begged him to quit whatever it was he was doing, to leave the poor people alone whom he was spying on. She pleaded with him to stop. She sounded as though she just might miss him, might have some bit of love left for him, way down deep in her unexamined self. Walter felt like he was going to cry. Sarah still thought enough of him to warn him about an impending and now accomplished ass kicking.

He sipped from his tequila. He stopped himself from crying. Then he let himself fall onto his old couch and screamed. Gritting his teeth, he let himself slide over the lip of seat cushions until his butt was on the floor again and his back was straight against the front edge of the couch. He took another sip from the bottle. He wanted a glass, but he didn't want to get up again to get one. On his next sip, he swished the tequila around in his mouth. It stung, but not the kind of sting alcohol makes in empty tooth sockets. His teeth were intact.

Walter straightened out his legs under the low coffee table in front of him and sat the bottle of tequila on the coffee table. Walter Boone had spent the better part of his life wrecking his life by heeding those desires that men are prone to. Money wasn't a desire, but it created the possibilities of wild male fantasies come true. Money could allow a man to indulge those fantasies and emerge with stories. And those stories were better than reality, because, if they were really good, if touched with art and charm, then they made all of that mean son of a bitch of reality bearable. So Walter had indulged. What he hadn't done was write the

131

stories. He sipped his tequila. Still, he had told some of his stories. He could tell a story to drinkers about Oscar and thus give poor Oscar some dignity beyond the indignity of his death. And with what two wives and several girlfriends, studio executives, administrators, and bosses had called his misguided and misspent life, Walter had made stories.

Walter needed, wanted some stories about him. But his money and his abilities at story making were gone. He was too old, his heart too weak to indulge in the male desires that made those stories. He sipped. He needed a new way to make stories. The green lights appeared back in the room. They made traces across the room, like the Marfa lights that he once watched with Sarah and a bottle of scotch. They criss-crossed his map of Mexico.

The light from outside and a muffled swoosh made Walter jerk, wince, pound the table with his fist, wince some more, and then see the front door slowly crack and then open fully. He tilted his head back to get a view through his glasses hanging on the end of his nose. He held his breath, back handed the tequila bottle neck, prepared to defend himself as well as he could. He glanced at the map of Mexico and prepared for what might be his last ass kicking.

Pooter and Dolph stepped into the room. Walter was relieved that he had started thinking instead of crying. It would be impossible for Walter and his drinking buddies to conduct themselves in any meaningful manner if Walter were crying. So Walter said, "You don't knock."

"Come on, let's get you to a doctor," Dolph said.

"Why would I want to go to a doctor?" Lights burst on. Pooter stood by the light switch, his forefinger still held out under the two switches.

"You could be hurt," Pooter said.

"I am hurt. I don't need a second opinion." Pooter nodded his head in agreement. Walter could communicate to Pooter through some weird philosophical sonar.

"Like hell," Dolph said. "You need to get to the hospital."

For a man with short legs, Dolph got across the room very quickly and reached down to pull Walter up, like he was some little doll. Walter winced, grunted, and wriggled away fom Dolph. "Goddamn it. No. Don't. It hurts like hell when I rattle myself around."

"What if you've got something really fucked up?" Dolph asked and reached, and Walter felt a sharp serrated knife stab into the underside of his shoulder, from the inside. When Walter gasped, Dolph jumped back.

Breathing heavily, feeling around his face, Walter said, "Look, look. It's not bad. Some broken ribs. My face hurts, but it's not broken."

"Your ex-wife. . ." Dolph started before Walter interrupted him.

"Which one?"

"The good one. The first one you talk about."

Walter let himself lean back against the couch and let his mind wander to Sarah. If only she would let him come back, he wouldn't need to go to Mexico. "Anyway, she called Jerri. And Jerri called me. And I figured the sons of bitches had jumped you."

Dolph went to a lamp and flipped on another light. Walter closed his eyes against the light. He heard Dolph from the other side of the room. "So Charlie wants to play it this way."

"Maybe it's the widow," Pooter mumbled.

"Of course, it's the widow. That viper. That bitch," Dolph said.

"It wasn't the widow and Charlie who beat me," Walter said.

Dolph was immediately up to Walter, "Who did?"

"Mostly I saw fists, but there was a little young guy with a shaved head, and a bigger guy with curly blonde hair."

Pooter walked up to Walter. "You let a little shaved-head youngster beat you?"

"It's hell to be a pussy," Walter said.

Pooter stepped over the coffee table and, daintily and gracefully for a big man, wiggled himself into a sitting position on he floor between the couch and the coffee table. When he had settled himself next to Walter, he held up his hand to reveal three shot glasses between his fingers. "While Dolph was pulling on you, I got us all some glasses for your medicine."

While one hand set the shot glasses down, Pooter grabbed the bottle and poured three neat drinks with his other hand. "Well done, sir," Walter said. "You are a gentleman, a philosopher, and a bartender."

Sipping his tequila from a shot glass, Walter watched as Dolph paced in front of him. Walter looked at Pooter, who, without making a movement, seemed to just shrug. Dolph, no doubt, placed some importance upon the ass kicking.

"To think," Dolph said and turned to Walter and then swung his gaze to Pooter, "that that fucker Charlie and that evil bitch tried to bargain all this away, not two hours ago."

"I think they're scared," Pooter said, and Walter was grateful that his disengaged mind was finally concentrating on something real. "Otherwise, why would they have started this?" With his left hand, the one not cradling the tequila, Walter gingerly patted his face with his fingertips: no protrusions, tenderness but no biting pain like his ribs. Walter held his fingertips in front of his eyes: not much blood. "You look like shit," Pooter said. "But nothing by itself looks real bad."

Dolph tramped closer to Pooter, "You're damn right, they're scared. That's why they're dangerous. But that's why we got them by the balls."

Walter interrupted, "Could you turn out the lights? I like it better in the dark. Somehow, it seems easier to breathe in the dark." Pooter rose, and the lights went out. "And for God's sakes, I have all kinds of liquor in the kitchen. Dolph, help yourself."

Walter saw the outline of Dolph, now lit by street lights from outside, squat in front of him. "I'm sorry."

"Why are you sorry? You weren't kicking me in the ribs."

"I'm sorry that I got you into this."

Walter shook his head. "I had some say about it, some choice. I liked being a detective."

Pooter showed back up with a bottle and tall glasses. He poured a sizable amount of Jack Daniels into the glasses. "Goddamn ice. Ice. You can't drink a gentleman like Jack without cooling him off," Walter said. He lifted his hand to touch his pacemaker. Dolph's eyes followed him. Walter had never told any of his friends about his sick heart. He pulled his hand back. Tonight might be the night that he revealed his pacemaker to his friends and thus got the concerned looks, the deference, the new considerations.

"So they called your wife?" Dolph asked. That question was for Walter. The next two were just Dolph's. "Where did they get her number? How did they know?" Dolph's mind was whirring in detective mode among causes scattered around like the fall pecans in the city parks. With his broken ribs and battered face, Walter's world was both slower and more complex than Dolph's. To cure the cancer eating out his ass, Walter had humiliated and humbled himself with chemotherapy and hospital stays only to see the cure kill his chances of a longer life. Walter's causes were the most ironic ones. A butterfly in South America flaps its wings and a tornado destroys Amarillo. In Walter's world, that butterfly was a buzzard.

Dolph looked at Walter as though he were actually communicating with him. "Your wife is safe. They won't bother her. And they didn't kill you. They aren't half as bad or as desperate as they think they are."

"That's encouraging," Pooter said. "We can relax."

Walter put his right palm over his pacemaker and studied his map of Mexico.

* * *

A low fog drifted through the trees and sleeping cows as Dolph pulled onto Jerri's property. "I can take care of myself," Dolph said to Pooter, who sprawled out in the seat beside him.

"Who knows? Maybe I feel a little unsafe. I live by myself too you know," Pooter said. The Nissan hit a chughole and bounced them both so that their heads hit the ceiling. Dolph had already replaced two struts, but he still wanted a car, not a truck. Way down, he knew it was best that he had Pooter to cover his back. For years, he and Pepper had watched each others' backs. Pepper was tricky and quick; Pooter was a bull with arms.

"Still, it's better to be either one of us than Charlie Montalvo," Dolph said. His ire was bubbling up. Charlie should have known that he didn't have the know-how or the balls to pull off a scheme like this. He was supposed to be smart. He had supposedly seen real criminals.

The fog was mesmerizing. Dolph couldn't help but stare into it. The beams of his headlights, which bounced off the fog and back into his eyes, kept his mind on the danger at hand.

"The cows are moving kind of funny," Pooter said. He was looking out the side window and pressing his index finger against it.

"What do you mean?"

"They're just moving, not sleeping. They're taking steps, looking around." Maybe Pooter was better than Pepper. Pepper would have had a beer and would have been bullshitting. But Pepper's bullshit usually relaxed Dolph. Pooter kept him wound up. Dolph looked for a cow to watch in the fog. They knew the Nissan. Maybe they were following it. Then Dolph hit his brakes when, not too far in front of him, expecting a late night snack, a heifer stepped out of the fog and onto the rutted road, lowered her head, and bellowed.

Dolph and Pooter pressed their butts into the seats and their backs against the upholstered bucket seats. They turned to each other to laugh, but just as he was about to honk at the cow, Dolph pulled his hand away from the horn, turned off the lights, and edged the car forward, bumping the cow and sending her shaking and waddling into the fog and the night. Dolph knew that Pooter wanted an explanation. "You're right. She should have been asleep. Maybe something is out there. Maybe we can surprise them."

"You sure we're not going to surprise ourselves?"

"We're invincible."

"We're fat, middle-aged, and past our prime."

"That's why they're picking on us. But they don't know our cunning."

"Do we know our cunning?"

And so they jested, Pooter proving that, for all his quiet and distraction, he had listened carefully to Dolph, Pepper, and Walter's bull-shitting. This bullshitting was why Dolph liked them. The bullshit distracted him, yet kept him calm and alert, made his mind work to keep up with them, but made it hold a chunk of anticipation and planning for the emergency at hand. Thank you, Walter, Pepper, and yes, Pooter.

Dolph braked in front of his cabin. "Don't open the door yet," Dolph said. He reached into the glove compartment in the console and pulled out his Taser. "Oh shit," Pooter said. "What do you aim to do with that?"

Dolph squirmed as he pushed the Taser into the back of his pants. "I aim to not kill somebody. But I kind of want to fuck with them too."

As he squirmed, Pooter said, "Be careful not to zap your own ass."

"Let's go on inside," Dolph said.

"Why don't I take a look around?" Pooter asked.

"Let's both take a look around after we go inside," Dolph said. "Make them think that we're inside, then sneak out."

So they got out of the car, both nervously looking over their shoulders, both hearing the swish of grass against cow or human legs, a heavy breath, a snapping twig. Dolph got his keys into the door and shoved it open. Once inside, he turned on the lights. Pooter followed him in. Dolph made his way through the cabin, turning on lights, turning on the TV. Pooter stood in the living room looking dumbfounded. Dolph advised, "We're not suspicious. We don't know a thing, don't suspect a thing. We're gonna have a beer and watch TV." Pooter nodded. "But really, I'm going out the backdoor and circling around to my left. Then you wait a little, then come out the backdoor and you circle around to your right." Pooter nodded again. Dolph touched the Taser in the back of his pants. "If you see anything, yell or run him down. If not, just squat down and look around for a while."

They stared wordlessly at each other while Dolph counted down to himself inside his head. When memories and anticipation wound his gut tight and stretched the scar across his belly, he knew he was ready. He nodded to Pooter and stepped out the back door. Dolph looked back through the open door at Pooter surrounded by light but blocking a goodly portion of it, smiling to encourage him and wish him luck, as though they were in a huddle and Dolph was the quarterback about to make a daring long throw and Pooter was about to be blocking for him. Dolph stepped out of the lights of the cabin and into the darkness.

Dolph tried to stare deeply into the fog as though to pierce it. Sister Quinn could probably have done it. She was the dead person who talked to him the most. In moments such as these, with his gut quivering, she guided him. Some of the other people laughed at him as though they were just waiting for him to join them in their oblivion. Dolph knew that, if he didn't keep his head about him instead of listening to the dead people, he might join them quicker than he had to.

He heard his own soft footfalls, rubber soles on the worthless rock and sand of this area, the swoosh of tall grass. Then a stereo effect: sounds to match his. Dolph stepped behind a short cedar tree, raised his Taser as though it were a real gun, checked around him, circled around the tree, straightened, and saw a hooded figure leaning against the side of the cabin.

Some of the nimbleness that he used to have from running down wets came back, and with light footfalls, he closed the space between him and the hooded figure. As the figure turned in slow motion toward him, Dolph called on the physicality and stealthiness that he still retained from his Border Patrol days. His mind and muscles followed the Border Patrol mantra, "Alto. Para las Manos." The Taser was in front of him. The hooded figure stepped back. Dolph pulled the trigger. The hooded figure began the jerky dance that the Mexican skeleton figures do during the Dios de la Muerte celebrations.

The hooded figure was on the ground. Dolph was saying firmly, "When you stop tingling, stay still." He heard a door slam, turned in time to see a big figure moving toward him. As the bigger figure got closer, Dolph's instincts told him to drop the Taser and raise his hands, for the bigger figure meant to run him over, stab him, or shoot him. But Dolph's mind told him that he had caught one. He squared his shoulders, waited to be rammed, tackled, stabbed. And squeezed the trigger of the Taser to punish the hooded figure for the damage he was about to take.

Instead, the big figure tripped. Dolph stepped out of the way as the big figure fell toward him and grabbed at him as he fell face first. Dolph squeezed with one hand, doubled his other into a fist, and swung, hitting only air. Behind the figure, slowly rising, was the pulling guard Pooter Elam, grinning, bruised, palms and nose bloodied. He had run up behind the big figure, and when he realized that he could not catch him, he flung himself forward, grabbing at the man's legs, to make a Dolph-saving tackle.

The big figure rolled away from Dolph and got to his feet. Maybe a former athlete himself, he side-stepped Pooter's next attempted tackle, and ran into the fog and the darkness. Dolph felt a tug at the Taser. Dolph squeezed the trigger before the hooded figure could pull the gun out of his hand.

Dolph and Pooter both stepped up to the hooded figure who gave one good jerk before becoming perfectly still as he welcomed back control over his body. As Dolph reached for the hood, Pooter switched on a flashlight and pointed it toward the hood. The face turned away, hands scratched at Dolph, then jerked some more as Dolph zapped him. "You gotta learn," Dolph said.

Even before the hooded figure stopped writhing, Pooter pulled the hood back and shone the flashlight into the face concealed by the hood on the sweatshirt. A bald head emerged. Silver piercings caught light from the cabin. "Izzy, you dumb son of a bitch," Dolph said.

"I say we just beat the shit out of him or zap him until he fries," Pooter said.

"You tell me now. My friend Walter. Did you and your compadre beat the shit out of him?" Dolph held up his hand to show Izzy that his finger was on the trigger. Pooter pointed the beam of the flashlight at the Taser to show Izzy.

"I ain't saying shit," Izzy stammered and stared at Dolph's hand. He couldn't get the tough words or attitude right.

"Your friend is pretty damn fast," Pooter said. "I don't think he was running to help you. I think he was just running away."

"He sure as hell is gone now," Dolph said. "I figure you've seen the last of him."

"Fuck you. Fuck you. You sadistic mother fucker."

"Aw, now Izzy. Do you realize that I could have brought a gun? Do you realize how fucked up you could be? Do you remember what I told you?" Dolph zapped him.

After he winced, Pooter said, "How much of that high voltage can somebody take before they start permanently drooling or their pecker falls off or something?"

With the flashlight beam in Izzy's face, Dolph saw that Izzy was indeed drooling. "Jesus, he is drooling," Pooter said. "You wonder if he'll stop." Bless Pooter, Dolph thought.

"Why don't you put that pussy, queer, goddamn thing down and face me like a man?" Izzy said.

" Cause I'm old, impatient, and can't spare the ass kicking no more," Dolph said.

Izzy sucked in hard for some breath. "Okay, okay, let me go then."

"Let's talk first," Dolph said. "No, wait. Check his pockets," Dolph said to Pooter.

"I ain't done shit," Izzy said.

"Good, you've already learned the most common refrain in any prison."

"Keep your goddamn hands off me," Izzy yelled. Dolph held up the Taser.

Pooter pulled back from Izzy with one big hand open in front of him. In it, in the beam of the flashlight, were keys, a wallet, and a cell phone. Dolph pinched the cell phone between his forefinger and thumb. Pooter shone the flashlight toward the cell phone while Dolph switched the Taser to his left hand and cussed while he tried to poke the buttons that he couldn't see without his readers. Pooter reached to Dolph's chest, grabbed Dolph's readers, and stuck the arms behind Dolph's ears. Tilting his head back, Dolph poked buttons on the cell phone with his right thumb. "Tell me, Izzy," Dolph asked. "Were you and your buddy planning on beating the shit out of me and Pooter?"

"You got no right to look at that cell phone. That's private property."

"You're standing on private property," Dolph said.

As he scrolled through the list of Izzy's phone calls, Dolph felt like zapping Izzy again when he saw Renee Montalvo's number. After beating up Walter, sitting with his buddy, whom he didn't know or care for, out under the trees in the fog, waiting for Dolph to return, Izzy probably got bored so gave Renee a call. Izzy, the would-be criminal, had her name spelled out right under the number. Next, he had called Charlie Montalvo, his name right under the number. "So did you ask Charlie Montalvo how long you should wait to beat the shit out of us?" Dolph asked.

"Looks like you and Charlie would have thought to have brought some more guys," Pooter said.

Dolph punched the buttons to call Charlie. When Charlie answered the phone, and said, "Izzy," Dolph said: "Charlie, this is Dolph Martinez. I'm standing in front of my house with the end of my Taser sticking in Izzy. He's twitching and drooling something awful. Some other guy just ran away. My friend Walter is just beat to shit. So how come I'm talking to you via Izzy's cell phone? Did you buy the cheap little shit the minutes?"

There was silence on the end of the line. After a while longer, came the lawyers' mantra, "I want an attorney present before I speak."

"Charlie, you are an attorney. Counsel yourself."

"I have no idea why some hoodlum is at your house. I have no idea why he has my phone number. I presume that he is a former client." After a few moments, Charlie added, "And I'm sorry about your friend."

"Do you think we're beyond circumstantial evidence?" Dolph asked.

"You got nothing. I'm a lawyer. I know."

"Charlie, whether I have any evidence or not, whether you go to jail or not, we both know that you fucking killed your brother."

Dolph clicked to hang up and turned his attention back to Izzy. "Fuck you," Izzy said. Dolph zapped him. Pooter said, "You think that you could maybe overdose him on electricity?"

"He's fried his brain well enough by himself for me to do too much damage," Dolph answered.

When Izzy stopped shaking, he looked at Dolph, seethed as he inhaled and exhaled, but did not say anything. "Okay," Dolph started. "I can see that I have your attention. Same as before. One, you stay away from Renee Montalvo. Your relationship with her is over. Two, what I've done is completely illegal. Report me if you want, but then you gonna have to tell the police why you were sneaking around on my property. . . ."

"I heard that speech," Izzy yelled.

"Don't interrupt. You know what happens when you interrupt. More electricity and your balls fall off." Dolph waited. Izzy did not interrupt. "So, three, pull those barbs out of your chest and start running."

"What?"

Pooter reached over and pulled the barbs out, and Izzy screeched. "Now just run."

"What about my phone and my wallet."

"I'm keeping those."

"That's robbery."

"So report me."

"You fucker," Izzy stepped toward Dolph.

"Now you stop and think. I could have called the cops. Then you'd be in jail. And you'd be facing conspiracy charges. I'm going after Charlie Montalvo, and I'm giving you one hell of a break. In fact, I may be saving your sorry ass from all sorts of ruination. All I'm doing is being a little bit of prick by making you get a new wallet and cell phone. I'd just like to have that information handy." Izzy's shoulders heaved. "And when you get out into that fog and you find your buddy waiting for you, you tell him that I just saved his ass too. You're bound to have a car somewhere around here. When you and your buddy are driving out of here, you two ought to just keep driving and hope that Charlie doesn't name you."

"What if my friend ain't waiting for me?"

"You should have chosen a better friend."

Izzy stepped sideways, inching away from Dolph as though he might yet bite or sting him. Pooter flicked off the flashlight so that Izzy became just a dark shape. Then the shape turned its back to Dolph and Pooter and ran into the fog and the darkness to whatever or whoever was or was not waiting for him.

After Izzy disappeared, Dolph pulled his own cell phone out of his pocket. He tried to remember the digits in Charlie's phone number. Putting on his readers, he punched the combination into his phone. Charlie answered with, "I'm not going to talk to you."

"Maybe you better." No answer, just breathing. "Look, that first time was for show. I was your brother's friend. For that reason, I'm feeling a little sorry for your sorry ass. Why don't I just call the cops, tell them what I know instead of going on with this pissing contest?"

There were several moments of hesitation, as though Charlie was making up his mind. "You can go to hell."

If he were really angry, Charlie would have hung up, but he didn't. "You sure, Charlie? La Mordida,' huh? A little arrangement. You're a lawyer, surely there's something we can bargain for."

"I'll call back," he said.

They hesitated and then hung up together. Pooter looked at Dolph for some comment. "He should have left this crime shit to professionals."

"We aren't professionals, are we?" Pooter asked.

Walking away from Pooter, stepping up on his porch, Dolph shrugged.

* * *

All sorts of needs drove Charlie to Lee Ann's house, once his brother's house, now looking almost like a tomb, with the drapes pulled, the lights on dim, the furniture gone. Standing in front of him, because she had nowhere to sit down, was Lee Ann in a business suit. If she would relax, whisper to him, just take care of his sexual needs, maybe then the other needs would wait in line for her to deal with them so he could get some rest. "Why are you here?" she asked without emotion, without a hint that she could take care of any of his needs.

"I didn't want to call. This is more important than a call."

"You aren't supposed to call me either."

"Then how am I supposed to get ahold of you?"

"That's exactly the point. You're not supposed to. You'll have all of me you'll ever need if you just stay patient."

Charlie rubbed his forehead. "Can't we have some light?" He curled his finger around a drape, pulled it back, and looked out the windows facing the back yard. Charlie saw a little light coming in from the streetlights and the lone light above the garage. "Can't we just go back to normal?"

"No, we cannot go back to normal. You by-god knew this full fucking well."

Charlie looked at Lee Ann's stern face. Twisted as it was, her face belied the work of her gifted surgeons and showed her age, worry, and desperate life. But even with a white blouse and a gray suit coat, Lee Ann revealed a hint of cleavage. Charlie tried to work up some interest. "Charlie, fucking look at me. Don't talk to my tits. Tell me what you are thinking about."

Charlie could only think that he had made an awful mistake. He had known from the start that he hadn't truly loved this woman—no one could, certainly not Ramón Burgiaga—but he could not recall the lust, the intrigue, the greed that had first seduced him into a conspiracy with her.

"I'm thinking that I'm tired and can't just live like this. I'm thinking that I can't run away. I'm thinking that I conspired to murder my brother."

"We've been over and around that."

"I've changed my mind."

"You chicken-shit, sniveling little pussy."

He reached for her. She slapped his hand away. "How can you do that?" Charlie asked. "Was there just nothing between us?" And Charlie knew that he was asking the question more of himself than of her.

"I've got a safety deposit box in Mexico, another in the Caymans. I've got a passport here with another name on it. I've got another waiting for me in Mexico. I'm changing identities. It's all just about finished. So the something between us was something between you and a different woman."

Charlie backed up against the wall and slid down it until his butt was pressed against the carpet, and he felt its bristles beneath his tropical wool slacks. "What are you?" Charlie asked.

Lee Ann reached into her purse. She pulled out a handkerchief and poked it toward Charlie. "Looks like you're going to cry, Charlie."

"I am not going to cry," Charlie said and waved his hand in the air to shoo her handkerchief away.

"You got lots to cry about." Lee Ann stepped toward him and poked the handkerchief toward him. "Ramón is talking."

Charlie looked up at her and started to push himself up. "He knows nothing about me. All he thinks is that I'm the lawyer."

"But Jerri Johnson can connect you."

Charlie remembered why he had come. Panic had sent him. "And now Dolph Martinez called me."

"So?"

"He called me on a cell phone of the thug that I sent to scare him."

"Oh, God. That Izzy character. Oh, God. Are you a total fucking idiot?"

"I don't know what he knows. I don't know if he can connect the dots. I don't know if there are any dots to connect."

"After all I told you. After all we rehearsed." Charlie looked up at Lee Ann for reassurance, for a sexual hint or innuendo, for some encouragement. All he saw was judgment. That judgment was that he was the little brother, never quite as smart, as accomplished, as ambitious, as capable as Oscar. "I can still do this," Charlie tried to say, but the statement came out sounding like a question.

"Honey, you are just one big pile of fuck up," Lee Ann said. Her shoulders slumped. And all the surgical work on her face and body seemed to slump, as if the elasticity that made it life-like was gone. "How'd it take so long to plan and yet fuck up so fast?"

"So what do we do now?" Charlie asked

"I don't know what you're going to do. I don't think you know what you're going to do. But I'm leaving the country."

Charlie looked around as though he expected to see cameras or the recorders hidden in the house, controlled by the spies watching from down the block. "I can get ready fast. Where should we meet?"

"You shouldn't have come here, Charlie. I told you not to come here."

Charlie stared at her sagging face. She smiled, and her face went back to its proper form. Another pang hit him. "You expect me just to idly go about my business without asking any qustions. See, I grew up with Oscar. It may be late, but it has just occurred to me that maybe I did something real wrong."

Lee Ann put a hand out and placed it gently on Charlie's cheek. It seemed like ages since the last time Charlie had actually touched her. He missed the excitement. Wrapped in her arms and legs, his head buried in her hair, he might feel better. "You just turned out to be shit on a cracker, Charlie," Lee Ann said as she massaged his cheek.

"No, no, no. Wait, I'll get ready."

"They're probably already following you." Charlie pulled his cheek away from her hand. He pulled the drapes back just a bit and peered out the window. Dolph was not there. Dolph could not be there. But where were the police? Why had Dolph not told the police?

When he turned and straightened, Lee Ann said, "You're not going with me, Charlie. I've changed my mind. You just wouldn't be able to handle it."

"Okay, good. Let's not go. Fine with me. We'll stay here. Take what we can. I am a lawyer."

"You're not going to surrender, to talk, are you?" Lee Ann smiled sweetly.

"Honey, no. Well, no. I don't know what I'm going to do. You leave me, and I don't know what I'll do."

Lee Ann backed away from him. She reached in her purse and pulled out a tiny pistol. Charlie's eyes focused on her and then on the door to the backyard. Something in his head told him he would be safe if he could make it out the door.

For a slice of a moment, before he charged, Charlie was actually proud of himself for not begging, for not crying. He knew he was about to actively oppose her. As he was charging, he saw Lee Ann's startled face, thought about slamming her with his head, but even though he lowered his head to make himself into a ram, he ran past her for the back door. "Charlie, ain't you a stud duck now," he heard her say. Then he heard a bang as he pulled on the back door.

Charlie got the door open and was stepping through the doorway when he felt the bullet. A rib seemed to grind against it. As he fell through the open door, he smiled at the light from the neighbor's yard, just beyond the backyard fence. The smile cost him some time.

Charlie was up and moving, toward the greenhouse, toward the back fence. He could jump it if he had to. Then there was a third shot. He ran without seeming to move. His legs were moving. He felt like he was moving. But the greenhouse and the fence seemed to be retreating from him. He reached into his slacks and pulled out his cell phone. As he did, he tripped. Lee Ann had not gotten rid of the lawn furniture. He made himself hold on to his cell phone instead of sticking his hand in front of him to break his fall. When he hit, a flame shot from his rib up into his throat. Grasping the cell phone as though it were a crucifix that would protect him, Charlie kept moving: elbows, then knees, then toes, until he was running again and holding his cell phone.

He was able to flip the cell phone open. He was able to fumble with the keypad with his thumb. He heard slight beeps. He saw the blue sky and surf on the background scene of the cell phone. His thumb pressed menu. He saw call history. His thumb hit menu. He saw incoming call. He pressed menu. He saw the number, twisted his thumb around, and hit *send*.

As the phone rang, he bumped his shoulder into the greenhouse, pushed himself off of it, felt the bullet grind against ribs, felt no other bullets rubbing against bone, fat, or flesh, and kept running for the fence. Over his shoulder, Charlie saw Lee Ann running toward him. Her high heels made her take small steps. With her hands in front of her, swishing from side to side, the right one with the tiny pistol in it, she ran like a girl. Surely he could outrun her.

He stretched out his hand, like he was trying to stiff-arm a tackler, hit ivy, then the wire pickets of the hurricane fence. He stuck a toe through ivy and into the picket. He pulled himself up, but his rib pulled the other way. There was a bang, and he felt his shoulder stuck with a hot poker then simply go limp. Climbing, twisting, grimacing against the pain in his rib and shoulder, he held the phone to his ear.

Lee Ann moved slowly but methodically toward him, the gun now held out in front of her in two hands, aimed at Charlie. She wobbled in her heels so that the gun swung from one side of Charlie's face to the other. Finally, a voice came on the phone; the voice said that it was Dolph Martinez. Lee Ann came to a stop in front of Charlie. Charlie, cell phone to his ear, said "Dolph, Dolph, I'm glad it's you." He stared at Lee Ann's stern face, said, "Lee Ann," into the phone.

"You just couldn't help but turn chicken shit and cocksucker, could you?" Lee Ann said.

Then Charlie heard another bang.

Chapter 9

Dolph couldn't coax himself to sleep, but Pooter commanded himself to sleep. So Pooter got several good hours before Dolph started screaming and cussing again. Evidently, Dolph's cell had rung again and set him off. "It was Charlie's number," Dolph screamed as he pushed at Pooter's chest and jiggled his arm, bringing Pooter into an incoherent early dawn netherworld. Then Pooter heard Dolph say, "I hear him say, 'Lee Ann,' then there's this dull bang." Pooter felt his eyelids flutter over his sore eyeballs. "I think the bitch shot him," Dolph said.

Dolph, when he was set off, was a dynamo. "We got to go," Dolph said again.

Without comprehension, Pooter got himself to his feet. He looked at twirling, twisting, urging Dolph and said, "I'm not going to even ask how you came by this information."

"You don't listen," Dolph said. "My phone woke me. Charlie must have punched the keys to ring me. Me! Why me? To let me know. Know something. Then he says, 'I'm glad its you,' then there's a muffled voice. And then holy fucking shit, there's what sounds like a shot."

"Do we call somebody?"

Dolph paced in front of Pooter as Pooter pushed himself to a standing position and looked for his pants.

"Jesus, help me with this," Dolph said in front of Pooter and continued moving. "What do we do?"

"You're the one best at answering that question," Pooter said. He found his pants. Still sitting he got his legs into the pants' legs, and shimmied as he pulled them up and over his butt.

"Well, let's go," Dolph said.

"Go where?"

Dolph was moving as Pooter was buckling his pants and looking for a t-shirt. "I'll figure that out in the car."

"Shouldn't we call the police?"

"And tell them what?"

As Dolph reached for the door, he abruptly stopped, hung his head, and while pushing the door open, turned to Pooter, "I'm just assuming you'll go. You don't have to go. I didn't even want you around here during the night."

"I'd say I was right about staying the night. I'm way fuzzy, but I'm guessing that I ought go with you." Dolph nodded. Pooter added, "To protect you from yourself. Like everybody says, 'you know how you get.'"

As Dolph drove north into the city, Pooter looked east at the top semi-circle of the sun rising up over a low flat field. As Dolph drove past trees, the sun sparkled behind them and sent rays through them; then it was up. Despite their mission, despite Dolph's babbling; the newness of the dawn was beautiful. But Pooter still had to get to work, and he hadn't had much sleep, and now they were looking for Charlie.

Dolph pulled into a convenience store and returned with two large cups of coffee and two small packs of vitamins. He handed a vitamin pack and a cup of coffee to Pooter. "Here, to stay awake," Dolph said.

"You tired?" Pooter asked.

As Dolph wove through the curved streets of Alamo Heights, Pooter began to brace himself for what he might see. "Where are we going?"

"Last words I heard were 'Lee Ann.' I figure we'll drop by Oscar's house first and check on the widow."

Dolph pulled into the long driveway that made its way through the sculpted front yard. Without a word, they were out and standing on the front porch, and Dolph was about to knock. "You're the backup again. You're the muscle. Go around back. Jump the fence you if have to, but make sure that no one runs away," Dolph said to Pooter. "And be careful. If you think it best, just run away."

Pooter backed down the steps of the front porch, saw Dolph step to one side and hold his hand across to the door. They exchanged nods.

Dolph knocked, and Pooter ran down the driveway. At the garage, he turned to his left and waited several feet from the gate to the backyard.

Pooter heard a loud knock, then banging. Dolph was giving the front door hell, and evidently no one was answering. Pooter stepped gingerly toward the gate and leaned over it. He stretched to try to get a glimpse of the back door, saw nothing. He squinted into the morning sun to look into the deep yard, saw only the plants, the fountains, and the flower beds. What he noticed was the smell of well-kept, fertilized spring grass. The St. Augustine had a vivid oniony smell, almost rank. He checked over his shoulder, saw nothing of Dolph, and opened the gate. He stepped inside, inched toward the backdoor, inched again and saw that it was shut. Blinds were drawn on all the windows, as though the house were sealed. Evidently, nobody was going to bolt out the back door. He really wasn't needed, so he relaxed and breathed in the pampered yard's smell. Sidestepping, he faced the backdoor, let his head drop, and saw a dried brownish spot in the fresh aromatic, early morning grass. He dropped to a knee, pecked at the brown color with his forefinger. He turned around and saw another dab. He followed a trail between the sculpted plants and saw the splotches. At the end of them was a crumpled body.

Pooter bellowed out Dolph's name even as he was running toward the body. He was not as fast on his feet as he had been. The body seemed to be receding from him, and he heard the gate open and close even before he got to the body. When Pooter jerked upright to look into Charlie Montalvo's open eyes, Dolph was beside him. Unlike Pooter, Dolph was still plenty fast.

Pooter knelt and saw a small hole in Charlie's chest. The blood seemed to have just leaked from that small puncture. Prepaid funeral, indeed, Pooter thought. Hell, prepaid death, only someone other than Charile had made the payments, just as Charlie had made the payments for Oscar's death. Symmetry, synchronicity, Pooter thought. He turned to look over his shoulder at Dolph.

"Poor Charlie," Pooter said.

Dolph stepped past Pooter and knelt in front of Charlie. The two of them, Dolph and the dead Charlie, seemed to exchange stares. Charlie's eyes seemed oddly serene and consoling, and his body seemed relaxed, not contorted, as though he had died quietly without any objections from his mind or body.

After a few moments, Dolph pushed himself up but continued to stare into Charlie's eyes. He looked at the dried blood that had drained from the hole in his chest. Then, his knees started shaking. The quivering made its way into Dolph's thighs. His face grew pale. Pooter turned away from Charlie and went to help Dolph. Grabbing an arm, Pooter eased Dolph into a sitting position to take the weight off of his legs. Dolph looked up at Pooter. "It's not right," Dolph mumbled. Pooter didn't know if Dolph meant Charlie being dead or Dolph's knees being weak.

"Take it easy. I guess I should call the police?"

Dolph poked his cell phone toward Pooter. "Donde esta Vincent Fuentes? Donde esta Sister Quinn," Dolph said succinctly as though questioning some one in his mind.

Pooter tried to hit 911 with his thick fingers but wasn't sure until he heard a dispatcher. "There's a body at . . ." He didn't know the address. "Dolph?"

Dolph looked up at Pooter, shook his head and mumbled the address. Pooter repeated the address, then knelt between Dolph and Charlie to wait for the police and whomever or whatever they brought with them.

* * *

When the phone call woke Jerri before dawn, the voice on the other end, as though unpracticed in making these calls, said only "He's very weak." Jerri blinked, breathed, tried to find her thoughts. The female voice on the other end said, "It's time. He's about to pass."

As she walked down the hospital hall to Palo's room, Jerri heard the squish of soft-soled shoes behind her and turned to look at the smiling, matronly nurse who wordlessly guided her into Palo's dark room. Looking already dead, Palo lay in the midst of bleeps, blinks, and flashing lines. Jerri stepped up to him. His eyes opened, then fluttered. Then the lines went flat, more bleeps sounded, the mostly dark room was lit by flashes of green and orange from the machines. Another nurse appeared, and then a doctor, and Jerri turned away from all of it.

She found the door and walked out into the hall. She had seen his last little flicker of life, but she had had no last conversation, no goodbye. If she had any family, then he was it. And she had let him euphemistically "pass." She should have taken note. She should have made more of a fuss. The old gangster was too weak and old to protest his mortality himself. Jerri should have done it for him.

Jerri walked past fellow sufferers who must have recognized in her twisted face the grief that awaited them. She stopped at a coffee machine, filled the thing with quarters, not even counting how many she needed, and watched the messy brown liquid pour into the Styrofoam cup. She gingerly lifted the hot drink to her lips, barely sipped, and pulled back from the foul mixture.

She saw a vacant padded couch. A woman scooted down from her to give her room. When Jerri sat, the woman sneaked one quick look back at Jerri and said, "I'm sorry."

Jerri knew that, if she let herself, she would cry. So she nodded her head at the woman and returned to her thoughts. She had not given Palo what he had deserved.

That "deserve" part caught in her mind. What had Palo deserved? What did anyone deserve? She thought of Angel, the poor peasant she had tried to help, doing a gainer into the hood of her SUV. She thought of Joe Parr looking up into her face and trying to find some time and some words to tell her that she had made his last years the best. They had both deserved better. There were others.

On the other hand, Palo had had better than he deserved.

Like his son, Vincent, the one Dolph saw shoot himself, Palo had no permanent shape. With charm, grace, and a smile, Palo, like Vincent, became what he needed to be. Professor or priest, thug or patrón, father and son adapted. Finally, they had always had what they wanted and needed: the sanctity of their own selves and the help of others. Not the blood of family, but the very blood in their very own veins, the momentary comfort, luxury, delight, happiness was what they lived for. They had made a god of expediency.

Jerri felt some warmth on her hand and a gaze on her neck. Her shaking hand had spilled some of her coffee, and the woman sitting down the industrial sofa from her stared at her. "Can I help?" the woman asked.

Jerri felt tears in her eyes. But she was crying from anger now. "No," she said.

She had wasted her attention, concern, care, and sympathy for too many years with Palo and Vincent Fuentes. To the detriment of her own family, she had let herself be concerned with them and for them even after Vincent was dead. She would not make that mistake with Palo. He had made her his daughter, he had made her his only family because he needed her. And she had broken the law for him. Palo's monumental selfishness had just worn him out, her too. Time to bury him.

Jerri wiped at her tears with the heel of her hand. "Sometimes, we just have to let the grief take its toll," the woman said. "I find comfort in Jesus."

Jerri's lip trembled. She was about to laugh. She nodded and left the woman with Jesus and walked down the hall to the elevator. By investing herself in Palo, she had lost time and friends and family. On the way down the elevator she wondered. Whom did she have? Who would watch her wind down toward infirmity and death?

When the elevator reached the lobby, Jerri spotted another sofa. On one end was Sandra Beeson. On the other end was Sandra's son, Dolph Martinez. Standing, leaning against the wall was Pooter Elam. Jerri walked to the sofa, said hello to Pooter, and sat in between Dolph and Sandra. She turned to Sandra first. "Call it a premonition, something. I just thought that this might be the time. He's dead isn't he?" Jerri nodded.

"Oh dear," Sandra said. "I called Dolph and told him to meet me here."

Jerri turned to Dolph. He truly looked like shit. Dolph said, "I had a rough night and rougher morning."

* * *

Renee had bangs across her forehead, and the last shallow pool of her milkshake rattled as she sucked it up her straw. She was a girl again, not a wayward adolescent with a drug and boyfriend problem. Dolph had met her for lunch at the Olmos Pharmacy, one of the last real pharmacies in the city, the only one with a soda fountain still intact.

She smiled at Dolph after she sucked up her milkshake. "I forgot how good these are. I really like ice cream." Perhaps the distance she had

154

purposely put between herself and her murdered father and uncle might protect her just a little longer before her cravings drove her back to her problems. She smiled, "Maybe I am cured, but as bad as you old guys are, Izzy is worse for me."

Dolph nodded. "I still like beer better," but he sucked out the last bit of his malt and felt a little bit of his boy's taste buds kicking in. He reached for the readers on his chest, stuck the arms over his ears, and dug in his pocket. He pulled out Izzy's cell phone, punched the outgoing calls, and handed the phone to Renee. "That's Izzy's."

"How did you get it?"

"I ran into him again."

"That *ran* sounds like maybe you drove a car over him or something."

Dolph pulled back from her. She gave him a defiant and coherent stare. She was improving. "Or something," Dolph said.

Renee looked down at the phone, "What am I supposed to be looking at?"

"It's yours. Throw it away or call any one of those numbers." Dolph stared at the table. "You'll probably be talking to some criminal or whore. I called several of them myself."

"You just don't like him."

"I might have saved him from doing a real crime."

Renee handed the phone back to Dolph. "I have class. I'm through with him."

"For how long?"

Renee had rehearsed being "a girl." She let her eyes drop instead of peering back at Dolph with a druggie's vacant yet pleading stare.

"I made a promise to your father."

Renee rolled her eyes. "So you said before. You, Charlie, and my father are troglodytes. You make each other promises. Yet neither Lee Ann, my mother, nor me figure into your 'promises.' Look where my uncle's and father's promises got them. Be careful where all your promises are going to lead you."

She did smile. Then pushed herself up. Dolph watched her walk away from him then focused back on his milkshake. He sucked at it. He longed to be at Big John's meeting with his drinking buddies. The night before, he

155

had sipped bourbon and tequila with Walter. And Walter hissed in his ear about Mexico until the red circles on Walter's map of Mexico started to glow. "When I saw Charlie dead, like when I saw Oscar dead, I just started shaking. It was like I couldn't think, feel, nothing. My knees gave way and my mind went numb."

"You drove smack dab, head first into what ails you."

"I've seen too many bodies."

"Up on this side of the border, we can handle death if we can account for it, wrestle it down, make it logical and reasonable. We like conspiracy stories because they give us reason. They give dark sinister forces the credit and thus give us a little comfort. What scares the bejesus out of us is the fact that death may just be arbitrary, absurd, scary. Some crazy fucker can strap dynamite to himself and take out half a city block. We need explanations, causes, villains." Walter's eyes shifted behind his thick glasses. Dolph could see that Walter was talking to himself as well as Dolph.

"Stop, Walter," Dolph said because he felt Walter's reasoning boring into his head.

"But in Mexico they celebrate fickle death. They ain't sophisticated like us."

Dolph got up and walked out to the sidewalk and stared across McCullough Avenue. What he had done when he saw Charlie was lose his shit. He could push and shove Izzy, but when he saw another grown human being dead, his shit went loose. He had given himself a break on Oscar's death. If he had known more sooner, then maybe he could have warned Oscar, threatened Ramón, shot Lee Ann. But the time between his knowing and Oscar's killing was a total of maybe thirty minutes. No one could have done better—not even Jerri.

But for Charlie, once again, he had all the pieces. Their edges didn't fit, but the pieces would have fit if he had shoved at them just a bit more. If he had been better, then Charlie would not have been dead. He doubted himself. His only penance, he reasoned, was to do something for what remained of the Montalvos, those two Southside boys who never could move away from the Southside inside them. All he could find was Renee. And the best he could do was to see her cleaned up and away from Izzy.

The night before, drinking with Walter and staring at his map, Dolph began to cuss Lee Ann for all the hurt she had caused everybody. Walter interrupted him, "Don't you see? Lee Ann made herself over or found someone to make her over. She changed destiny. She got herself to where she wanted to be. Her method just didn't include any moral bearing." Dolph wanted to tell Walter that he was full of shit, but he got to thinking about what Walter had said. "In Mexico," Walter added. "They work with what they got. They're used to destiny." Dolph wondered if Walter had ever even been to Mexico.

Lee Ann might not have gotten away. Someone might find her, and most countries would extradite her, but that would take years, and maybe half-a-dozen years was all that she wanted. And Dolph would not be the one to retrieve her and set the matter straight for Oscar and Charlie.

After helping Renee, Dolph figured that he had to do something for himself. Maybe what he needed was in Mexico with Walter. Call it God. Call it fate. Call it just desserts. Call it Pooter's Spinozistic logic. But what made Dolph's knees shake was what was after his ass. Charlie and Oscar Montalvo, Joe Parr, Vincent Fuentes, and Sister Quinn were warning him that his ass was standing right in the way of that god or monster. Dolph was thinking that maybe he ought to run away with Walter and get out of its way.

* * *

Jerri watched Rodney bring the tips of his fingers together and stare over them at Ramón. "We've done some research. A Lubbock probation officer reported that Lee Ann Montalvo, before she became Mrs. Montalvo, besides the obvious problems she had with the law, pretty much had problems with everybody. The psychological counselor decided that she was sociopathic and issued a report that she thought Lee Ann might be dangerous."

Ramón sat on the other side of the short table. Because Rodney yelled and screamed, the police excused him from talking to his client from behind a Plexiglas window. So in his orange suit, handcuffed, Ramón got very private consultation. "What's sociopathic?" he asked.

"Fucked up," Rodney said. He got up from the table, walked up to the chair where Ramón sat with his cuffed hands in front of him, and gave him a comforting slap on the shoulder.

Ramon hung his head and said, "I don't want to do no prison time." He raised his head to look at Rodney Lee. Jerri, from her vantage point, saw Ramón's eyes and the rest of his face just droop. He had given up. He was afraid of going to prison, and he was humiliated that he had let himself be duped.

Rodney Lee held his fingers in front of him and then slowly brought them together, his back to Ramón. "A confession, a smoking gun, and now a conspiracy make for a hard defense. All we got now is for you to be appropriately remorseful and for me to make the judge and jury cry for a poor misguided boy."

Ramón looked at Jerri. "You eat with the devil, you better use a long spoon," Jerri said.

"The bitch, it was that bitch, look at how she done me," Ramón said.

"Would you rather have been Charlie?" Jerri asked.

Rodney Lee chuckled. "That's good, Jerri. I know why I like working with you." Rodney bounced his fingertips together then straightened his bright purple tie and the lapels of his shiny suit. He looked at Ramón. "You got better than you deserve or can afford, which is me. And even better yet, I feel sorry for you. Who knows who might succumb to the wiles of that bitch?"

Jerri had done the research and made the call. She could have come up with just as good a defense as Rodney Lee. But because she could never simply dismiss everything outside her own ego, she could never perform like Rodney Lee, any more than she could behave like Vincent or Palo Fuentes. In more ways than she cared to think about or admit, she was more like Ramón. And in reality, she was what she was in part because of Palo and Vincent, but also because she always felt some need to help the Ramóns.

"So you gonna get me outta this?" Ramón asked Rodney.

"I don't think there's much getting out to be done. But I'm going try to make sure that the punishment ain't near as great as the crime." He was performing for Jerri. For Rodney, Ramón wasn't even in the room.

As they left, and Rodney again patted Ramón's arm, Jerri thought of her son, J.J., and then of the boys that she was indeed trying to raise: Dolph and his buddies.

Outside the jail, in dampness left from an early morning shower, just a bit of steam on the hot asphalt, Rodney started to mumble, "I don't know. I don't know. They take a dim view of murder for hire. This boy could be getting the needle."

"And that would look bad for your career."

"Look even worse for his." Rodney slapped his palms together, forever the optimist and said, "I'm going make 'em cry for the poor boy."

"You do that," Jerri said. And walked away from Rodney.

"Hey, you want a ride?"

"I'm three short blocks away, and I like the steam."

"Celebrate the fresh air." Rodney turned away from her and leaped up to grab at some air.

As she trudged down Dolorosa, so familiar to her because of her work and her men, the wet air seemed filled with her consciousness. Others had come down this street: generals, invaders, killers, conquerors, Comanche chiefs, reformers, politicians. She was a part of this place and its history. And it was so goddamn pungently male. The air had filled with the smell of men's locker rooms. The men had squeezed all else out but their egos. And she had joined their strutting parade.

As she got close to her office, Sam Ford's old place, she gasped for some fresh new air, even though it came from an air-conditioner and not from the city streets. The men she had chosen and the choices they had made her make had pushed her into a life of association with criminals, on both sides of the law. She had been on her way to becoming a teacher, an artist, a gentlewoman, but she had become an accomplice in the disgusting business of keeping an appearance of legality.

Jerri longed for comfort, leisure, refinement, for long discussions about the theoretical or hypothetical, instead of the self-absorbed expression of male egos and criminals. As she opened the door to her office, with her head pushed back by the cool air, at first she did not see Dolph, standing to one side, waiting for her, ready to plead his case.

In her office, Dolph told her his intentions. At first, Jerri almost laughed at the complete absurdity of following that borderline loony

Walter Boone to Mexico to cure Dolph of his moral obsessions. Jerri reminded herself that most of Dolph's friends were looneys, and again she reviewed the men around her. Dolph was not that different from Vincent, Palo, Joe, and Rodney, none of whom could outrun their own obsessions. But Dolph's obsessions expanded outward from his sense of justice. Dolph could actually lose his ego or maybe just lend it to others. Rodney, Vincent, and Palo had firm, inflexible egos. For them and so many others, helping and using were the same. Jerri had to feel for Dolph.

The air got heavy between them. Dolph was not in her office just to tell her that he was leaving; something else, something momentous to Dolph, had brought him there. When Dolph's ego stretched to others, those others often got hurt. This is what made Dolph hurt. Jerri didn't want to see Dolph hurt. She wondered if she were about to hurt.

To break the heaviness, to pull it off their shoulders, they both glanced out Jerri's window to the pedestrians: tourists, city and county officials, panhandlers, lawyers. Out there, south of Main Plaza, for nearly four hundred years, ever since the town was San Antonio de Béxar, preening males had bartered away their souls and the lives or livelihoods of women and children. And when the bartering stopped, there was often killing. Jerri turned to stare at Dolph. The air was still heavy. "This whole Mexico idea is ludicrous, absurd. You are not goddamn Hemingway or some shit. And Walter sounds like he's delusional."

Dolph fidgeted and kept looking out the window. "Absurd doesn't scare me as much as delusions. And here, in San Antonio, I'm hearing voices again."

"Those voices are your conscience."

"Well, my conscience talks loud. I want to run away."

"To what?"

"To something else."

Jerri let her head sag. She realized that, though she had never invited him to barge into her life, she would hate to see him leave her life. "So what would make you stay here?"

Dolph shifted and looked at her. His eyes went out the window for as long as it took for his eyes to flicker, "I'd stay if you asked me too."

"You're my best private eye. Of course, I want you to stay."

"I don't mean for that reason." Dolph's eyes dropped as though he were thirteen. "Seems like we've been playing cat and mouse for a long time. It's time one of us catches the other. Thinking of that gives me some hope. Other than 'toying' with you, only Mexico gives me hope."

When Dolph forced himself to raise his eyes and look at Jerri, Jerri dropped her eyes to her desk. "A lot of the men whom I get involved with get killed. I'm a little snake bit."

"So am I."

"I just don't think I can give you enough of what you want." That was true.

"I don't want much."

"I don't know that I can give anything." That wasn't true.

"That's 'absurd,' 'ludicrous,'" Dolph said.

Jerri's hand started shaking at the same time that Dolph's hand started to twitch. "I wish I weren't this way," Jerri said. "I wish I could tell you something else." Dolph seemed to suck his chest and his gut in. Jerri added, "Maybe someday I'll be able to tell you what you want to hear."

Dolph lowered his head and shook. "I wish Mexico wasn't so attractive." Dolph raised his head to look at Jerri. "I wish I felt like I had time to wait for you."

They both stood at the same time. Jerri walked around the desk and up to Dolph. She was the one who took him in her arms and started the kiss. Dolph was the one who stopped the kiss. When Dolph left, they were both confused.

* * *

It was a real switch; Dolph was drunk and Pepper wasn't. Dolph babbled about Jerri, but because he had started drinking well after Dolph had started, Pepper couldn't quite absorb all that Dolph was saying. But on the other side of him, having started sipping gin at the same time Dolph had started, Joan was just as drunk and thus able to keep up with Dolph. Joan pulled herself up to a sitting position in the reclining lawn chair on Pepper's back porch, twisted her whole body to look at Dolph, and said, "Jerri Johnson is full of shit. From what you say, you can see that she's hiding behind several layers of pretend." As she spoke, Joan pointed at

Dolph with her forefinger while still holding her gin and tonic in her hand. It was spring, mosquitoes were starting to come out. Malaria season. Take precautions. Drink quinine. Thus gin and tonic for all. Pepper sipped a beer.

Dolph had come by on his way home from a visit with Jerri. Joan was home from school and so had let him in. Pepper was still on the job. By the time he had gotten home, they had twisted open the second bottle of gin. She was indeed a pistol.

"You should stay. Any fool could figure out the symmetry between you two. If you can adjust and straighten yourself out, then you should stay. You owe it to yourself," Joan said.

"I've adjusted. I've twisted," Dolph said. His head wobbled, but he held his gaze at Pepper. Pepper looked into his backyard. Behind a row of banana trees was the San Antonio River. Downriver was Big John's. Upriver was the tourists' Riverwalk that was moving its concrete banks toward Pepper. A couple of centuries before, fields of corn would have lined the banks of the river that surrounded Pepper's house. He and Dolph had always settled on the banks of rivers in vacant corn fields. They were attracted to the oldness and wildness. There was plenty of both in Old Mexico.

Joan shakily stood. As she rose, pushing herself up with strong thighs, she beamed at Pepper. She really must have appreciated him. And for Pepper, a woman's appreciation was an aphrodisiac. There had been his first wife, the one from Maryland. Then there was that whole litter of wives between then and now. You would have thought he could remember what a woman's need felt like, but he had forgotten it or suppressed it until he saw Joan smile at him. "I better go to bed," she said at Pepper, but then she turned and repeated herself and her smile to Dolph. But Pepper was sure that Dolph did not get the same smile that he got. Just to make sure, he jumped up and kissed her as she staggered into the house.

Sitting between Dolph and Joan, Pepper had felt like a cat with two tails under two rockers. Pepper knew that Joan was probably his last chance for his better self. But he knew that Dolph might mention or bring out his worse self, which he missed. He had to learn how to relax more, instead of just feeling grateful with his better self. Still, he was glad as Joan turned her shapely middle-aged behind to him and left him with Dolph. There were things to be said that were best said by Pepper's worse self. So Pepper and Dolph sat in the dark and stared out at the San Antonio River. He and Dolph, like so many times before, were negotiating with their futures. What was scary now was that neither one had that much future left.

"So just what the hell you think you gonna find in Mexico?" Pepper asked after checking to see if Joan were indeed in the house.

"My youth," Dolph said. "Or maybe my old age. An old man can have some dignity in Mexico. Because you can buy dignity in Mexico. And an old American with some money can buy himself a nice niche."

"Goddamn it, Dolph. Sounds like you're buying yourself a tombstone."

"I hope to live a long time down there."

Pepper twitched in his chair and sucked out some beer. "Ain't this about as ironic as shit. I'm supposed to be the one running to Mexico to evade responsibility and myself. Not you. You're cocksure. You're the government, the fucking Border Patrol. You're responsibility, right thinking, the tried and true all rolled up in one. You're fucking Dolph Martinez. And you know how you get, so just forget this whole scheme."

"Aw, fuck it all to hell anyway," Dolph said and waved his empty glass in front of his face. He had even sucked the ice out, so only a lemon slice rolled around in the bottom. "It's a dream, hope."

"Well, you, by God, have seen where hope and dreams got me. Hell, you're the fucker threw me in prison for following my hopes and dreams."

"Yours were stupid and self-destructive."

Pepper gasped. "I ain't even about to comment if you can't see the bold-face, red-assed hypocrisy and stupidity of what you just said."

Dolph stood and started walking across Pepper's lawn to the river. Pepper pulled another beer for himself and another one for Dolph out of his ice chest and followed Dolph down through the banana trees to see the tiny trickle of the San Antonio River. In town, the river was really a canal. Here it was more of drainage ditch, redirected to flow the way engineers wanted it to. Texans had done that to most of their rivers. Pepper lowered himself onto his butt beside Dolph and then handed him a beer. They both gazed at the trickle of dirty water. It seemed to Pepper that they both saw the future in that murky water. "Walter Boone talks shit," Pepper said. "Like you your ownself said, he's like the snake in the garden, hissing out evil. If you pay him too much mind, you're gonna find yourself kicked out of the garden."

"Maybe the garden is in Mexico. Jerri doesn't understand, and I'm afraid to say it because I'd just get a lecture. But goddamn it, there's just something about Mexico that set old Sam Houston and John S. fucking 'Rip' Ford into charging into it and wanting to take it over. Jerri wouldn't understand. It's the fucking garden."

"Maybe it's here. Maybe that garden is here. And maybe those nineteenth-century fuckers were full of shit and your goddam study of history ain't done you no good. Maybe the fucking garden was back in West Texas. Goddamn, you're too old and saggy to go charging into Mexico, telling Texas to kiss your ass and Mexico to kiss your balls."

"That's probably the most fucking profound thing I ever heard you say." Dolph waited. Pepper waited while Dolph asked the obvious, "You gonna go?"

Pepper wanted to go, but he said, "I'm thinking."

"You followed me here."

"That's because I didn't have nothing left out in the Big Bend."

"You had history and family. Here you had nothing. What's the difference between here and Mexico?"

Pepper knew the god's honest truth. It was the same it had always been, yet this time, because he was older and had actually weighed and judged, he said, "I don't have a woman in Mexico."

Dolph tsked. "Jesus Christ, in Mexico, you'd have *women*."

"But you goddamn well know that there's women make your hand shake the bourbon out of the glass. And then there's *women*."

"And you goddamn know how much we suffered because of them."

"Well, I got another one."

"Shit."

"You fucking asked Jerri to ask you to stay. She did no such thing. Now I got too much respect for you to keep you from going to hell after your own fashion, so I ain't gonna tell you what to do, but I will by-God try to save you from yourself, just as you was always trying to save me from myself, and tell you to keep your sorry ass right here on this side of the border."

"So you're not going?"

"I'm old enough so that I don't have to make all of my decisions based just on my hormones. So besides my hormones, my mind is telling me stay here. Because Joan might just be the last best chance I got." It was the same impasse they had come to before when one of them chose a woman over what was obviously best for the two of them. But because of the weight and heft of years, because of the hope that maybe they had both gained something resembling wisdom, they both knew that, though the answer was the same, this time it was different.

"Well fuck," Dolph said, downed his beer, and threw the bottle toward the trickle of river.

"Damn it, don't do that," Pepper said. "It's littering. Don't mess with Texas. Don't you listen to all those Texas celebrities telling you that on the T.V.?"

Pepper pushed himself up, set his feet sideways as he inched down the incline to the edge of the trickle, and picked up Dolph's beer bottle. When he looked up, he saw Dolph staring off into the night. "What it was is that I lost my shit," Dolph said into the night. "Jerri might be enough to make me stay, but that ain't gonna happen. You got Joan." Dolph shrugged. "I need to run away."

"We'll miss you," Pepper said as he inched up the slope. "Who knows but what you'll be back."

"I hope I can stay in Mexico," Dolph said.

Pepper hoped that he could stay with Joan. He hoped their arguments and tantrums had run their course. Charlie Montalvo, the cause of their friction was dead, and his death made their arguments look silly. "Then I hope you can stay in Mexico too," Pepper said to his compadre. It was funny, Pepper thought as he walked back to Dolph: we start out as little boys or little girls and we like only our own kind, other little boys or little girls, but then we get stiff dicks, at least the boys do, and we end up chasing the girls, but we get old, our dicks get soft again, and we settle with our own kind whether our own kind are males or females. Pepper hoped that Joan was his own kind.

* * *

Three months later, just after five pm, waiting for the rush hour traffic to slow down before making their ways home, three friends sat in Cappy's bar getting a head start on nursing their liquor into the hot Texas dusk. The three women had formed their own habits and meetings. Sandra Beeson, Joan Phelan, and Jerri Johnson met to wind down from their days and their obsessions just as Pooter and his friends had met at Big John's. Behind them, behind the bar, Pooter wiped the bar with a bar towel that resembled a baby's diaper. He tried to eavesdrop. If he could somehow decode their conversation, he might discover some secret in femininity. But he never quite got all of their conversations. That was all right too. They met here because it was safe, because Pooter was there to watch over them.

Witnesses said Rodney Lee was brilliant at Ramón's trial. *The San Antonio Express* said he was flash and dazzle yet sympathetic. Poor folks reasoned that Rodney Lee was a compassionate man concerned about every layer of society, just the sort of young intelligent man who ought to be mayor, and why stop there, who ought to be governor or senator even if he couldn't get Ramón completely off. Pooter read about Rodney Lee's political rise.

Ramón got fifteen years and was eligible for parole, and with Jerri's help, he got an appeals lawyer. And Pooter admired Jerri for driving to the Huntsville unit to see Ramón. Lee Ann Montalvo just got away. The Bexar County Attorney's Office figured that she was in Mexico or the Carribean. They could get an extradition, but they really didn't have the patience, the pressure, or the price to bring her to justice. Renee Montalvo made the honor roll at San Antonio Community College. Charlie was buried at Mission Park cemetery, right across from Big John's, right next to his brother Oscar in the family plot.

Pooter missed their old gatherings at Big John's. Once in a while, if he got the itch, he would go by for a beer. But the expanding houses and businesses sprouting up all over the Southside had surrounded Big John's. Then the dead mesquite finally fell onto the picnic table and crushed it. Besides, Oscar was dead, Dolph and Walter were in Mexico, and Pepper was content with Joan. Pooter might be able to find another place, but he couldn't find another group of buddies. Pooter, of course, saw a big crash coming for Pepper. Joan was socially and politically too far away from Pepper. She'd ride with him for a while, but eventually she'd jump out of the car.

Pooter hoped that Dolph's future with Walter was better than Pepper's with Joan. Dolph's e-mails described big-breasted American and Mexican women, all-night drinking binges, great seafood, horny tourists, newlyweds, monkeys, iguanas, poker games and fights at cheap bars, celebrities at better bars. Dolph, Pooter figured, was probably lying to himself.

Joan's eyes caught Pooter's. A smile lit up her face. She turned from Sandra to Jerri. "To Pepper," she said loudly enough for Pooter as well as her friends to hear. Then she added, "And to Pooter." Sandra and Jerri joined Joan in hoisting their margaritas to Pooter.

"And Dolph too," said Jerri.

Pooter surely did miss his friends' gatherings, but time moves on, things change. So he took delight in the new group of drinking buddies, sipping their margaritas, while he wiped his bar and watched over them.

Chapter 10

Walter looked at himself in the mirror behind the bar. He was gaunt and yellow. His thick lenses caught some reflected light and bounced the beam between his face and the mirror. Walter shook himself to clear the light beam out of his eyes and head. He had lost count of how many beers he had drunk. He tried to calculate how much he owed, but he was still no good with Mexican money. Though he couldn't remember what he had drunk, he could remember why he had come to the bar: he had decided to drink away the morning. It was now afternoon. The beer should be making him fat, but instead his belt was in the last hole, and still his pants sagged. Even his straw hat drooped, but his head hadn't shrunk; the straw hat had gotten wet.

Rather than blink against the glare and think about himself, Walter swiveled slightly on his barstool and looked out the large window. Outside, standing in the rain, Dolph curled his toes over the edge of his rubber flip flops and pushed them against the curb. When he saw his chance, Dolph jumped, slapping his flip flops into the puddles as he ran across the street. Dolph had lost some of his gut. His forearms and calves were bronzed and toned. Playa del Carmen had been good for him.

It was the rainy summer season. Now that the tourists were gone, Dolph and Walter ventured away from the bars close to the highway and made their way to the tourist bars on the beach, to Señor Frogs. Dolph tried to miss a puddle and nearly tripped himself. Walter thought about joining Dolph in the rain. It was the only relief from the humidity, the dampness in the air finally turning to actual water. Walter turned back to the mirror and caught another face looking in the mirror. He turned and

169

saw that the woman's eyes were on him. He glimpsed a slender nose, puffy lips, taut cheeks. Probably she was no tourist at all but one of the weird expatriates who had come to Playa del Carmen to live cheaply in the tropics. But as Walter had found out, a comfortable life here wasn't as inexpensive as advertised. Maybe she had come for the cheap surgery. Maybe she was gay. Playa del Carmen was one of the world's gay havens. And here were Walter and Dolph living together. Walter smiled. She smiled. He tipped his wet, wilting straw hat. She smiled. Dolph burst into the bar, dripping.

The older he got, the more Walter understood time. The seconds, the minutes, the hours, the days deliberately make their way into years and to your end. For all the romance, in spite of relativity and existentialism, our lives are simply the ticking off of seconds. We do what we will to avoid hearing the ticking, but Walter had stopped being able to turn it off. At times the ticking was a pounding in his chest. Sometimes he could muffle the ticks with his nitroglycerin tablets and liquor. He smiled at the woman, counting the moments he had lost, while Dolph walked up to him.

Dolph plopped on to the barstool next to Walter with his back to the door, his face to the mirror. He spoke to the mirror. "We got the rest of the summer's rent."

"So how much longer you figure we got in paradise?" Dolph asked.

"I've got another account in Hollywood. Sarah has the information. I'll have to call her."

"Walter, my salary just ain't adding up to expenses," Dolph said. The bartender set a happy hour beer in front of him.

"Your worries will soon be over," Walter said.

"Jesus, Walter, you sold your car." Dolph was right. Walter rode a Moped, just like the locals, piling groceries on his lap while he steered in and out of traffic with one hand.

Walter didn't answer. He wanted desperately for time to slow down, to stop, so that he could take stock of this second, this moment, the minute, the hour, the afternoon before it slid into eternity. And at the same time, he wanted to hide from the ticking. The awareness of his own inability to mold time for his own comfort made him want simply to get through the ticks to eternity or doom.

Dolph shook his head and then sipped his beer. "What a country, huh? What a fucking country! And I should have known. Me, more than anybody, with all those years squatting in the desert, catching the wets, taking 'em back across the border, only to arrest them again. I should have known. What the hell? What the hell did I think they were running from, huh? Poverty, man, poverty."

When they got into town, Walter and Dolph snuggled into the the tourist community with cobblestone streets and fake architecture close to the beach, the suburban franchise stores and the local failing businesses out toward the highway, and the expatriates' condo community inside their gated residential area. Then reality crept in. They got jobs. Walter sold Mercedes and Audis to rich people, few of them Mexicans. But after seven months, he just grew too weak to get to work. His veins and capillaries groaned as they tried to move his blood along. Dolph gave tours on buses that drove tourists down to Toulum and Xel Ha. His Spanish came back to him. He radiated health. He seemed to fit in with the locals. Walter didn't know why Dolph was so pissed off. All he didn't have was money.

In the mirror, Walter saw the woman behind them rise and walk toward them in slow motion. She had an unbuttoned light cotton or silk blouse over her shoulders. The opened front revealed her ample breasts covered by a slim tank top. A delicate, silky pair of shorts that matched her top stretched across her hips but draped softly against her thighs. Her lavender toenails poked out of white sandals. "Can I buy you guys a drink? I'd like to hear a little English," the woman said with a bit of a Texas accent.

"Yes, you can. Beer and English is always good," Dolph said.

The fortyish woman lowered her eyes and then her head. "I'm not usually this forward, but I just want to hear some Americans."

"Did you miss the tourist season?" Walter asked.

"Hell, we ought to go ahead and annex the Yucatan. I'll bet they'd be willing to secede from Mexico," Dolph said.

"I was right. It is good to hear Americans."

Even if the new lady could not feel Dolph's eyes on her, Walter sensed the lonely Dolph eyeing this prize. Only the liquor and beer had been plentiful, not the money or the women. And in truth, Walter and Dolph were getting older and well beyond any glamour. But now, after two years of forced celibacy, they both wanted to ease their loneliness as much as indulge their weakening hormones.

The conversation remained pleasant and nostalgic. She was originally from El Paso, she said, though she couldn't recall any of the landmarks Dolph mentioned. She stumbled over some Spanish words and even some English words. Walter thought her mind stumbled too, but her smile and her tight smile and body made up for those weaknesses. Eventually they drifted out to the porch, to sit in wicker chairs facing the Caribbean Sea and its accompanying breeze that blew a mist into their faces. And for the rest of that afternoon, for Walter, the moments stopped their ticking.

* * *

Over the course of two weeks, Allison, as she called herself, courted Dolph and Walter. Weak, counting his ticks, Walter left Allison and Dolph alone some nights to lie in his bed and try and account for all that he could.

With more weakness and more time his bedroom, Walter started to read more. Mostly he reread books he could order from the internet or find in the library. And the bought and unreturned books piled up around him. And sometimes he watched videos on his greatest extravagance, a high definition TV. Meanwhile, like Prufrock, he listened to the voices from a farther room: Allison and Dolph. Walter then turned to arithmetic. He added up some images and memories and fact. The sum was Allison. He worried for Dolph.

When Dolph came into Walter's room one morning and said that Walter didn't look so good, Walter decided it was time to tell Dolph why he had really come to Playa del Carmen. He explained about the operation that had helped his colon but shrunk his heart. Walter thought he told that story well. He liked it. It was full of irony. If you were going to die, a good ironic, slightly absurd, totally human cause would leave behind some stories and memories. Dolph's face turned red and his lip and hand quivered. Walter couldn't tell if he was frustrated or angry. Walter wouldn't have been surprised if Dolph had beaten the shit out of him. "And so why the hell did you have to bring me?"

"I didn't want to be lonely."

Dolph started shaking again. But instead of beating the shit out of Walter, he turned to go to Allison, leaving Walter in his room.

Several nights later, as Dolph and Allison finished a cheap pizza (money was getting even scarcer), Walter looked out the long window across from the foot of his bed and tried to make sense of his life.

He wasn't looking for excuses. He wasn't even looking for meaning. He sorted back through moments and tried to assess whether or not he had wrung every bit of enjoyment from those moments. He tried to attach years and context to those moments to see what excited him about him. But he was no good at autobiography. Not only could he not recreate, he could not account for years or context or intensity. They were just pleasant, clear, and timeless. But he wanted to know that he knew that they were going to be timeless when they happened. That he could not do. So he punished himself for not concentrating on beauty.

He punished himself for not making the time stand still back when he still had the time. Why had he not grabbed more? As he watched the ceiling fan over his head, connected images kept coming back to him. They were all of women. All of them pleasant. All of them moments that made his life happy. Most of the moments were filled with Sarah. Even the memories of her chiding him seemed pleasant. Maybe all these memories were just colored pleasantly by a Yucatan summer and the whirring ceiling fan. Hume, Locke, and Newton were right. Space and time trap us. Free will is nothing more than a little wiggle room within our time and place. Spinoza must have been right, and Pooter, back in San Antonio, must have been right about Spinoza, but then his thoughts of Spinoza were interrupted by Charley Pride.

Dolph and Allison were listening to Charley Pride wail "Is Anybody Goin' to San Antone?" Walter remembered that song. He was with Sarah when he first heard it. The memory of young Sarah with young Walter became clearer, and Walter was suddenly back then and here too and also everywhere in between. He was out of space and time. He commanded himself to freeze this moment. It was going to be one of the good ones.

Charley Pride drew Walter out of the bed to his bedroom door. He reached for the handle, and his mind went before him, slowing time and imagining what he might see as he stepped into the living room. What he did see was a whiskey bottle, a pizza carton, and Dolph and Allison entwined in each other.

Allison drew back and stood, not apparently knowing that her blouse had fallen around her waist, revealing her perfectly symmetrical, perfectly shaped breasts. Dolph leaned into the back of the couch smiling, saying with his eyes that he did not begrudge Walter the opportunity. "This is one of my favorites," Walter said. Allison tiptoed up to him, and Walter grabbed her and two-stepped her around the living room.

Walter was okay. The ticking had slowed, then gone away. The moment was frozen, would live forever, so after the dance, Walter let Allison pull him into his bedroom. Dolph followed, not to interrupt but to witness this moment. He stood at the open door and stepped into the frame. Allison pulled off her shorts and stepped into Walter's bed. Charley was singing "Kiss an Angel Good Morning." Dolph was closing the door to close himself out. Walter was in his bathroom.

The ticking countdown, ticking both in Walter's heart and in his head, was subdued. His life had been full—to hear his ex-wives, girlfriends, and bosses tell it—of debauchery and physical excess, but Walter couldn't but think that he had missed excess. He had some noble joys. He almost cried when he thought of his first years with Sarah. His mind smiled when he thought of his son Michael. But in the sentimental and the debauch, he could remember no real act of sheer, purified beauty. Other motives than the aesthetic had been involved. He could not remember doing something solely because it would appear beautiful, nothing bereft of morality or meaning, just pretty. It was writing. He had not written in years. Tonight, he would write again. And he would leave this writing to those who might choose to remember him.

But there was logic too. Walter had long since figured out who Allison was. Dolph probably should have put the totals together too, but like most men, Dolph, for all his detective work, couldn't do the math when women were involved. And even though way down deep Dolph knew who she was, Walter knew that you just couldn't tell a buddy to dump his latest woman, whether she was a wife, a lay, a flirtation, or an enemy.

So Walter could save Dolph from what Allison might have in mind for him. His death would leave a beautiful and tragic, albeit absurd, memory. And it might save Dolph's life. This was beautiful. This was logical. Sara might even love him. He swallowed the Viagra, took a drink from the faucet, then he put one of his nitroglycerin tablets under his tongue. If the others were too slow or dense to understand, then surely Pooter would when he heard the story. And Pooter would make sure that people heard Walter's stories told beautifully.

He came out of his bathroom to find the voluptuous Allison spread naked across his bed. She was magnificent. Walter hoped that Dolph could hear her screams. And as he waited on the last ticks of his slowed heart, he said to her, "Was it okay for you, Lee Ann?"

Allison's face showed just a glimmer of recognition, then became its usual tight blankness. "Who is Lee Ann?" she asked.

Walter stared up at the ceiling and folded his hands across his bare chest to feel the last ticks of his heart until it finally exploded or gave out. "You've had your revenge, Lee Ann. I'm dead. Now leave Dolph alone."

Chapter 11

The little Ford Focus squeezed in on Dolph. The contents in the Focus, what possessions Dolph couldn't sell and didn't leave in Mexico, pushed against the back of his seat. The little car grew smaller and smaller. The empty Arizona desert baked it, shrunk it. From inside the car, Dolph knew that he and his little tin shell were just a speck in the desert. He yearned for the air-conditioned protective bubble that his old Border Patrol S.U.V.s provided. This whole little car could be punctured like a tire by a saguaro needle.

He wished he had gone with his first instinct and bought an older, bigger, cheaper car for road trips and a motor scooter to get through the narrow, crowded streets of Playa del Carmen. But Walter had argued that a smaller car was more practical and saved the planet. At that point, Dolph didn't give a shit about the planet.

He zipped by the spot on this back road where Tom Mix crashed his convertible and died. Dolph was going too fast too, just like Tom Mix. But he wanted to get there. *There* was officially Prescott, same as Tom Mix's destination, but Phoenix would do, anyplace would do. Speed was important.

He wanted to feel better about the desert, but it wasn't his desert, the Chihuahuan desert. The fragile-looking Sonoran saguaros scared him, as though they were ready to fall on him, as though they knew him to be an intruder. Even the Focus was scared. It shook sideways. He slipped his hand inside the opening of his shirt and wrapped his hand around the vial of a silver blue liquid. Sister Quinn had told him to hold it when he had been gut shot and nearly dead. It gave him visions back then. At times,

Sister Quinn, though dead, talked to him now. He didn't believe the curandera shit behind the vial, but he had kept it anyway. Now, what could he say, he had been in Mexico and was running away again from voices, memories, premonitions, and another dead man.

Like any desert, the Sonoran was full of plant life, plenty to see, just like his Chihuahuan desert, which he had spent years learning, and he liked it better than trees, better even than the Mexican beaches, so he wanted to step out of his tiny tin cup of a car and look at the delicate flowers, weeds, and cacti. But driving was all he could do, just as he had been doing for two days, with stops only along the sides of Mexican highways, a few winks and then another amphetamine. He needed to drive. He let go of the vial, pulled his hand out of his shirt to use both hands to drive.

"See, see there, you son of a bitch. See what you done to me," Dolph yelled at the corked urn in the passenger's seat. "Died. You fucking died. What the hell is that? What good could that do anybody?"

Playa del Carmen was like a Mexican Disneyland—too Mexican to be American but too American to be Mexico. Everyone hustled the tourists, who were everywhere, even crowding the public beaches. Like the locals, Walter and Dolph got pushed inland, away from the beaches and into the hot, humid jungle brush. They made okay money by Mexican standards, but were poverty stricken by American standards. Walter sold cars. Dolph served as a tour guide. The Mexican tourists thought him strange because he spoke Spanish with an American accent, but the Americans tipped him well because he spoke English "without an accent." Like everyone else, he had hustled and chanted and barked at the tourists. And Dolph, like Walter, watched his savings and his retirement dwindle.

Their nest eggs went into a pleasant condo in a walled off suburb. They each had a bedroom, with a third for stayovers and privacy. They drank decent beer and whisky but nothing extravagant. After the first visit by a whore, they both just got bored with hiring women. They found no girlfriends. They were lean but comfortable. Then Walter died.

Walter was as much a hustler and barker as any of the dealers outside the small shops selling T-shirts and cheap jewelry in Playa del Carmen. He had made Mexico sound too good to be true. It had been good and true until Walter told Dolph that he had really come to Mexico to die. And then Playa del Carmen turned untrue and bad.

That morning, Dolph had gotten up for some orange juice and coffee to chase away the slight hangover from the night before. Walter wasn't up. An hour later, nearly nine o'clock, well past the time that old men wake, Dolph stepped into Walter's room. Walter lay on his bed and looked out his window. "I'm just tired today," Walter said. "Just so weak I can't move." Walter then told him the whole story about his wishes, fantasies, and delusions that he should die in Mexico.

When Dolph asked why the hell Walter brought Dolph with him, Walter told him that he just wanted somebody to watch him die, somebody to bear witness that at one time he had been alive in the world and reacting with it. "But why me?" Dolph said.

"You were the only one willing to come down here." Dolph had seen too many friends die. Turns out what Walter really wanted was just what Playa del Carmen was: Mexico, but not too exotic, good cheap hospitals close by in Cancún, and if no lover was available to ease him into death, then a friend to get him there.

"I'm sorry, Dolph. I'm sorry I didn't tell you. The doctors said it was coming back. I knew it. And I was tired of fighting it. Better to go out living it up rather than slowly withering. It was cowardly of me to want someone with me. But I'm glad it was you."

Dolph wondered, cussed, and watched more saguaros whizz by his Focus. Why him? Why had he not seen? Why had Walter chosen this? "Goddamn, Walter. I feel sorry for you. But what about me?" Dolph yelled at the urn.

So Dolph had known about Walter's weak heart and his few remaining ticks when he squeezed Allison's shoulder and pushed her toward Walter. What greater love hath one old drunk for another than backing away from the best woman either of them could have found in a foreign land? She left in the middle of the night, and Dolph had wakened early, checked on Walter, found him dead.

Walter's will, made out by an American lawyer and probated by a Mexican notario, stated that all his earthly remains, literally the ashes in the urn and the three-year old cashier's check for $30,000, should go to his first wife Sarah Boone, the most prominent chainsaw sculptor in the United States. Evidently, he had decided on cremation and an urn and had written the cashier's check when he first learned of his condition. The notario said that Walter had deemed Dolph his angel of tidings, his messenger, the executor of this will, so whatever money was left was to go to Dolph. After Dolph sold what parts of Walter he could, Dolph's part of Walter came to $25,000. Dolph knew that this money was to be his fee for the delivery of the cashier's check and the urn.

Walter had brought Dolph to Mexico, and then had delivered him from it. So Dolph had zipped through Mexico and was cruising at 90 in a tiny piece of tin past the site where Tom Mixed crash, burned, and died, toward Prescott, Arizona, the new residence of the best chain saw sculptor in the world. Dolph turned to the urn. "Damn it, Walter. Why didn't you talk to me, give me some hint, explain something before you fucked yourself to death?"

After Walter died, Allison called. Dolph told her what happened. And then she dropped by Dolph's empty condo. He had sold what he could. The Focus was crammed full. Allison looked around. "Where are you going?"

"I'm delivering Walter."

"You're as fucking spooky as he was," she said. She seemed a little upset herself, like something spooky had taken place there in the night with Walter.

"So what did happen?" Dolph asked.

She said, "It's just freaky. He was perfectly good, you know. Then alls of a sudden, well, just, shit, well. He stops breathing. I just left. You were asleep, and I didn't wake you up. And I'm not even sure what happened until now."

"You shouldn't blame yourself," Dolph had said. "He just had his ways." But then Dolph said what Walter, Pooter, and Pepper would have wanted him to say. "Jesus, you fucked him to death."

She laughed, but uneasily. Then Allison looked at Dolph like she was sizing him up, like she was trying to decide what to do with him. And Dolph, in turn, was twisting his mind all up trying to decide what to do with Allison. She scooted closer to him, kissed his ear, ran her flat palm up his inner thigh. Dolph's mind raced, got jammed. He panicked. "I got to deliver Walter to his widow."

"What about me?"

"I can't help you," Dolph blurted out. He left Allison in the condominium and started drinking and found the amphetamines. When he returned, Allison was waiting for him at the condo. She trembled, at first, Dolph thought, with desire. But it was anger, "Fuck you, Dolph Martinez. And fuck Walter Boone. He got what he deserved. I'm glad I fucked him to death. And now, I'd fuck you to death to if I didn't have to actually fuck you again."

"This condo has been sold," Dolph said. "I got to go. I've got a mission."

"I hope you and your mission go all to hell," Allison said.

Playa del Carmen had been a mistake. Dolph missed San Antonio. He missed Big Bend. He missed Jerri. He missed Pepper. He missed Pooter. Walter could tempt him but not guide him, not like Jerri. He needed guidance. He needed penance. He needed to finally complete his mission. If he could just properly dispose of Walter, properly deliver Walter's memory into the right hands, he would be resolved. He could get on with what he had left of his life. Dolph sped towards Prescott, Arizona. He wanted to honor Walter's last request, but he also wanted to know why Walter did what he did. It was clearly not an accident. Now Dolph needed a beer and a rest, and ahead of him was a small wooden and tin building.

Dolph glanced into the rearview mirror and saw a row of four motorcycles behind him. He hadn't noticed them while he was zipping forward. He put on his blinkers. He turned into the old wind-and-sand torn desert convenience store. The motorcycles pulled in after him. "You want a beer, Walter?" Dolph asked the urn. It didn't answer.

Four motorcycles pulled up to one side of Dolph's car, and he nodded at the pot-bellied leader. Dolph grabbed the urn, got out, and walked with the bikers into the store. One biker had on black leather chaps, and Dolph wondered just how hot he must have been and how sweaty the back of his legs must have been. Surely riding in an air-conditioned tin can was better than riding through the desert dressed in leather, even if something exciting was between your legs. The biker also had on a black leather bandanna pulled around his head. He must have shopped at a biker specialty shop.

Dolph and the bikers milled around the store, Dolph a little dizzy from standing up. He bought a six pack, plastic wrapped strips of beef jerky, and a bag of corn chips. The bikers lined up behind him as he paid. Then he went back outside, and under the wooden awning of the convenience store, his butt on wood, his feet on gravel, he sipped from his beer, gnawed the jerky, and talked to the urn beside him. He almost expected, certainly wished, the ashes inside the urn would answer.

"What the hell you talking to?" a voice said. It was a biker whose curly blond hair hung down in strands over his eyes. He shook his head to clear the hair from his eyes. In one hand was his helmet; in the other was a beer.

"Nobody," Dolph went on to say, "What the fuck is it to you?"

"You know, you're kind of a spooky dude," the biker said.

The blond biker sat to Dolph's left, the urn was between them. He looked out at the desert, and Dolph thought he recognized the ruddy red face and the mop of curly sun bleached hair. The man looked like he lived in the desert or some place with lots of sun and no humidity.

"Does that jar ever answer you?" a voice said from Dolph's other side. He swung his head. The biker with the leather do-rag had sat next to him. Dolph figured his senses were shot. He hadn't heard or felt the man move closer to him.

"What kind of jar you talking to?" A voice said from behind him. Dolph turned and saw the biggest biker behind him. He had on cut off jeans, knee protectors, and tennis shoes. He obviously couldn't afford the designer black biker apparel of his buddy. The fourth biker was also behind Dolph. This one had on a leather vest. His bare shoulders were shining bright red through the sun block he had just bought and was spreading on them.

Dolph looked at his car, not that much bigger than the bikes, then turned his attention to the blond biker on his left. He gazed past the biker at the desert, as he often used to do when he was with the Border Patrol tracking for signs. The biker's stare was uninterested and bored. He was just going through the motions.

"You guys obviously don't give a shit about my urn or what's inside."

"What's inside?" Dolph heard from behind him, but the man to his left didn't move.

Dolph looked up, "In this urn is a Mayan god. He's not the main one, just a minor deity. He's the god of flood control." Walter would have been proud of Dolph's answer.

"What the fuck?" the man with the knee pads and cut offs said.

"Chased him in here with some candles. Once he was in, I corked up the urn, and there you see it."

The man on his left turned to him and smiled. The man with the cutoffs reached for the urn, but Dolph pulled the urn away and rested it in his lap. "I wouldn't fuck with him. I let him out, he's gonna be pissed."

"You're talking shit," the man with the black leather bandanna said.

Dolph shook his head, then held it still. The paunchy middle-aged bikers who were creeping up on him were still there. They were husbands and fathers out for a noonday spin, trying to relive some youth by buying an expensive toy, trying to be cowboys or bad boys. They were not Hell's Angels or Bandidos. They were not bad people. You wouldn't expect them to be dangerous.

Not this time, Dolph thought. He would not let these guys get the jump on him. He would not let their innocuousness mislead him. He was no longer a Border Patrol agent. He would give them no deference. He would not resist action. He would not be wary. He would make the first move. But then he felt himself growing light headed. And even though he was sitting, his knees started to shake. This was not someone else about to get hurt; this was him. No more, not again, get ready.

The man with cut-offs and knee pads bent over to grab the urn. When Dolph could feel the man's sour breath on his shoulder, he reached up, grabbed what he could, and flipped the man over. The biggest biker did a forward roll then did several sideways shakes as he tried to right himself. Dolph swung his right hand out and caught the leather do-rag biker in the face. Dolph was up with the urn in his hand. "Now, you fuckers just back away from my fucking urn. Otherwise, I'm letting him out."

The man with the sunburned shoulders raised his arms and shrieked. Then Dolph felt a breeze and looked up just in time to see the blond man swing his helmet at his face. He leaned back instead of trying to duck forward. The helmet just scraped his nose. But then his knees buckled. He was on them. Someone had tackled him and knocked him all the way over.

183

He looked up to see the blond man's fist coming. He got a hand up and kept the full blow away from him. He swung to the side to just barely miss the swing. This, Dolph realized was not just suddenly happening. It was not provocation. It was premeditated. They had come to beat the shit out of him.

Dolph tried to swing his right hand, but the urn was in it. He dared not break it. With his left hand, he starting beating at the man who had tackled him: the leather bandana biker. The cut-offs and knee-pad biker, scratched and skinned, was moving toward him. The sunburned biker watched. The convenience store operator appeared at the door and looked right at Dolph, long enough for Dolph to scream, "Call the police," before the blond man could hit him. "And an ambulance," Dolph said as the blond man pulled his fist out of Dolph's face.

Dolph's face swung to the right and he dropped the urn. He kicked and got to his feet. He felt a fist just at the base of his neck and another on his forehead. His readers swung on his neck from one side of his face to the other. Maybe he ought to slip his readers on. Before they just totally beat the shit out of him, he wanted to get one or two blows in. He flailed, tripped, looked up, saw the blond man. He looked a little like a lion with the shaggy blond curls in his eyes. The blond man swung. The blow sent Dolph's face to the right. He did not go down. He got to his feet. He tried to decide whether to swing or run. They circled him. Then one of them grabbed him from behind. He saw the blond man step up. His fist smashed Dolph's face. He didn't go down or lose consciousness. But he was fuzzy. He got a fist back into the blond man's face.

Then they all started in on him. Before he lost consciousness, he saw the blond man's face in front of his. "Fucker," the man said and hit him again. Before he passed out, Dolph remembered seeing this blond man over a year before in a near showdown on the banks of the San Antonio River at Big John's Ice house. And he knew who Allison was and felt ashamed that it had taken him so long to figure out what Walter knew right away.

* * *

When Dolph's consciousness returned to him, he heard the swaying rhythm of "Appalachian Spring," smelled the antiseptic hospital, and saw a beam of light from a single window across from him. The beam of light settled on him. "Appalachian Spring" swelled. He looked at the curtain to his right, and his memory kicked in. He was not in heaven, hell, or just dead. He was in a Phoenix hospital. On the other side of the curtain, a man had just returned from prostate surgery, and his wife waited with a boom box, so that her husband could wake with the sense of melancholy yet triumph that his favorite piece always gave him. Thus, Dolph and his roommate were regaining consciousness to "Appalachian Spring" at the same time.

Dolph felt sorry for the couple. Dolph wanted to say something, but his mouth wouldn't work. He tried again, and a sharp pain went up the side of his face. Once more he tried and found that someone had muzzled him. Dolph remembered a little. The middle-age bikers had broken his jaw in two places, and the doctors at the Phoenix hospital had slit Dolph's jaw and stapled and wired his mouth shut. The bikers had also cracked a rib. The doctors could do nothing for the rib.

Dolph knew that he was in Phoenix. He had come to his hospital room from his ass kicking in an ambulance and had looked at the signs on the freeway. He had realized that he was going to Phoenix. But he didn't know much else. The pain medicine mixed with what he had taken earlier had put him in limbo. He remembered asking the paramedic about the urn, but when he tried to work his mouth, he felt as though someone had jabbed a rusty nail up under his jaw. And the air he tried to breathe in order to talk seemed thick and heavy, and once inside him, the air expanded, for he felt it pushing out from inside him, about to blow right out of his sides and chest. Was this a heart attack? Had he caught a heart attack from Walter? A paramedic pushed him down. "Be careful. You've probably got a broken jaw and broken ribs. Your face is crooked and you're leaning to one side." But Dolph tried to ask about the urn. The paramedics just shrugged. Then he sorted through some haze. He remembered an image coming right before blackness. He had seen the blond biker pick up the urn and take it to his bike.

The door opened. "Appalachian Spring" swelled again. And a figure stepped into the light from his window. From his confinement in physical and mental limbo, Dolph expected God pissed off.

God introduced herself. "I'm Sarah Boone," she said. As the paramedics were pulling him up off the gravel parking lot, they had asked Dolph whom he wanted them to call. And he was somehow sharp enough to give them her card that he had stuffed in his wallet.

Dolph had been looking forward to this moment. He had expected to see Joan of Arc, Helen of Troy, Queen Elizabeth I, or the goddess Venus before him. But Sarah Boone was small, tanned nearly cooked, and just a bit curled forward at the shoulders. "Are you in pain?" she asked and stepped forward, following the light into Doph's room. "Appalachian Spring" stopped.

"They gave me something," Dolph said and tasted blood.

Sarah's eyes followed the tube from Dolph's arm to a drip. "Morphine," she said.

"I should feel better, then," Dolph said, but the words came out jumbled.

"Maybe, you shouldn't talk." Sarah opened her purse, dug into it, and pulled out a notepad and pencil. She handed these to Dolph. "The doctors said your jaw is wired shut."

Dolph reached for the notebook, but his side felt like it was going to explode from the inside. "The doctors say that you broke a rib too." Sarah laid the notebook on the small table to Dolph's left.

"They are going to check you out. Do you have anywhere to go?"

"Do I have a car? Did they find any money on me?" was what he tried to say, but it sounded nothing like that.

Sarah had smile lines etched into her face. Her hair was dyed a reddish brown. She had the ubiquitous Southwestern turquoise and coral around her neck and wrists. She didn't seem like the sort of woman who could send Walter into deliriums of regret, but Dolph could see that he was going to learn more about her. She stepped out of her beam of light and sat in the chair in front of Dolph. "Your car is safe. You have a few bills in your pocket. They broke a window, probably looking for something valuable."

"The urn. They got the urn," this time Dolph was able to push the words out through his teeth. Dolph could taste blood.

"The urn?"

"The urn with Walter's cremains. They got Walter." Talking just took concentration.

Sara pulled back just a bit from Dolph. "You had 'Walter?'"

"I was bringing his ashes to you. His last request. That's why I called you. You've got an urn and a cashier's check for . . . " Dolph stopped when the words got caught on the wire in his mouth.

"Oh God, I didn't believe that whole cock-and-bull story. Just like Walter. Maybe I chose not to believe it. But that's just like Walter. Is that some literary idea leaving me his ashes? God," Sara said.

"I'm going to get them back," Dolph said and felt a click inside his mouth along the line of his jaw.

Sarah stood back up into the beam of light, walked to the door, returned, stepped out of the light, and looked at Dolph. Her sculpting had sculpted her. Nearing seventy, she had taut skin and muscles. "Forget it. Walter is a lunatic. When he loses his mind, he loses it in ways that are peculiar to him. God, this is absurd. Why couldn't he be normal crazy?"

Dolph was beginning to see just a little of what Walter saw in her. "I promised." Now there was pain in his mouth.

"This is the worst kind of macho, male-bonding posturing. Don't you see? It is some kind of joke. Walter's last act is to fuck around with everybody. You, me, the world at large. He will gain several more hours, days, even years by being as annoying as he possibly can. And he will live even longer by giving us all a lasting memory of just how crazy, how annoying, how singularly peculiar he was."

"I'm going to get it back." Blood and pin pricks filled his mouth. But he fought the pain, "Is the cashier's check in the car?"

"The police found it. It was in an envelope with my name on it."

"It's yours. Get it."

As the white vinyl curtain separating the two beds pulled back and the poor man's wife peered out at the disturbance, Sarah stepped into the beam of light from the window and walked in it, stepped back to the chair, and sat down. "Walter, you must know, is a world-class flake."

"Why are you still so pissed off at him?" Dolph asked, but he was sure the answer was that Walter had just become a part of Sarah's skin, her DNA, that she could not shake him, as though she had gotten used to a crooked nose or broken tooth and just didn't dare to have it cosmetically fixed.

"Walter Boone gave me a good name but took away a lot of years," Sarah cupped each hand around the opposite elbow and sighed. The woman from the other side of the curtain looked on. "He's, he's, he's like a tumor." The woman with the suffering husband grimaced. "A good looking, appealing tumor." Sarah smiled.

"Why didn't you go see him?" Dolph wanted to say more, but he ran out of air to push the words through his teeth. The blood in his mouth tasted really bad. He reached to the table beside him and grabbed the notepad and pencil.

Before he could write anything, Sarah had grabbed the thermos of cold water with the straw in it and held it front of Dolph's face. "You look like you're hurting. Maybe a drink would help." The cold water didn't help. In fact, Dolph had to slam his heel into the mattress a couple of times. Sarah pulled the thermos out from under his face.

Dolph glanced to the bedstand beside him and grabbed his readers. When he put the glasses on, they felt heavy, and the pressure on his ears made his jaw grow hot. Dolph scribbled on the notepad. "You could have helped him. You must have known. Would it have killed you to have taken him in instead of letting him go all the way to Mexico?" he wrote and held the pad in front of Sarah.

"As bad as Mexico might have been, I could never have matched the idea of it. I was past for Walter. I was memory for him, not one of his dreams. He couldn't have died with me. He had to die with a failing dream."

"You could have done something," Dolph said.

Sarah dropped her head. "Look, you're going to rip your jaw loose." She reached and gently touched the side of Dolph's face. "You've even got a little blood there." She shook her head at Dolph and smiled. "Why don't you stay with me until your jaw doesn't hurt? I've got a nice house on the side of a mountain."

Dolph pulled his readers off and threw them back on the table, held the notebook well out in front of him, and tried to write with the opposite hand. "I've got to find the urn," Dolph wrote.

"You know that Walter is fucking with you."

"Of course he is. That's not the point," Dolph wrote.

"So stay with me until you feel better. I'd like to talk to you about Walter. I think that maybe you might have gotten to know him better than I did."

"Mountains, coolness," Dolph hissed and then nodded, raised his hand to the bandage at his side. His jaw felt as though it were a rusty hinge. He rubbed at it and it hurt.

"Well, then," Sarah said and pushed herself up into the beam of light. "I'll look after your things." This, then, was the goddess Dolph would serve. He would retrieve Walter's urn for her. "Appalachian Spring" started on its crescendo, but it was playing only in Dolph's head.

* * *

Dolph spent an hour and a half playing with his jaw trying to move it against the wiring, tasting blood, moving his lips, practicing making sounds then words when another visitor came to see him. This was a short man whose muscular torso put so much weight onto his legs that they bowed. In back of him was a long pony tail. In front of him, on the tip of his pug nose were a pair of thick glasses. He glanced around the room—Dolph's roommate and his wife were already trying a walk down the hall—and followed the sunbeam down to the chair in front of Dolph. The man sat down and extended his hand. "Johnny Yield," he said and offered his hand.

Dolph jiggled his rib and winced, but he shook Johnny Yield's hand. The postoperative medication was wearing off, and Dolph was tired of the morphine. He wanted to be clearheaded. He had a mission. He could take the pain. He had before. "Wow, you must be fucked up," Johnny Yield said.

Dolph tried to talk, but blood and bone-against-bone grinding filled his mouth, so he held the notepad well out in front of him and wrote. "I've been worse," and held the notepad in front of Johnny.

Johnny smoothed the black hair on the sides of his head, pushing it into the loose pony tail. "Me too," Johnny said. "You get in fights. You break ribs, knuckles, noses, cheeks, and jaws. So I'm glad to see you ain't bitter about this." He picked up his right foot and rested it on his left knee. He rubbed at the leather top of a thick-soled boot. "But you see, I am bitter. That's why I'm here." Dolph started to scribble. "No, don't trouble yourself. I'll explain a little."

Dolph leaned his head back against the back of his bed and nodded. Johnny Yield started: "I'm Mescalero Apache. Inn of the Mountain Gods in Ruidoso, New Mexico. You heard of us? No wait, don't answer. Let your jaw relax a little. It'll hurt the first day but then you get used to it." Johnny paused and pushed his glasses up his nose with his thumb. But because of the pug, because he had no real bridge to his nose, the glasses just fell to the tip. "Now some of us got a motorcycle club. That's how I'm here. On my bike. And we like to cruise over to the White River Apache Rez and then cruise around the area. We get from up around Four Corners to El Paso to Yuma. Sort of an old-style raiding party." He laughed. "Only we raid convenience stores and bars. Same as a lot of biker groups. Only we're old school. From back when bikers were the bad guys, Hells Angels and Bandidos and shit like that. So a lot of people in this area like to blame every little bar fight and petty crime on Apache bikers. So the Pima County Deputy Sheriff's Department has been asking about why we beat the shit out of you. They want to know what we stole, why you pissed us off."

Dolph held up his hand and scribbled. "You didn't beat the shit out of me."

Johnny nodded and thus had to push his glasses up with his thumb. "They always blame the Indians," Johnny Yield said.

"These guys weren't Indians. I gave a description," Dolph wrote.

"Nobody is gonna believe you. How would you know? You were drinking and full of illegal home-grown Mexican substances. You're lucky you're not in jail."

"Sons of bitches," Dolph wrote.

Johnny Yield nodded. "I can see we gonna get along fine, partner."

Dolph scribbled, "I've got no partners."

"Oh yeah, you do. See, I got scouts out, just like in the old cavalry days. And we're going to spot the boys beat the shit out of you, and then we're gonna lead you right to 'em. And we'll even help you beat the shit back out of them." Johnny dug into his pants pocket and pulled out a cell phone. He held it up in front of Dolph. "These are marvelous. We got Apache scouts all over the biker haunts. When we spot 'em, I'm getting a call."

"What about the police?" Dolph wrote.

"Dipshits have already blamed us. Which of course is why we are helping you. Call it Native American pride, or something like that. We may not be able to convince anybody we're innocent of this one, but we're gonna let somebody know we're pissed off."

Dolph wrote down his cell number, tore the page out of the notepad, and handed it to Johnny Yield. He figured there was no reason to argue. And deep down, beyond just wanting to trust Johnny Yield, he just did trust him.

Johnny nodded. "I got this nice Indian. Fuck Harleys. They're technologically backwards. Fad pieces of shit for white boys. Got a picture of that old photo of Geronimo on the back fender of my Indian. They can see me coming, or going. You can see me around."

As Johnny pushed himself out of the chair and his glasses up his bridge-less nose to his forehead, Dolph wrote again and handed the note to Johnny.

Johnny smiled. "You wouldn't understand my real name. It's kind of sacred, you know. So a lot of us name ourselves after something you whites value. You don't seem to pay much attention to 'em, but you put up a lot of yield signs."

So like General Crook, Dolph had his Apache scouts.

* * *

A breeze that must have passed over mountain water and come through a canyon struck Dolph in the face and his hot jaw cooled. He had gotten used to pushing his words out between his teeth with his tongue, but he had talked too much and the wires on his jaws had grown hot. Across the small backyard were several long, large pine logs. And beside them in various forms of development, as though displaying the evolution of chainsaw art, were raw and polished creatures: eagles, bears, mountain lions, Indians, and cowboys.

Just days before, Dolph had been in Playa del Carmen soaking up the steam coming off the puddles in the street. A little over thirty-six hours before, before getting his jaw broken and rib cracked, he had been in blistering desert heat. He liked this coolness without humidity. The breeze lifted him back to the Chisos Basin in Big Bend. Sometimes, after patrolling the desert lowlands, officially or unofficially, he drove up and got some coolness and breeze in Big Bend.

Sarah Boone's art bought her this house on the edge of the mountain. As he sat with her and felt the breeze and gazed at the Aspens twitching green then silver, he thought that this place was a haven from Walter Boone and his residual influence on people. Dolph began to think that maybe he should just let the blond-haired biker and his middle-aged, middle-class gang keep Walter and his urn.

Sarah Boone's bare feet rested on the wooden railing that looked out over the backyard beneath them. She sipped her margarita. Dolph sipped his from a straw. Earlier, he had sipped his enchiladas from a straw. Small chunks of tortillas were still on the wires wrapped around his teeth. Brushing his teeth had become very important to Dolph. "Prescott may be on its way to becoming another Santa Fe, in which case, I'll have to move again. But not yet. So you can stay if you like. It's a nice place. It's got shot-gun-style bars. The type Walter would have liked," Sarah said.

"So how long did you know about Walter's condition?" Dolph hissed and squeezed out of his mouth. He was sort of getting used to talking this way. The movement had all but stopped hurting.

"Right away, as soon as it happened, Walter called me. He must have had a drink in one hand and the phone in the other."

"That shouldn't happen to somebody like Walter."

"It's ironic, stupidly ironic. It's perfect for Walter."

"You should have come to San Antonio. You should have come to Mexico."

"Yeah, I should have."

Dolph touched his jaw. He was running out of money. He had even less now that he had to pay the deductible for his medical expenses. Luckily, he hadn't let his insurance drop in Mexico. He wondered how long he could stay with Sarah.

"With Walter, you always had the unexpected." Sarah sucked at the last of her margarita. "I would have loved to see Walter. But the unexpected just scared me. He would have done his magic, and there I would have been, in Playa del Carmen or San Antonio, watching him die, instead of you. So maybe that's why you're here. I feel like I owe you."

Dolph felt glad to be there, but he had friends back in San Antonio, and he had told them where he was and what all had happened. His friends didn't take long.

Prescott's distinguished old courthouse sat in a large square. In front of it, across the street were boutique shops and restaurants. On another side were the original buildings that had once housed the old whorehouses and saloons. These were now bars and cheaper restaurants. At dusk, retirees promenaded around the square. After a full day of sightseeing, of chainsaw sculpting demonstrations—Sarah wielding her chainsaw like a welder does his torch—Dolph and Sarah sat in the cool mountain breeze on the courthouse steps facing the bars. The promenaders, some hand in hand, moved like the gentle cows on Jerri's farm. Dolph felt good in this pleasantness. Then like that scene in the Wild Bunch, the scene where one member of the bunch then another rounds the corner of an old adobe, all on their way to the climactic showdown to rescue another doomed member of the bunch, coming around the corner of the courthouse were Jerri, then Pepper, then Pooter, and finally, limping a little behind them, Dolph's mother.

He had listened to Walter every day for over a year, and before that, he had listened to him nearly every day for three years. Walter's preaching had nearly converted him. He knew even before the ass kicking that Walter had given him a mission, had shown him what to do. Now, with an ass kicking, getting rescued by Sarah, and his friends coming to help him, he knew that what he had to do was right. Walter had a certain logic to his illogic.

Chapter 12

As soon as Dolph stood up, Jerri hugged him, and she kept her palms on the sides of his shoulders when she pulled away from him. Pepper figured that they ought just have mounted each other right then and there and done it like city cats in an alley. Neither one had the good sense to do what he or she just goddamn ought and had to do.

Next, Sandra hugged her son. And then Dolph stood straight and shook hands with Pooter, then Pepper. Dolph's eyes were blackened, making him look a little like a hungry racoon. The slits under his jaw line had dried blood on them. His nose too had bruises and looked a little misdirected. "You look like shit," Pepper said.

Dolph with his mouth shut hissed, like Walter used to, "Glad to see you too." Then he looked over at Sarah Boone and said, "Why didn't you tell me I look like shit?"

"I thought you would look in a mirror and see for yourself," Sarah said. Pepper liked her already.

"So how's Joan?" Dolph asked Pepper.

Pepper felt all the eyes turn to him. He caught Pooter's gaze with his own. It said that he should have known better. "That didn't work out so good."

"It ain't too good for her," Pooter said. "She's drinking a little." Pooter then shrugged, like he knew it was hers and not Pepper's fault.

"Your hand's shaking the bourbon out of your glass" was what Dolph said, though no one but Pepper understood that was what he said.

"Good to see you too," Pepper said. He remembered the fights, the cussing, and the final big boom inside his head that said, "this ain't so bad.

I had worse." He looked at Pooter. "Naw, for once in my life a woman is shaking the bourbon out of her glass because of me. I kind of got used to the whole movie. I've seen that same old ending so many times it don't upset me no more."

Dolph looked surprised.

"So, my God," Sandra Beeson said. "It's been two years; we're standing in the square of a strange city instead of sitting with a new acquaintance in front of us, my son with a caved-in face, and what do we talk about? Pepper's love life. Shouldn't we have some introductions and a few drinks and some pleasant chatter?" Pepper agreed. He always seemed to agree with Sandra. Somehow he and Dolph's mother made better partners than he and Dolph.

Pepper looked around, saw the long rows of bars across from the square, and pointed, "there." In unison they moved away from the courthouse, across the street and into one of the long shotgun bars. In the bar, they were lucky to find a vacant round table, and while the shadows of mountains darkened the streets outside, they talked until the night darkened the bar. Pooter stood behind them because there were only five chairs and fetched pitchers of beer and filled everyone's glass. Open doors let in the cooling night. The lamps, which were imitations of old kerosene lanterns, made a purposeful golden glow in the bar. The smell of beer and grilled steaks surrounded them. And from upstairs from over the railing, from years past, Pepper could almost hear the laughter of whores. The mountain night air might have given these old Texans who lived in humid nights or scrub desert a slight chill, but still, Pepper felt familiar in the scene. For Sarah and Jerri had taken Oscar and Walter's places, and Sandra was along to watch and to direct their attentions. "Variations on a theme," as old looney Walter used to say.

And Pepper listened to Dolph. Even with his lips sealed, because his jaws were wired shut, Dolph told a story better than he used to. His words hissed and at other times seem to squeeze out his lips, so he was hard to understand, but still, he chose the words better, waited in the delivery, cocked an eye, motioned with his hand. Pepper took it as a compliment that the time sitting at Big John's with him and Walter had made Dolph a better story teller. In the past, Dolph could make some smart-assed remarks, but he could not really bullshit well. He never seemed to have the time for it. But now, as he told Pepper about Mexico and Walter, Pepper could see that he was enjoying the telling. Pepper especially liked the part that concerned Lee Ann Montalvo or Allison Richardson or whatever the artificial face and titted woman's name was at the moment.

"So you mean to say," Pepper started just like he was back at Big John's with Walter and Oscar in with them, but then he caught himself when he saw Sandra, then Jerri, then Sarah. Certainly not Jerri or Sandra and probably not Sarah would mind the vulgar barnyard word or the gist of what he was about to say. They looked at him.

"You mean to say what?" Pooter asked.

"You mean to tell me you did Oscar's old lady?"

"Pepper?" Jerri scolded, but then her look at Dolph scolded him too.

Dolph just nodded. "So how was it?" Pepper asked, and he felt the stares. But Pepper knew that that was just exactly the question the drinking buddies of old Walter, Oscar, Dolph, Pooter, and him would want answered.

"Hell," Dolph said, and even with his wired jaws, he smiled. And maybe, Pepper guessed, it was the first smile in a long time. And Pepper waited for Dolph to go on. And Pooter leaned forward to hear. And the ladies all listened. Holy shit, Jesus, but Dolph had indeed learned to tell a better story. Pepper didn't even need to listen now, but he wanted to hear what Dolph came up with. And Dolph said, "Hell, it killed Walter."

"Dolph!" Sandra now scolded. Then Sandra thought, "I don't get it. Of all the places in the world she could have hidden out, she chose Playa del Carmen and bumped into you and Walter?"

Pepper and the rest of them waited to tell her. But Sandra's eyes lit up before Dolph could say, "Mom, she tracked us down. She was going to kill one or both of us."

"Why didn't you stop her? Report her?" the naive yet practical Sandra asked.

"Because, at the time I was doing her, I didn't know it was her," Dolph added.

"How could you not have known?" Sandra asked.

" I was a tour guide. I was retired. I wasn't detecting for anybody. My thoughts were elsewhere." The way Dolph ducked his head but kept his eyes switching between his mother and Jerri, he seemed to be apologizing to them like he was a bad boy.

"What a wonderful mother-and-son conversation," Sarah said, but her smile kept Sandra from pouncing on her.

"And ain't it all just some goddamn great poetry," Pepper said. Dolph finally understood. Maybe, all his causes weren't worth a shit, but talking about them was better than the doing of them because, in talking about them, you were reliving them in front of different people and thus creating a slightly different story that had to be repeated so that the next time you could put just another thin layer on them with slightly different folks—variations on a theme, as Walter used to say.

Pooter, standing behind them, nodded, "Romantic. It was what Walter would have wanted. It's how Walter would want us to remember him."

"Yeah, right," Sarah said. "Remember with all your misplaced, false, silly sentimental male bonding bullshit." Jerri smiled too. Pepper had seen that look before. Jerri looked like she was on Oprah and wanted to shout to Sarah, "You go, girl." So Sarah, of course, continued. "The fact is that Walter is dead. And he all but killed himself. Not just now, not just with that evil bitch, but with the whole way he led his life."

Pooter interrupted. "Ain't that what life is? Just preparing to die."

Pepper was getting excited, "Right, brother Pooter. You ought to leave something pretty behind. And the best thing to leave is a good story. And Walter has written himself a whopper."

"And obviously, we got some disagreements about what is pretty and what is a waste," Sarah said.

Pepper liked this old lady. What's more, he really truly was over Joan. That thing with Joan had happened and now it wasn't happening. This was the first time that Pepper felt that way in regard to a woman. Pepper was having fun. He wanted to tease Sarah, so he said to Dolph. "Are we going to get some Mexican villagers and go track down and burn the Frankenstein monster?"

"No. We're going to destroy her later. But first we got to find that evil henchman of hers, that blond bastard that was at our parley with her and Charlie back at Big John's. We're going to get Walter's urn," Dolph said.

Pooter's eyes and smile lit up. Jerri dropped her smile. Sandra tsked. Sarah shook her head, and Pepper watched her. "He pisses me off worse than she does. She's just being her corrupt evil self, what she has to be. He's doing it for money."

"That ain't natural or right," Pepper said.

"And how are we going to find this evil bastard?" Jerri asked.

"My Apache scouts are out looking for him." Pepper switched his attention from Sarah to Dolph. Dolph told another good story, this one about Johnny Yield and the remains of the Apache nation.

* * *

That night, Pepper was in Sarah's kitchen cutting carrots and listening to Sandra. But he glanced out the kitchen's plate glass view of her patio and the sculptures in the back yard. In the light, Pepper could see Pooter walking around the wooden creatures as Sarah pointed out details.

At the bar, the smell of steak had gotten to all of them, and they decided, to save money, to cook at Sarah's house as she graciously offered. Hell, Pepper worked in a kitchen. He would have bought them all a steak. Talk about spending money. They had just bought four one-way plane tickets from San Antonio to Phoenix and rented a minivan to cart their expensive asses up to the Arizona highlands to rescue Dolph. What was a steak, especially one seasoned and grilled by hands other than your own? But Sandra had taken charge. Just as she was now in charge of the kitchen. No one stayed to listen to her except Pepper.

As she chattered on about the chickens they had bought and the best way to cook King Ranch chicken, a recipe she had gotten all backward and wrong, one that any self respecting Kiñero would have laughed at, Pepper cut the carrots that shouldn't go into King Ranch chicken in the first place. Sandra took a turn at the celery, but she cut it all wrong. She did not place her forefinger or first two fingers over the dull, flattened side of the blade to guide her slicing. Instead, she clumsily chopped. But Pepper was not about to tell her.

But the easy rhythm of cutting soothed Pepper. Only Sandra's barking orders upset him. If she would leave, he could get on with what he had done for so long without knowing it. Back when he and Dolph lived in the desert, Pepper had cooked chili for the deputies and custom agents coming to arrest him. Then, in prison, with shiny aluminum vats and long grills, he had cooked for prisoners. Back out of prison, in the bed and breakfast he dreamed up with Sandra, he perfected his recipes and created new ones. And when he went to work, he worked as a chef. In truth, cooking had become as soothing as a tall glass of good bourbon on ice and more trustworthy than any of the women Pepper had known.

Pepper looked up to see Sandra toiling. "Just in case you don't know, I figure I should be so lucky as to have a momma as good as you," Pepper said to Sandra because he figured she never heard much about that.

"No, Pepper. I sucked as a mother. Now, Jerri, there's a good mother."

After dinner and drinks and more boasting and one-upping and collecting and recreating old times, Dolph got a call. Johnny Yield, Apache scout, had spotted some Texas bikers headed from out of the Arizona White Mountains. Their bikes had a name of an Odessa dealership written on the frame around the tag. They drove to Silver City, where they checked into a motel and spent the night drinking. In the morning, Dolph and his team would fire up the minivan and chase the bad guys.

The new adventure didn't cheer Pepper up as much as talking about it did. Staying, cooking cheered him up. He sat on the porch looking into the dark at the outline of Sarah's wooden monsters and thought that maybe it was his adventures with Dolph that had fucked up his life. Well, of course, Dolph's previous calls for adventure and revenge and capturing the bad guys, like a plot from old John Wayne movies, had fucked up his life. Pepper had always known that. It was just that now, chasing the bad guys didn't seem like fun.

As he was contemplating this new way to look at his life while passing the old side of middle age, Sarah slipped open the plate glass door and gave him a margarita. "I don't sleep much," she said.

"Neither do I," Pepper said. "I never have."

Sarah sat down next to him and looked over her creatures. "There's my life. A bunch of silly pieces of wood. So I haven't done much better at making something of myself than you, your buddies, or Walter." Pepper smiled way in the back of his brain. "I had ambitions to be a real artist. Not what I've become. But then there probably is no such thing as a real artist anymore."

"Maybe there never was," Pepper said.

"So you cook. Is that an art to you?"

"No. It's a job. A pretty good one, but it's way on this side of art. If you want art, you got to think of Walter. He told a good story."

"The last thing I want to do is to think about Walter."

The margarita was good, and the ice all but burned his throat as he swallowed a big glob of it. "This place of yours reminds me of places of mine. I seem to have fucked those up . . . or followed Dolph out of them. Not that what I got in San Antonio is so bad."

"So don't follow Dolph after this urn," Sarah said. Pepper shook his head. He had been talking to himself and maybe the margarita, not to Sarah. "I enjoy having company. I've lived alone most of my life, even while I was married to Walter."

"No, the urn is Walter. I got to go."

"The urn is Dolph. Or maybe it's Walter's fantasies. I want nothing more to do with Walter's fantasies."

Pepper stared into his margarita. So be it, he had drunk enough. He would listen to Sarah but talk to his margarita. "No, Dolph wants it. I usually help Dolph go after what he wants." Pepper thought. "Then when we get it, he don't want it."

"Sounds like you're arguing yourself out of it."

"I deserted him once already. Because a woman, just like you, whispered temptation to me and bad-mouthed Dolph. I should have gone with him to Mexico. I could have helped with Walter."

"Please. You honored Walter by staying with the woman. Think about Walter. You think he'd run off from a piece of ass?"

Pepper snapped to. Maybe talking with Sarah was better than commiserating with his margarita. "I got the idea that he was running to Mexico for the ass."

"And how did that work out for him?"

"Well it didn't work out so good for me either. She's gone."

"But you played it to the end, didn't you?"

Was Sarah a witch, like old Sister Quinn, who still sometimes spoke to Dolph? She was hexing Pepper, confusing him. She went on, and on, in a seductive kind of way so that Pepper could see just why Walter wanted his ashes delivered to her. Finally, she said, "Why don't you stay a day or two?"

* * *

In the middle of the night, Pepper made his way through the dark living room. Jerri was lying on her back, asleep on the couch. Pooter had rolled himself into a ball and was in a corner with an eagle overlooking him. In the first bedroom, he found Dolph, making a weird snore through his wired jaws. In the next bedroom, he saw Sandra. He made his way to her bed, sat down, and gently shook her. She blinked her eyes and awoke looking a little like a child. "My God, Pepper," she said. "What is up?"

"You know what Dolph is going to do?" Pepper asked.

"Stop him," Sandra said.

"You know nobody is going to stop him. He's got a mission. Walter ordained it to him."

"Then you watch over him, Pepper."

"Sandra, you know you can't go along."

"And I don't want to. I don't want to see it."

Pepper smiled. "Tomorrow, I'll drive you back to the airport and get you back to San Antonio."

"And what will Jerri do?"

"She'll go with Dolph."

"And what will you do?"

"I believe I'll stay here for a while."

"I wish you were there with Dolph."

"I'd like to stay with this lady awhile and see Prescott."

"I know what you want to see," Sandra said.

"So do you really mind if I stay instead of following Dolph?"

"You've done it once. It's a change for you. First time didn't work out for you. Maybe this time will be different." Pepper smiled in the dark to himself. He knew why he liked Sandra and why he had asked her before telling Dolph.

And the next day, as they loaded the van, Pepper, once again, with the weight of his last desertion bowing his shoulders, went to Dolph and said, "How about I stay?"

Dolph looked over his shoulder at the loaded van and then returned his racoon eyes back to Pepper. "Look, I spoke to your momma. I'll get her to the airport and back to San Antonio."

"How?"

"Sarah and I will take her."

Dolph's eyes dropped then raised. "Not again, Pepper. Not again."

"It ain't like that this time. It's not for a woman. It's just that this seems like a place to stay. It just seems like for once I ought to stay." Dolph nodded. "Look, we got to get your momma back. And you got your Apache scout, Pooter, and Jerri. Hell, anymore, Jerri's twice the man I am. I couldn't get my cane on the plane. What good can I be? I'm short and gimpy."

"You can stay. But you're always good to have around."

Pooter wished on his soul that Dolph wouldn't have said that last bit so as to make him start all over with ifing and shoulding and would-having. It was a terrible place to exist in. But Pepper watched Dolph get into the back seat of the van. And he waved good bye to Pooter as Pooter stuck his head out of the driver's window to ask what the hell was going on. He shrugged to Pooter and kept waving as the van drove to the dirt road that connected to Sarah's driveway. And he turned back to two fine old ladies and looked forward to a day with the two of them.

Chapter 13

So the guy that they were after was the guy that Dolph had missed with his Taser, the guy Pooter had almost had to hit while they were in the back of Big John's ice house, back when Big John's was still whole. Incidents have a way of unraveling in a Spinozistic sense. The problem in connecting the dots was that the dots were scattered around time and space. That was a big job, and Pooter was never sure that he was truly up to it. So he became a lineman, and then a bartender. They were both fine occupations.

Up ahead of Pooter, whizzing along on his motorcycle right by the center stripe, was Johnny Yield. He had braided his pony tail in Comanche rather than Apache fashion and the two ends, caught in the draft of the speeding motorcycle, stuck straight out behind him. From behind him, Pooter heard Dolph grunt. Earlier, Dolph's jaw had been hurting, so he crushed two Advil in a plastic cup, added some coke, and then sucked up the mixture with a straw. Jerri glanced back over her shoulder at Dolph. In the mirror, Pooter saw Dolph try to smile. There was more to know about all of this. Pooter watched the road and pushed his mind.

Pooter agreed with retrieving the urn, but their attention was on it, not on remembering Walter. Without the intervention of God or some miracle, one of the few ways to preserve any meaning or dignity was to remember. The urn was only important in so far as it recalled Walter. And when Pooter thought of Walter, he thought of Oscar and then Charlie Montalvo and then of his best buddy, Bailey Waller, the ex-wishbone quarterback at UT. Then he recalled Sister Quinn, who had given him some of her visions. His life was filling with memories of dead or missing people, and there would be more. The goal for retrieving the urn should not be to grant

Walter's last request but to create one more story that connects to Walter so that all of Pooter's friends would tell the story a few more years, and thus, for a few more years, Walter would be kept alive. And then there would be an outside hope that Walter might live several years after them because a minor league legend about an urn, a trip to Mexico, an evil enchantress, and a band of modern day Apaches riding motorcycles instead of horses to attack some Odessa, Texas cowboys would still be told in some out-of-the way bars. But that was still not the full legacy of Walter.

Dolph's ringing cell phone's disrupted Pooter's highway concentration, the kind that only miles and miles of straight interstate across empty land can create. Dolph answered his phone, and up ahead Pooter could see Johnny Yield talking into the mouthpiece that came out of his ear. Dolph mumbled. But what he said was that the Odessa bikers had come down out of Silver City and were now headed east, probably toward home, toward Odessa. Somewhere along the way, the Apaches would pounce. Scalps would be taken, horses stolen, women violated.

The plan was a gamble. They had taken I-17 to Phoenix and then raced east on I-10 to avoid the Arizona mountain ranges. They figured that the bad guys planned a slow return to Odessa. Meantime, Johnny Yield's Mescalero pals were tracking the Odessa bikers.

Pooter returned to his thoughts. When Joan came over and cried in Pooter's apartment this time, she had obviously made progress. True, she had a drink, but it was her first one, and she had not been drinking to find the courage to come see Pooter and cry all over him. "It's not so much Pepper being gone that is the problem. It's not even that yet another in a long series of relationships ended. But now it seems like this may be the last one," she had said.

Pooter had sat with her on his couch, dared to reach across and stroke her hair, and then said, "Maybe there's comfort in that."

Joan giggled, "You're a monk, a mystic. What would you know about growing beyond sexuality or just losing it?"

Pooter gulped for some breath. Maybe he should take comfort in the fact that that was how his friends saw him. He would have to think about himself later, for that particular night Joan was demanding his attention. "You knew, given you and Pepper, that it wouldn't last."

"Why couldn't you and I last?" she asked rhetorically.

Indeed, Pooter thought. He knew that it was impossible because Joan would always be looking for a star, a quarterback: Baily Waller, the rich married mayor of Austin, various politicians, the famous political science professor, Charlie Montalvo, and now Pepper. With his ability, he might have very well adapted. But Joan would never allow him into the lineup that made up her team. So Pooter didn't tell her that he could indeed last with her, but not her with him.

Joan lifted her head to look at him. They had been through this scene so many times that they should have just tugged and pulled each other onto the floor and shed clothes, caution, and concern. "It some ways, I'm disappointed that I'm not more disappointed. Maybe I'm growing use to it, getting callous. I've just got this revolving door that men spin around in and then leave."

"You need a hobby," Pooter said.

"What?" Joan straightened up to look at him.

"You're a little self-absorbed right now. You used to have politics, then teaching. Now you need something to absorb a little of you."

She started laughing, so she and Pooter went out for some late night drinks. Pooter drank less than all his friends and held his liquor better than all of them. So when Joan passed out, he got her home.

At work that day, Pepper took a seat by the bar and said, "You know Joan and I done split?" Pooter nodded. "Hell, it was the distance. Driving between my house and hers costs too much gas money and was taxing on my nerves. Let's just count it up to that."

"That sounds like a really good reason. I'll tell her." But Pooter didn't get to tell her. Joan had stopped coming to the afternoon sessions with Jerri and Sandra, and Sandra even asked about her, tried to call her. It had been four months. Maybe Joan had found a hobby.

Pepper had gotten e-mails from Dolph full of references to booze and women, and he printed them up and showed them to Pooter. But then the tone changed. Pooter caught it first. "They're not happy," he said. "He's bitching now."

Pepper read through it again. "Maybe we ought to go get him?"

Then the e-mails started about Walter mysteriously dwindling, then an angry one that said Walter was dying. "Let's go," Pepper said to Pooter. But they waited.

There was one last message that said that Walter had died, that Dolph would deliver the remains to Walter's ex-wife, and that eventually he would be back. They had a ceremony at the bar to honor Walter. Sandra, Pepper, and Pooter sat at the table closest to the bar and told stories about Walter and Dolph, hoping to keep Dolph healthy and Walter in some way alive. Pooter had called Joan, but she didn't show for Walter's ceremony. Then Jerri ran into the bar saying that Dolph had been hurt. Pooter's mind switched immediately from keeping Walter's memory alive to keeping Dolph physically alive. Pepper said that he would go to Phoenix come hell or high water. Sandra refused to stay home. Pooter would go to watch over all of them and to remind them not to forget Walter and to somehow, if only in his own mind, make sense of this.

Jerri checked over her shoulder again at Dolph. "I know that it does absolutely no good to even try to get you to change your mind."

"Then don't try," Dolph mumbled. In the rearview mirror, his face showed that he was tired and in some pain.

"What are we supposed to do?"

Dolph shrugged, then said, "Just get the urn. That's all I want. No return ass kicking. Though he deserves it."

Pooter could feel Jerri look at him. "And what about you?" she asked.

"What?"

"Why don't you just pass right on by these guys and drive us back to San Antonio?"

Pooter could do nothing more than shrug. In the hierarchy on this mission, Dolph was quarterback. "You know it's my money we're all spending," Jerri tried again and got no response.

They were heading east and Deeming was ahead. The land they drove through looked baked and scarred. Pooter had never been this far west. This landscape seemed emptier, a drier and even more rocky West Texas. He wished that they could pull off the interstate and drive into the rocks and get a first hand look at them. Interstates always seemed to lull him into first laziness and then sleep. So he started to think, and then to talk. "Dolph, so why aren't we after Lee Ann?"

"That's a good question. Why aren't you telling the F.B.I. about her?" Jerri asked.

"Yeah, like anybody really gives a shit," Dolph mumbled.

Watching Johnny's braids wave up and down, Pooter pushed his thoughts and his questions. "So you want to get her?"

Pooter checked in the rear view mirror to see Dolph fidget. "And do what? Kill her?"

"You'd wouldn't think about killing a man," Jerri said.

Dolph looked at Jerri as though scolding. "I've had enough of killing," Dolph said, holding his chin down to his chest and mumbling so that Pooter and Jerri had to guess what he said. He raised his head. "When I found Walter dead, all I wanted to do was to get out of Mexico. And it wasn't until that big guy hit me that it finally dawned on me what happened."

Dolph stared at Joan, not at Pooter's eyes in the rearview mirror. He said to Jerri, "I was scared. I just wanted to run. And so I did. I still feel like running."

"So run somewhere other than after this guy."

"He has the urn."

Jerri pulled herself away from Dolph, to sit up straight in the front seat, facing the windshield. She crossed her arms, and stared out at the highway. Pooter's mind went back to work. "So is it true that Walter literally killed himself fucking?"

"Doctors confirmed it," Dolph said.

"Did Lee Ann force him?"

"Right," Jerri said.

"Did he put up a struggle like poor Charlie Montalvo?"

"Or did he just do what he was told, willingly?" Jerri interrupted again. "Like Ramón Burgiaga, still doing his time?"

"It was Walter's idea. He came into the living room and got her. Took her away from me."

Jerri twisted around in the seat to look at Dolph. "So she could have killed you."

Dolph returned Jerri's stare.

"Yes," he said.

Pooter's mind raced ahead of the would-be-but-still-not-yet lovers. "So Walter took a bullet for you."

"What," Dolph and Jerri said together.

"Walter died for your sins," Pooter said. "Walter didn't just do some wild, romantic, sentimental gesture—whatever you want to call it. He saved your life. We should remember and honor Walter."

"Come on, Pooter," Dolph said. "Walter was horny and hadn't had any a while."

"But he had a heart condition, and he was tired of living like that," Pooter said.

Jerri was leaning over the back seat to face Dolph, "When did you figure out who she was?"

"Like I said, I didn't even suspect her until that goon of hers beat the shit out of me and kind of knocked some sense into my head."

Pooter was so excited that he started to bang the steering wheel with the heel of his hand, "Yeah, yeah, exactly. Walter was smart. One of the smartest but weirdest people any of us ever met. He doesn't want to go on living like he has, just waiting. And Dolph is too busy being horny to notice her, but Walter does. So he has a graceful, slightly pleasurable, but ultimately dramatic and poetic death. One that we can remember and thus remember him. And she, she's now gotten Walter not Dolph. Don't you see? Walter sacrificed himself so that Dolph could go on fucking." Pooter was proud of himself. He saw the logic before he felt it. Now, more than believing this story, he had faith in it. Pooter, always content to ponder but not solve, had solved the mystery of Walter. Pooter had become a quarterback. "No, Walter prepaid for his death—and his funeral, which is us together, right now, looking for his ashes."

"Good goddamn holy shit," Dolph said.

"Now the point is that the urn doesn't matter. Remembering Walter's sacrifice does. We got to interpret the story right. Lee Ann didn't kill Walter. Walter saved Dolph."

"Holy, Halle-fucking-lujah," Jerri said. "So let's turn back or keep on driving to San Antonio."

"Can't do that. We still need the urn," Dolph said. "It was part of Walter's last wishes, part of what he said."

Pooter could feel Dolph's eyes on him, then he could feel Jerri's. "Dolph's right. We got to get it. We maybe can't see why now, but we got to have faith that there is a logic in getting the urn."

Dolph banged the armrest and then groaned. Jerri looked at Pooter and groaned.

Stunned, they drove on. At Deming, they got a report from Johnny. At Las Cruces, they got off the interstate and turned up to Alamagordo. Pooter could look at some scenery. He kept Johnny Yield in front of him and studied the pockmarked landscape, true badlands, and then imagined Walter with him when they got to the White Sands. They rolled through the clean high mountain town of Cloudcroft and came down out of it through the apple orchards in the valley east of it. Then they rolled down out of the high plains toward Texas. And just on the other side of Artesia, they followed Johnny Yield into one those dusty, deserted New Mexican bars that had to serve drinks as well as sell liquor. In front of the bar/liquor store were four bikes with license plate frames that said, Cowboy's Harley. Standing by their bikes, arms crossed, were two squat Apaches. They shook hands with Johnny Yield. Pooter, Jerri, and Dolph got out of the van to join Johnny, he pushed his glasses up from the tip of his nose and said, "These are my compadres," he said. "The advance scouts."

Dolph mumbled. "Let me do the talking."

"Easy for you to say," Johnny Yield said, and all of the Apaches laughed.

"Look," Johnny said. "We probably been in a few more bar fights than you two, and we're a lot younger. So you guys watch first and see where you can help."

"Why does there have to be a fight?" Jerri asked.

"Just 'cause," Johnny said.

"Cowboys and Indians," one of Johnny's friends said.

Pooter couldn't help himself. "We're with the Indians, right?"

"At least when it starts," Johnny said.

"Whoa, whoa, wait," Dolph hissed. "Let me get the urn first."

"Grab the urn and get out," Jerri said.

"Okay," Johnny said. He breathed deeply, bowed his head for a moment, as did his friends, and then said, "Show time," and pushed his glasses off the tip of his pug nose.

Pooter stepped in front of Johnny and held out his hand to stop him.

"What the fuck?" Johnny said.

"We'll fuck or fight," Pooter said. "But remember this ain't about fucking, fighting, or the urn. It's about Walter. Remember Walter."

"Who is Walter?" one of Johnny's friends asked.

"He's the guy in the urn," Dolph said.

"What urn?"

"I didn't explain the whole story," Johnny Yield said.

Then, Dolph's face dropped. He got a forlorn look on his face, and he forced out the words: "I wish Pepper was here."

Pooter held the door open for all of them. The last one to go in was Dolph.

Pooter knew his place. He waited until they all got in. And then he stepped in and planted himself by the door.

Inside, Pooter noted the layout and got ready to grab, squeeze, block, or absorb fists or bullets. It was game time. He watched Dolph. As they had planned in the past, at past events, so that they needed no coaching now, Pooter took the door. No one was going to leave through him.

Jerri was in front of him. Pooter stuck out his hand and gently eased her to one side so that he had a clear view of Dolph's back. Johnny Yield and his two friends moved down the wall across from the small bar in the small saloon. A dusty juke box was playing Elvis's "Jailhouse Rock," maybe an original 45 rpm. Behind the bar, a mousey bartender with a bushy black moustache eyed all of them. On the other side of the bar, eight forearms rested on their elbows with their palms wrapped around beers. On the forearms were cheap tattoos going all the way up to some of the shoulders. The heads swung toward Dolph. One biker had on a leather do-rag. Another's shoulders and forearms shone bright red. Another had placed his helmet in front of him, and another had hiked his bare leg on the bar rail. It had new snakes and dragon tattoos, the ink hardly dry, the scabs hardly healed. The biker behind the helmet had blond curls. Pooter made his mind sort through files of memory. He was the blond man they missed. He would be the dangerous one and the first one to move. Pooter, the old pulling guard, did not have the pull or the speed to get to him. But after the first moves or blows, he would move as quickly as possible to the leader and try to thrash him.

As Dolph moved forward, the biker with the blond curls in his face straightened and eyed Dolph. Dolph eyed back.

"So just what you hoping to do, coming strutting in here like that with your posse?" the blond biker asked Dolph. "And don't it look like a pretty ragged posse?"

Johnny Yield tilted his head back to see through the glasses on the tip of his nose and said from his wall, "We were the last ragged band to surrender. Two countries sent armies after us, and still Americans begged us to surrender."

In unison, the biker's faces swung behind them to see Johnny and his scouts. If the bikers were smart, if they had been in many of these fights, they would have spread out a little.

The curly-headed biker turned to face the bartender, and the others turned their attention toward Dolph, and Pooter could see that Dolph had left some marks on them. "Ain't you had enough of your shit beat out of you?" the blond biker asked.

"Where's my urn?" Dolph said from between his teeth.

The sunburned biker grimaced. "Speak up," he said. "I can't hear you."

"Bust your jaw?" the biker with the leather do-rag asked.

"Just what you thinking on doing?" the leader asked.

"We're thinking about defending the reputation of the great Apache nation," Johnny Yield said from behind them.

The man behind the bar scooted from behind the bar to the juke box and unplugged it. Elvis suddenly stopped singing in mid-sentence.

"Before anybody starts any kind of shit," the bartender said, "let me just say I got 911 dialed. Cops'll be coming."

Dolph walked toward the blonde leader, and Pooter tensed. He looked at Jerri to see her eyes begging him to do something.

"Keep on coming, you want," the blond biker said. "But just one punch from any one of us, and you ain't got a jaw." The Apaches moved up from behind. Pooter crossed his arms across his chest and followed a ways behind Dolph.

"Where's the urn?" Dolph asked.

"I ain't got the urn," the leader said. "But I got some whup ass you still want it."

The leader scooted down toward the end of bar. The other bikers looked at each other with confused looks on their faces. Their tattoos seemed to shrink. The three Apaches moved in on them. The bartender said, "Please. Y'all are going to be paying for whatever you break."

Dolph stopped moving toward the leader. He straightened. Then froze. Bikers and Indians froze. This was a ritualized moment of negotiation. Up until now, Pooter, and probably Dolph, had not realized that the bikers had suffered too. They weren't up to these fights. They weren't professional criminals. In the heavy air, with the twitches and dropped glances, Dolph's team, bikers, and Apaches were sizing each other up, deciding if they would fuck or fight. At this point, to Pooter, either might please Walter. Open to debate was whether they had all had enough, whether they could continue out of the bar with dignity intact if they did not have a fight. And if they did have a fight, they debated whether they could get out of the door at all without being wheeled out on a stretcher. It had come down to Walter's urn. That is what his memory demanded. Then, again, once more, there was Charlie and Oscar. And tangentially, way down the line, as victim and cleric of this ritual were Pooter's best buddy, quarterback Bailey Waller, and Sister Quinn, and so many others.

But suddenly, Jerri was screaming. "Nobody's going to do any kind of childish, bad boy shit." In front of Pooter, Jerri squatted, let her hand drop to her ankle, tore some tape with her left hand, bit her bottom lip to fight the pull of the tape, and came up with her tiny gun in her hands. She pointed the gun at the biker with the blond curls. As she had explained to Pooter, Jerri had packed her tiny little .22 in her checked luggage. She brought her permit and her identification. She had unpacked it at Sarah's. And just as she had done when she was chasing bail jumpers and illegals, as she had shown Pooter, she had taped it to the flat side of her leg just above her ankle. "I shouldn't have this gun. I shouldn't have it in here. I would be in deep shit if I let a round go. But so help me, I will shoot, and I'm starting with you," Jerri said.

They had been on their way to some kind of dignity for everyone.

214

Maybe someone would have been hurt, maybe badly. On the other hand, maybe they would have all gotten out with jaws, noses, and limbs in place. But Jerri did not believe. Despite her life among men, despite being trapped in these positions by lovers and husbands, Jerri wanted only to avoid violence or harm. So she had tipped the scales and destroyed the negotiations.

"Good deal, lady," the bartender said. "Everybody just relax."

Jerri looked over at the Apaches, "Sit down." She looked over her shoulder at Pooter, "You too, Pooter." The bikers at the bar giggled when she said "Pooter," so she pointed the gun back at them. The giggle continued. They had been serious; now they were laughing at silly names and sounds. "All of you. All of you fuckers, with your little boy games, and teasing. You're a bunch of little pussies. All this cowboy shit. All this pretense. Well, here is a real gun. And I'm just a girl, so I got to shoot because I just can't keep up with your macho bullshit." Jerri stomped her foot, "Go ahead, just do something. Make me shoot." Pooter smiled and stepped up so that he could keep anybody from rushing her.

"No, lady," the bartender said. "You don't have to shoot anybody."

"Let me just get the urn," Dolph said.

Jerri almost pointed the gun at him. "What is this stupid game you're playing. Haven't you seen enough dead people? Haven't enough people died around you? What good is getting that urn going to do anybody?"

"Walter . . . " Dolph started.

"And Walter is dead. And no silly, macho, romantic promises are going to change that. We are here," and then she turned to look at the bikers, "And they are here because you are just hiding from anything serious." She lowered her arm with the pistol. Dolph and Pooter both took their eyes from the bikers, risking a surprise rush, and went to Jerri. She looked into Dolph's eyes, not a tear in hers, and calmly and plainly said to Dolph. "Think about the deaths you've seen. Think about your wounds. Don't you know that death is just the ultimate goddamn indignity? That is all it is."

Dolph looked like he would cry. He couldn't speak. So Pooter, keeping one eye on the bikers, stepped up and said, "Yeah, you're right." Dolph looked at Pooter, and Jerri turned her head to Dolph to look at him. "But Dolph is trying to give it some dignity."

Jerri jerked her head to look at Pooter, "By causing a goddamn bar fight in a no-count bar in a lost fucking town in back fuck New Mexico?" Jerri all but screamed.

"Lady," the bartender said. "Liquor licenses in this state are rare and limited."

"We could have this philosophical debate without the gun," the biker with the golden curls said. Of course, Jerri was right, Pooter thought, but we can make some meaning. We can stand the awfulness and indignity of the cessation of our consciousness if only we could give people left behind something to remember. And this scene, with Jerri holding a gun on working-class bikers out for a Saturday spin and ass kicking, was something to remember. Maybe Jerri, not Dolph, was proving Walter right.

Dolph turned his back to her and walked up to the bar. Pooter saw forearms, biceps, and tattoos tighten. The biker said, "The lady is right. It does no good for any of us to go through with this little circus." He looked at Dolph. "Why can't you just take your ass whipping and forget it?" Despite Jerri's outburst, or maybe because of it, the ceremony of negotiation between the two chiefs had begun. Good statesmen, they had recovered from Jerri's disruption and were now horse trading.

"Why did you have to whip my ass?"

Jerri, her pistol still in her hand, moved closer. Pooter came up behind her. The Apaches came up. The startled biker looked around him. "Ain't you figured it out?"

"Lee Ann, or Allison, or whatever her name was," Dolph said.

"She knew you wanted the urn. She paid me to whip your ass and take the urn."

"She didn't pay you to kill me?"

"She knew I wouldn't do that." And again the biker with the blond curls faced away from them with his elbows on the bar. "I'm tired of this shit." He looked down the bar at his friends, "What about you guys?"

The guy with the leather do-rag said, "It ain't been that much fun or that much money."

"Fuck them," the guy with the helmet under his arm said.

"Watch out who you include in 'them,'" Johnny Yield said. Pooter stiffened and braced himself.

The blond biker looked around, then started: "I see no reason for us to puke and piss on each other while we're breaking more noses and jaws." He held his palms up and looked at Dolph. "I mailed the urn to my house in Odessa. A present for my wife. So I just ain't got it."

"Oh shit," Jerri said. "She know what's in it?" She stared at him, then turned to look at Dolph. He looked haggard and tired. "So what did you do? Attach a nice note, 'Here, Honey, look what I picked up. Pour out the ashes and put some flowers in it?'" Pooter was the only one to giggle. But by god, funny was funny. He relaxed. They could all relax and have some fun.

"I'll give you my address and directions. It takes three hours to get there."

Pooter was growing curious. He asked what they all wanted to know, "So why Lee Ann? You know what happened to Oscar and Charlie. What are you doing with her?"

"You guys aren't cops, right?"

"Even if we were, there's nothing we could do with what we're hoping you'll tell us," Dolph mumbled.

The blond biker looked at his buddies first. "I knew Lee Ann back when. She was skinny, morose, an outsider, nobody liked her, but I always liked girls like that. Something about her made you want to help her. Me and her, we just always had an understanding. And she paid me well for me to look tough."

"Some kind of temptress," Jerri said. "I thought you guys liked tits, ass, and high hair. Which is why I thought she bought herself a surgeon then a body."

"She may have had her faults. But she had her reasons," the blond biker said.

"People usually do have reasons for killing people," Jerri said. Pooter stepped up. Jerri might now be leading them into a fight.

"How did she contact you? This last time I mean," Dolph asked.

"She phoned me.

"Give me her number," Dolph commanded.

"No, this has gone on long enough."

"What's your name?"

"Bo."

"Give me the number, Bo," Dolph said.

Jerri stepped up to help Dolph. "What good has she done you? What has all this done but cause a lot of shit."

"She's used you. She used Oscar Montalvo," Dolph added. Jerri and Dolph could indeed gang up on people. They could also be very entertaining.

"She used Ramón," Jerri interrupted.

"She used Charlie Montalvo," Pooter found himself saying.

"Walter, me," Dolph continued. "You."

"Me? How me?" Bo asked.

Pooter couldn't help himself. He wanted to be a part of the play too. "For instance, look what you're doing now. Risking broken teeth, more broken noses and jaws, and puking and pissing, for the sake of the wicked witch of the west." Pepper would have been proud of the last part. Pooter found himself wishing Pepper were here too.

Bo sputtered out a number. Then he slowed down as Dolph pulled out his cell phone and dialed the number. Dolph waited, and then he looked up at them and smiled. He whispered to them, "It's her voice recording." Then he turned back to the phone. "Lee Ann or Allison or whoever you are. This is Dolph Martinez. I'm having a beer with Bo. We've had a real long talk . . . "

"Hey," Bo said.

"I just wanted to say 'hi' from all of us. Wanted to say that we're all thinking about you. Want to say I'm forwarding this number to the F.B.I. You best keep on running, Lee Ann. Have a nice day," Dolph said. He was beaming.

Jerri smiled at him, then shifted her head to smile at Pooter. Then she turned to Bo. "Cheer up, Bo. Just think, nobody really got even with anybody, but your temptress, the wicked witch of the west has to get a new phone, a new country, and a new lover. The least she could do, wouldn't you say? And she'll leave all of us alone."

"She had her good points," Bo said.

Pooter decided that decisive action was needed. So he said, "Three long hours to Odessa. I could use a beer. And look where I am."

"Now, you're talking sense," the small bartender said and licked his moustache.

After more than "a" beer, the bikers moved on. Dolph and his team had two more beers. As they walked out, Johnny Yield stopped Dolph and said, "Our work is done here, white man," and adjusted his glasses and pushed his braids back over his shoulders.

"What? This is it?" Dolph asked.

"All we wanted to do was scare them." Johnny's two friends nodded.

One said, "You're going to Texas, and Texas ain't a good place for Indians because they think we're Mexicans."

They saddled up their motorcycles, and Pooter watched as they rode off into the sunset. It had been a fine day so far: full of meaning, full of redemption for Walter and some others dead or damaged, and full of entertainment. Pooter had been Spinozistic, connected the dots, found links, solved the case, figured out the mystery of Walter's final act, and had thus made the rest of their lives just a tiny bit clearer. And by the end of the day, Pooter would see his hometown, Odessa, Texas, again. It would have been a good day for Walter to tell about over a couple or three beers.

Chapter 14

Odessa, like most West Texas Cities, had a famous landmark: the world's largest fiberglass rabbit. So Pooter, Dolph, and Jerri stopped to look at it. It had one ear broken off. Odessa had the country's only presidential campaign museum. Jerri argued against stopping to see it. Pooter wanted to stop, but Jerri was already disappointed with the rabbit and wanted mostly to get business done. Dolph wanted a drink. For the first time since Jerri had been around him, Dolph complained about his jaw. He said that he felt like the wire in his mouth was on fire, and he wanted to cool the wire.

Besides the rabbit and the presidential museum, Odessa had a meteor crater. To keep Dolph out of the bar, to humor Pooter, Jerri did agree to go to the meteor crater. After you bought your ticket from the guy at the card table and folding chair, you could walk out into the gravel and shrubs, squat, look sideways, and see that all around you was about a six-inch rise. You were standing in the meteor crater itself. Pooter laughed. Dolph tried to smile. And Jerri just urged them on toward Bo's house. And then a smell rolled in. "What is that?" Jerri asked.

"It's good when you smell that. Means no poisonous fumes are getting out. It's hydrogen sulfide. All oil fields smell like rotten eggs."

They were still early and killing time, so they looked around. Odessa had wide, seemingly deserted streets running perfectly straight and making a grid of the city. It had pumpjacks scattered throughout the town. It had city parks with a few weak and delicate mesquite trees and grass burrs mixed with the sparse grass. It was home of Permian High School, famous throughout the state for its champion football teams. It had red sand blown against the sides of the curbs to make little packed red gardens of scrub plants. It had a mall and a Super Walmart. The sun was a hot red ball in the western sky that did not want to go down. Pooter said, "This is my hometown," Jerri and Dolph turned to look at him. Jerri was surprised and knew Dolph was surprised, that they had never asked, never wondered where Pooter was from. For Pooter seemed never to have been a child or even a teenager. He just seemed as if he had always been what he so consistently was as an adult. "Then after college, I spent seven years living here and selling cars in Midland with my best buddy, former UT quarterback Bailey Waller." Pooter was getting reinvigorated by the city in the middle of miles of flatness and scrub. "The city has changed a little." Then Pooter smiled, "The land hasn't."

Dolph said, "Pepper and I sometimes partied here. It feels a little like home."

Jerri said, "I could see why a woman might murder her husbands if she was raised here."

They found their way to Bo's house, three blocks south and then a left down from Permian High School itself. He lived in a row of 50s-style tract houses, with water coolers—"a swamp cooler," Pooter said—sticking down into the houses from the roofs. They unloaded. Dolph, rubbing his jaw, led the way to the front door. Jerri hung behind them, wanting this all to be over. It was starting to feel like a cheap Catholic wedding for the kid of some relative you barely knew: no meaning, just empty, perfunctory ritual.

Bo answered the door and held it open for them. "My wife and kids went to get supper," he said when they got in. He had showered and shaved. His long golden curls were pasted back over the top of his head. He had, Jerri noted, transformed himself into a well-groomed worker after work.

As they walked through his small living room with ancient wood paneling, Jerri noted the desperation in the ornamentation: blown up photos, a painting from Walmart, an off-brand high definition TV hanging from chains from the ceiling, not attached to the wall. But after the 100 degree dry heat, the ancient swamp cooler did send some wetness circulating around the room. As they walked into a bedroom, with an unmade bed and dirty clothes scattered around the floor, they saw a bookshelf with knickknacks displayed on one shelf. Up on top, next to but taller than the state play-off trophy, so much like the holy grail that Jerri thought Dolph would kneel before it, was Walter's urn. Because he was taller than Dolph, Bo stretched on his toes and reached to the top to get the urn. Dolph held out his hands as Bo placed the urn in Dolph's hands. Pooter slapped Dolph on the back. Jerri turned her back to them and walked back into the small, cramped living room.

After Oscar Montalvo's physical and personal makeover of her, Lee Ann must have seemed exotic to Bo. Somehow he must have cussed himself for not having taken more advantage of her when she was the loner, the outsider, the gawky teen. Jerri could understand how she might have just bored a hole into the marrow of Bo's soul, but she did not understand how he could not have just said "no" at some point. Pepper and Walter were like him. Pooter could reason himself to safety. Dolph could probably have avoided her. Jerri wished she could have seen Bo's wife and kids. She looked around the house and at the pages torn from coloring books, the vases, the artificial flowers. There were more traces of a wife and kids than of the goon for hire.

Soon, Bo came back into the living room, followed by Dolph and Pooter. Bo took a left into the kitchen. They looked at each other. Dolph looked at the urn in his hands. He held it toward Jerri. And to see if the focus of all their efforts actually had weight and heft, Jerri reached out with both hands and took the urn. It was indeed surprisingly heavy. She looked at Dolph and said, "It is heavy."

"That's because you got what's left of Walter piled up inside," Pooter said. "There was a lot of Walter." He wasn't meaning to be that funny, but Jerri laughed. And then, because laughter was infectious, Pooter and Jerri turned to watch as Dolph shook while he tried to get his laugh out of his wired-shut mouth.

Bo came back with an open beer bottle in his right hand and the necks of three bottles of beer between the spread fingers of his left hand. He stiffly held out his left hand, like Frankenstein, and each of them took a beer.

Bo lowered himself on the couch, put a coaster on the coffee table, and put his beer on it. "Y'all have a seat. Drink your beer. Then, I'd prefer it if

Jim Sanderson

y'all was gone before my wife and kids got back."

Dolph and Pepper looked for a chair, found none, and then lowered themselves on the couch on either side of Bo. Jerri looked around and chose the bean bag chair. She had heard that they were coming back into style, but this one looked like an original.

Bo grabbed the remote and flipped on the high-definition TV to the High Def Discovery channel. Jerri caught a glimpse of the show about boat people in Thailand.

Bo took a long pull at his beer and then tried to articulate his thoughts. "I figure now the two of you was kind to me back in San Antonio when you had that little shaved-head pinché shot with your Taser. I figure you could have pressed charges. So I didn't like beating you up."

"Nobody forced you," Jerri said.

"I figure y'all want to know why. So I'll save Dolph the effort of working the jaw that I busted." He nodded the neck of his beer toward Dolph. Dolph nodded the neck of his beer back at him. Jerri winced behind her fake smile. "See, the best thing I ever was was a guard on Permian High School's playoff football team."

"I was a guard too. Only I went to Odessa High, the one that loses." Pooter said. "It ain't bad. You get used to it. And I know about the thrill of playing on artificial turf." He looked at Dolph. "I still am a guard." Pooter broadly smiled. He was having a grand time.

"Lee Ann was a nobody, but we were engaged." Bo stared at the top of his beer bottle. "We were both oil field trash. My momma and daddy didn't get married until I was two years old. Her momma and daddy never did get married. And her daddy disappeared to Alaska and then Saudi Arabia, or where ever there was good roughnecking wages he could piss away. Same as my daddy. I hadn't planned nothing. I was just glad to have played some football on artificial turf. But Lee Ann went off to Lubbock. Lubbock had a medical school and a university, and she thought she could be an LPN or RN or something with Ns in it. And from there, she just started to talk and look different."

"As Pepper might say," Dolph said, "she'd make your teeth itch."

"Kind of like that," Bo said. "After football was over, she was the best thing I had ever had. So I kept up with her." Bo hung his head. "Even after

224

I was married."

"You sound a little like me," Pooter said. Jerri didn't think that Bo sounded at all like the big philosopher filling up the living room. "But I got to U.T. Later I got an education. You should have found something like that."

"Instead of Lee Ann," Dolph added.

"All that's over now," Jerri said. "She's all over. You better concentrate on what you have and try to make that the best thing ever happened in your life."

"Easy to say. You ever tried it?" Bo said. You could see him fidget from their glances, which were forcing him to go on. "You see, so here's me. Look around. I'm in this old house without steady welding jobs, and there was Lee Ann, moving right up, from Lubbock to San Antonio high society."

"At least she didn't ask you to kill anybody," Dolph said. And Bo, with not even a smile, just nodded. "So how much did she pay you to beat the shit out of me?" Jerri winced inside her head because Dolph wanted to push his finger into Bo's deep wound. But then again, that was what Bo had done to Dolph.

"Not nearly enough," Bo said and switched his eyes between them. "But it wasn't about money. I just wanted to help her. And I guess she figured the worst I could do to you was steal that fucking urn and beat the shit out of you."

"What about your buddies?" Dolph asked.

"I promised them all the beer they could drink, a hundred dollars, and a good time."

"You know I had a cashier's check and cash in that car."

"We aren't thieves," Bo said incredulously.

From the bean bag chair, Jerri tapped her beer down on the floor, and they turned to her. She could feel her face flush, "So I guess not a one of you can see how stupid, how misguided . . ." The lawyer in her made her bite her lip to keep her from tipping her hand. She looked at their good ol' boy eyes. "Didn't you even weigh the consequences?"

"Sure," Pooter said. "That's the point. It's silly if there ain't no consequences." They all looked at Pooter. Bo and Dolph nodded. Jerri turned from him and stared at floor, feeling that she had been excluded

225

before she even walked in the door. Then Bo, as evidenced by his stuttering, said to them all, "I guess I thank you all."

They finished their beers and left Bo to welcome his wife and kids home. And just as the sun finally did sink, they checked into a La Quinta, one room for the boys and one for Jerri, and later that night, as Pooter watched TV in his room, Jerri and Dolph dangled their bare legs in the La Quinta swimming pool. Jerri looked at her legs and saw varicose veins and some stretched, wrinkled skin where taut muscles used to be. She had always had short stout legs, but they seemed to have gotten thinner. Dolph, from years in the desert, like the Apaches, had grown bow legged. He had scars on his legs. The Carribean sun had cooked him to a golden brown. "How did we get here?" Jerri asked mostly to herself.

"Came east on I-10, then over through Artesia and . . ."

"I mean, to this time in our lives."

"Didn't pay attention, I guess," Dolph said.

Dolph was sucking the beer out of the bottle with a straw. He had just taken two Advils. In a year or two, his thick hair would be all gray. Physically, he was a compact mixture of Sandra Beeson and the wild Mexican man she chose as her husband and her son's father. Maybe their short, tempestuous marriage made Dolph as he was. His only contentment was his next job, his next assignment, the next patrol along the border. Sometimes, Jerri got the idea that he was uncomfortable in his own skin. And his mind was certainly not an easy place to live. Dolph flutter kicked in the water. "It's almost cold. I miss this. Out here, without humidity, once that 100 degree sun goes down, things cool off really nice, the water cools. Well, in the Big Bend, nothing is cool until well after midnight."

Jerri concentrated on the air around her. With the sun down, Odessa was still ugly but you couldn't see as much, and with the cool water and the cooler night, it felt nice. Dolph scissor kicked in the water, and though it hurt him, he smiled at the splashes he made.

The whole time Dolph had been gone, Jerri had worried about him. And when Sarah Boone called and said that he was beaten, Jerri felt her heart lodge in her throat and try to strangle her. She wondered why she should feel such a way about Dolph and not any of the others who worked for him and thus for her. It made no sense. Worse, it was dangerous. Jerri could not explain that to Sandra. Sandra Beeson had pushed, no, she had shoved, and perhaps she had been right. But Dolph was like Joe Parr in that he was such a male, such a cop, such a fundamentalist in terms of law, fairness, and rightness. But she had truly loved Joe Parr. My God, she needed a shrink, immediately.

Jerri turned to look at the splashing and slurping beside her. Dolph seemed calm. "You've got the urn. Are you happy now?"

His wiring caught his smile, "Yes."

"You know, surely, that this whole chase over that stupid urn is another of Walter's misguided, misplaced wishes. Sarah doesn't want his ashes. Walter was never concerned about his remains. He'd as soon you stuffed his ashes in a beer bottle and smashed it on the bow of a cruise ship or thrown it in the Carribean."

"Those were second and third choices," Dolph mumbled.

"And then Lee Ann. Good God. You two, you, you two. You diddled her."

"'Diddled?'" Dolph tried to laugh.

"You two are on the far side of middle aged and ought to be thinking about nursing homes, and you let a . a . a. a strumpet like Lee Ann kill Walter and kick your ass. How can the trip to Mexico, and the worry it caused all of us, and all the ways it twisted in and out from under you be worth it?"

"'Strumpet?'" Dolph smiled, "Did it cause you worry?"

The soft blue lights from the pool danced around on Dolph's dark face.

"Once a week my stomach did flips worrying about you and Walter."

"Walter?"

"Okay, then, you."

They should have lunged toward each other and then fallen into the pool and then groped and rubbed, and then "diddled." But on this evening, they had both turned too thoughtful and too deliberate to do something so young. In truth, they wanted something more than cool water on a nice night on their naked bodies. Diddling was okay for the likes of Lee Ann; Jerri wanted more or at least more to accompany it. They breathed deeply, and each waited for the other one to do something. When neither one did anything, they waited some more and sucked in air.

"When Walter gave me this stupid assignment, he knew I'd do it," Dolph said.

"And he got your jaw and your ribs broken."

"Exactly. It was all worth it."

Now Jerri wanted to push Dolph into the pool by himself to cool off the delusional fever that must be in his head. Dolph held out his thumb. "One, I did finally do something right. You think about my cases." He looked at Jerri for a moment then muttered, "our cases. Joe was dead. Vincent Fuentes is dead. Charlie and Oscar are dead. I've never done anything right. Sure, I found the bad guy, but nothing turned out right. This time the ending is right."

"But you're beat to shit."

Dolph kept his thumb held up and then pushed out his forefinger, "Two, I did get the shit beat out of me but not through my own mistakes. This time I saw it coming and got in some licks. No backpacker with his pack full of marijuana or some poor fake old lady working as a bank teller or some big-titted Frankenstein monster got the drop on me and shot me."

"But . . . "

"Three, I didn't get anybody hurt. Pepper still has his other knee intact. I didn't get any friends dead or hurt."

"So you found the Holy Grail and returned it to the fair damsel."

"So I will in the morning."

"This doesn't make sense."

"I didn't say it made sense. That's too much to ask of it. But like Walter used to say, 'it makes for a beautiful story,' especially if you chase it with a beer."

From way back in her past, from a time when she first started running and hiding with Vincent Fuentes, a wild, secret abandon seized Jerri. She sat her beer down and lunged at Dolph, wrapped her arms around him, and pulled them both, beers and all, into the cooling La Quinta pool. Under the blue water lit by the single lamp next to her face, she saw Dolph's grin and the bubbles coming out of his wired-shut mouth. Kissing underwater is hard to pull off, especially kissing a man with a wired-shut jaw.

* * *

The Midland/Odessa airport was more like a bus station than an airport, but the oil brought the big jets and thus access to the outside world. Pooter, Dolph, and Jerri waited for the people on the flight from Phoenix to unload. Like parents and friends around them, they just couldn't help waving when they saw Pepper and Sarah emerge from the tube that fed the passengers to the plane. Pepper shook Dolph's hand and said, "Your Momma's safe back in San Antonio." Sarah nodded. She and Pepper seemed a bit wary of each other. They should be, Jerri reasoned, he had spent two days with her. Of course, after the night before, when they politely emerged from the pool, she and Dolph became wary of each other.

Jerri took a step back as though she were a video camera and needed to record this. She wasn't sure if the scene to be played out would be pathetic, tragic, or comic. But Dolph pulled the urn from the paper shopping bag where he had stashed it, wriggled his lips to say, "Here's Walter," and handed the bag to Sarah.

Pooter and Pepper stood on either side of the them, and the four of them stepped out of the way of the departing passengers. Jerri too stepped to one side and saw Sarah grab the bag, then reach inside of it to pull out the urn. Strong as she was from lifting chainsaws, she could not pull it out of the bag with one hand. So while Pooter held the shopping bag, Sarah reached inside and pulled out the urn. When she saw it, her nose wrinkled—as Dolph, Pooter, Pepper, Walter, ol' Joe Parr, and the rest of the old drinking buddies would say—like she just smelled a turd. And then Jerri heard laughter from dead people, not Dolph's dead people who laughed inside his head, but her first dead people laugh. It was Palo. She had forgotten about him, but somehow, from beyond the grave, he delighted her and was delighted once more.

Dolph stepped back and smiled. And Jerri saw a shimmer around him and heard more laughter from Palo. When Sarah's fingers touched the urn, Dolph had finally completed a mission. Though Sarah looked like she smelled a turd, Dolph had finally found some peace, especially with women. Jerri was at first glad for him, then envious, and then her heart sank because, though she could feel happy for him, she could not feel his elation.

On Pepper's suggestion, they drove to Midland, followed a back road to an out-of-the-way Mexican restaurant. Dolph insisted that they eat outside because beer and Mexican tasted better outside. Pepper and Pooter agreed. So they sat under the wood-beamed awning, which made enough shade to keep them from boiling in the dry heat, and they gorged on Mexican food and Carta Blanca: Pooter and Pepper reminisced about great Mexican food meals that they had eaten. Sarah sat nervously with the urn resting in her lap. Dolph enjoyed the enchiladas and beans that he pressed between his lips. Jerri over-ate and over-drank and grew envious and curious about her boys.

As the afternoon stretched on and that contented haze that accompanies a big Mexican dinner demanded a siesta, they drank more beers, and all of them caught little dozes in the afternoon heat. Dolph's lips started working and all of them shook their heads to clear away the haze and listen to Dolph's sealed-lip sermon: "All y'all know I hear voices of dead friends. But way back, on the day Oscar was killed, I was feeling people."

Sarah stopped, "I'm new here. You talk to dead people?"

"I just listen."

"Has Walter started talking to you?" Sarah asked.

"Let him get on with it," Pepper said.

"That day when Oscar was killed," Jerri said because she wanted to hear what Dolph wanted to say.

"On that day, I wasn't listening to Walter because I was watching the river in that old part of the city. There at Big John's were the old Spaniards' fields. And the Spaniards and the Indians they were Christianizing weren't talking to me, but I could feel them around me."

"Me too. Me too," Pooter said.

"And up on the edge of Balcones Fault, up on the very edge of the hill country, were several Comanches looking down at these strange creatures and the Cohuelticans who had given up being Indians to become fake Spaniards."

Jerri leaned forward because, though the talk was crazy, this was the most that Dolph had talked since he had broken his jaw. She could see him take a swallow to keep his jaw working. Beside him, Sarah looked on astonished at all of this. "You are a friend of Walter's." Sarah said.

"And I think the Comanches were drinking spring water and eating buffalo jerky or pemmican because they had not yet tasted liquor."

"Savages," Pepper said.

"And the Cohuelticans and the Spaniards were drinking wine or home brewed beer and were finally feeling good about each other, maybe even trusting one another."

"Like Walter and me," Sarah butted in, seeming to enjoy the story.

"And the Comanches didn't know enough yet to really be concerned about them," Pooter said.

"And then there was Oscar, Walter, and us three. And in Playa was Walter and me. And here we are with Oscar and Walter gone, but Sarah and Jerri are here . . . And it is almost like Bo and Lee Ann should be here."

"Dolph, you're getting spooky on us again," Pepper said.

Pooter actually got excited, "No, Dolph is right. We're here because of Walter and Oscar, and way back, we're here because of those priests, ranchers, and Indians. It's all connected. It all fits."

"Makes for a good story or a good joke," Pepper said.

"Makes me bored," Sarah said, not in a mean way, toward Pepper. "You forget, I lived with Walter and that kind of thinking." She stopped for a moment. "It is kind of fun."

And Jerri felt a little numbness in her mind. What Dolph was saying was what Joe Parr might have tried to articulate one night while they had sat in their underwear in their backyard and watched the deer nibble at the tender St. Augustine grass. Or what Dolph said might be what Palo had tried to say as he stumbled over and searched for the English words. Once, when she first met him and he still had promise, before he became just a voice in Dolph's head, Vincent Fuentes had said much the same to her. She didn't want to understand what Dolph was saying.

Dolph turned toward Jerri, "Like you said in that bar, death is just the great final indignity. But stuff goes on."

Pooter and then Pepper looked at the urn in Sarah's lap. "I think that I'm going to throw this in that large waste can over there," Sarah said. "The way you talk, I'm thinking Walter's going to haunt me."

"Maybe he has all these years," Pooter said.

"It's your urn," Dolph said and smiled with just his eyes because his mouth was obviously tired. "Walter wanted you to have it. Do what you want with it."

Sarah grew fidgety. Jerri withdrew. The boys had another round, and then another. And then, still sleepy, they crammed into the mini-van and returned to the airport.

They waited with Sarah until she got in line to board the plane. Sarah, then, pushed a wad of bills into Dolph's hands, "I sold your Focus, like you asked." She attempted a smile of thanks, but instead it looked like a smile of relief. She went back into the tube that fed into the gullet of the plane. Pepper did not board with her. No one asked Pepper anything. He just followed them as they exited the airport. Nothing but flat land filled with mesquite and creosote surrounded the Midland/Odessa airport. In the distance was a barbed wire fence, seemingly built to catch the tumbleweeds and the litter. Jerri looked around for some other people and saw and heard only cars zipping down I-20 far away in a horizon that you could indeed see in this city. All of West Texas must have been lonely, Jerri reasoned. And that must be why Pooter, Pepper, and Dolph were the way they were. That desert loneliness must have made them feel at home. It must have made them feel long-dead people they never even knew hovering in the air. In the slow, methodical, wry way that West Texans spoke, Dolph spoke first, "You not going back?"

"My welcome and I both wore out," Pepper said.

The conversation continued in some telepathic West Texas male way that Jerri couldn't understand, couldn't even hear, but could just note on the twisting expressions of Pooter, Pepper, and Dolph. "I know these bars," Pepper said.

Pooter said, "I bet I know the same ones."

Jerri went with them to try to see the fascination. And for a while, Jerri seemed to have lost twenty years as she felt the delight of drinking in disreputable places with boys albeit old boys who should know better and should grow up. She felt herself with Vincent and Palo Fuentes and Joe Parr.

Well after sundown, Jerri dropped the boys off at their room at the

LaQuinta and went to her own room. But she could not shut down her mind. It churned over and around the image of Dolph smiling at Sarah when she gave him the money from selling his Focus. With his mouth wired shut so that he couldn't show his teeth, Dolph painfully lifted the corners of his mouth, to smile at Sarah. Even as the corners of his mouth dropped to make his mouth its usual straight line, Jerri could see a restlessness ease out of him and a newfound contentment fill his eyes and the corners of his mouth. And maybe, Jerri thought, some of that contentment was left over from the dip in the pool the night before.

She pulled herself out of the bed, walked out of her motel door, not even minding that she wore only her negligee—who would even care to look at a middle-aged woman with short legs—walked around the corner to her boys' room, and knocked. Dolph opened the door, mumbling from between the wires. She asked him to come to her room. He was not too old or too changed to turn back to face Pepper and Pooter, drinking beer and watching a basketball playoff game, and smile and gloat at them. And they returned dirty, little boy smiles. Jerri turned her back and led Dolph back to her room and knew that he swaggered behind her.

They got in bed together and just held one another. Then after fumbling, groping sex—no bells, no whistles, just great need and relief—they held each other some more. They rolled away from each other, laying on their backs staring at the ceiling. Jerri turned first to look at Dolph. He rolled his head to look at her. The gazes locked, and Jerri both heard and understood some of that telepathic West Texas, male communication. "Finally," Dolph said. Jerri chuckled.

In the morning, the rotten egg smell of hydrogen sulfide was in the air again. Jerri called the car rental agency in Phoenix and got the okay to return the van to San Antonio. So she would return home instead of back to Phoenix. As they all began to load into the van, Dolph fidgeted in front of Jerri with his Focus money in his hand. Pepper and Pooter stood behind him, Jerri stepped out from the car to look at the three of them. "I think I'd like to stay for awhile," Dolph said.

"Why?"

"I'd like to see how Lee Ann was brought up. Maybe, I'd like to see Odessa some more," and then he shrugged. "I'd like to drive around in

West Texas and look at the horizon."

Pooter nodded his head in agreement. Pepper said to Dolph, "I'd of thought you had enough horizon staring. It's what made you crazy in the first place."

"What are you going to live on?" Jerri asked.

Dolph held up the Focus money. Then he said, "Ask my mother to wire me some money. I'll send an address later."

"Then keep the van. You'll need a car."

"I'll rent or buy my own," Dolph held up the money again.

Jerri looked at Dolph, then out the windshield, then remembered Pepper and Pooter. "What are you two going to do?" she asked them.

"I'll stay," Pepper said.

"What about Joan?" Jerri asked.

Pepper and Pooter both exchanged glances. "I was born here. It's awful. There's nothing to do. I think I'll stay too," Pooter said. "After all, what can my boss say?"

"I guess I wouldn't mind looking at a little more horizon and getting crazy again," Pepper said.

"What about you?" Dolph asked. "Need a vacation?"

"In Odessa?" Jerri said.

"Can you think of anyplace better?"

"Or a closer place?" Pooter asked. "You know what Johnny Yield, though an Apache, would tell you about the Navajos. They say there are seven directions: east, west, north, south, up, down, and the most important one here."

The telepathy was going on. Jerri could hear and see it. "I can't," she said.

"We're going prepay our funerals," Pooter said. "We've already made down payments on our deaths."

Jerri got into the van knowing that it was useless to argue, knowing that this was a new Dolph, knowing that she might not see him again, knowing that she might have lost a really good team for Sam's Investigating Services, knowing that she would cry on down the road. Jerri now understood just a little. They were still on the youngish side of old. They had some itch they had to scratch. They wanted one last chance before facing some inevitable future. She wished, she prayed, that she could stay with them.

As she had many times before, she drove off, leaving some aging men staring at their nearly certain futures. But this time she left without bitterness or regret. Maybe this time they would find something, and she would be pleased for them. She had the desire but not the temperament to stay, so she glanced up to see her boys and Odessa in the rearview mirror.

In the thirty years that Jim Sanderson has been writing seriously, he has been given many labels. He went from being an "aspiring writer" to a "working class, Texas" writer when he won the Kenneth Patchen Prize (92) and had his short story collection, *Semi-Private Rooms*, published (Pig Iron Press, 1995). With the publication of his essay collection, *A West Texas Soapbox* (1998, Texas A & M Press), he became a Texas humorist and essayist. When he won the 1997 Frank Waters Prize (given for the best novel about the southwest), he was a new "rural Southwestern literary writer." When the novel that won that prize, *El Camino del Rio* (University of New Mexico Press, 1998) came out with his editor's label as a "mystery" and was subsequently reviewed in the *Washington Post* and *New York Times* as a mystery, he became a mystery writer. With the University of New Mexico Press's publication of two more novels, *Safe Delivery* (2000, Violet Crown Award finalist) and *La Mordida* (2002), he became a "literary mystery writer." With the publication of *Nevin's History* (Texas Tech University Press, 2004), he became a "historical writer" or a "Western writer." With *Faded Love*, he returned to being a short story writer and was honored by being a finalist for the Jesse Jones Award for the best book-length fiction by a Texan or about Texas, sponsored by the Texas Institute of Letters in 2010. Sanderson lets others choose his labels, but *Dolph's Team* is another in his literary-mystery series.

CPSIA information can be obtained at www.ICGtesting.com
Printed in the USA
LVOW070806050112

262493LV00002B/111/P